WENDY DAY

Killing Cupid

Second edition

ISBN: 978-1-7371669-0-0

This book was professionally typeset on Reedsy.
Find out more at reedsy.com

For anyone who has been told they are too much or not enough.
You are fearfully and wonderfully made, just the way you are.

Acknowledgement

"Follies and nonsense, whims and inconsistencies, *do* divert me, I own, and I laugh at them whenever I can." - Pride and Prejudice by Jane Austen.

This book is 30 years in the making. Actually, I just started writing it a few months ago, but my friends and family have had to hear about my book ideas for years. And I could never have finally finished a book without them. I won't torture you, or them, with rehashing my many failed attempts. Instead, I want to thank them, most ardently, for their love and support.

This book is only possible because of the love and patience of my amazing husband, Kevin, who has helped make all my dreams come true. And thank you to my children, David, Erin, Allison, and Brady, who tolerate my shenanigans and lack of cooking skills. I am so proud to be your mom and love you more than you know.

Thank you, Mom, for always having my back and being willing to fight for me. Thank you, Gene, for sharing with me your clever wit and love of fishing. Dad and Davie, I miss you both so much. Thank you for teaching me to dream big. And to my extended family, who have helped shape my life and my imagination, grateful thanks.

Much love to my best girlfriends; you never doubt my wild ideas and are always willing to go along for the ride. Our girl gang could take over the world *if* we wanted the hassle of running it.

Thank you to my Keller Williams Living family for your encouragement and for letting me talk incessantly about my book between selling houses. You make real estate fun.

My heartfelt thanks to my editor, Melissa Dawdy. Your insight, encouragement, and friendship are a blessing. Thank you to Heather Aeschliman, who made sure I didn't kill off Jayla, and Lisa Roose-Church, who is hilariously honest in her proofreading.

And most importantly, I owe everything good in my life to the one true God for whom I strive to live. All glory goes to Him.

1

Was Jane Austin Wrong?

Sunday, January 2

Dating sucks. Seriously, what happened to good old-fashioned courting? Hand-written love letters or a light brush of fingertips to set the world on fire; that's what I want. I thought it would be easy to meet men in Chicago. Big city, great nightlife, fabulous roommate to bash about town with me. I was wrong. Cupid has most certainly fallen down on the job. And if he's given up on love, what chance do I have?

Even dating apps are no help. I tried to paint myself as an exciting, fun, up-for-anything kind of girl, which I'm not. Mostly, that got me unsolicited dick pics and late-night hook-up requests.

Then I decided to be honest.

Introvert from Indiana who loves Jane Austen; doesn't exercise much; would rather stay at home and drink wine; can't cook and has the fashion sense of a goat.

Since that wasn't netting me any eligible men either, I decided to make things up three months later when I filled out the subsequent questionnaire.

What do you like to do for fun?
I like to hunt Sasquatch on the weekends.
What do you do for a living?
Growing up, I worked in a whale fat candle-making factory.

Jayla had rolled with laughter and was sure I would scare off any potential suitors. It turns out there are a lot of men who also like to chase Sasquatch on the weekends, which resulted in invitations for several weekend hunting trips (all of which I declined). Another guy sent me a sample of candles he made using fat from a source he wouldn't disclose. I deposited the gift into the trash with a shudder. I was done with online dating.

I met Tom at work. He is way too practical for Sasquatch hunting. We've been dating for a few months; what I feel for him could not be characterized as true love, not by Jane Austen's standards. I'd rather fantasize Mr. Darcy is at the door with an armful of roses. I can almost smell the fresh English blooms. I push the thought away. After all, there's nothing wrong with Tom; he's decent-looking with sandy blonde hair and is the ideal three inches taller, so I can wear heels. He's nice, predictable, and a practical choice. The pain-in-the-ass Elizabeth Bennet inside my head scolds me not to settle for a boring routine. She craves adventure, romance, and genuine passion. Dating Tom, she pouts, is settling for something less.

"I hate Elizabeth Bennet and her Mr. Darcy," I say as I struggle to zip up my favorite black dress with the cap sleeves and cinched waist. "I mean, why should Elizabeth and Darcy end up passionately in love when the rest of us have to settle for some mediocre imitation? It's rude." I slip the pearl earrings Tom got me for Christmas into my ears.

Jayla, dressed in her silk robe and holding a pair of fabric sheers, pokes her face around the corner to laugh at me. "Girl, you may say you hate Elizabeth and Darcy, but I've seen your sorry-ass, dog-eared collection of romance novels."

I frown at my reflection. Maybe it's irrational to hate fictional characters in a book. Still, it's also entirely unfair that Elizabeth and Darcy should find love while I, a perfectly above average twenty-three-year-old in Chicago, am stuck with Tom from accounting.

Jayla interrupts my thoughts. "Hey, gorgeous, your makeup looks fine; your true love is knocking at the door, and I need to use the bathroom." She wiggles her eyebrows and glances at the toilet.

"Sorry." I slide open the drawer and sweep my makeup into it, giving my hair a final look before scooting out of her way.

I slip on my favorite pumps, compose a pretty smile, and swing open the door. Tom steps over the threshold, bringing the familiar scent of woodsy shower gel with him. I lean in gracefully for a kiss, but he turns his head, and my lips graze scratchy jaw stubble.

"Ready?" he asks, flashing a brief smile, rocking on the balls of his feet.

"Sure," I say, reaching for my black coat and sliding it over my shoulders.

We bypass the ancient elevator and take the stairs to the lobby. Tom managed to grab a parking spot right out front and holds the door open for me as I carefully navigate the slush and snow, sliding into his SUV.

"I thought we would check out an Italian place." He pulls into traffic and switches lanes to turn left.

"Really? That sounds great." I snuggle into the supple warmth of the heated seat. We ride in comfortable silence. That's what I like about Tom; he's a friendly, easy-going, regular sort of guy. He isn't Mr. Darcy, but maybe what I need is a Mr. Collins anyway.

He eases into the parking lot of a quaint, brick building with a red check patterned awning across the front. We are serenaded by the low, sweet sound of a singer's voice piped through speakers as we enter.

We settle into the booth as leather-bound menus are placed in our hands with a promise of wine to follow. The air is thick with garlic and freshly baked bread. Tom silently picks lint off his jacket sleeve as I consider the dinner options. I peek up at him. Is he nervous? He looks nervous.

"Did you say something?" he asks, meeting my eyes then shifting his gaze sideways.

"I didn't say anything." I'm smiling and tipping my head to the side. Is reliable Tom about to become surprising Tom? The waitress appears at our table and pours us each a glass of red wine, and then Tom orders for both of us.

Lifting the glass to my lips, I contemplate why he could be acting so weird. There are only a few choices. Then it hits me. No, there's no way; it's been only four months. But he did say he loved me. Oh, no. No, it's just a nice restaurant. We hadn't even talked about marriage. I set my wine glass down, almost tipping it over.

"Careful." Tom reaches out to steady the glass. He still isn't meeting my eyes.

Tearing off bites of soft Italian bread, I chew and try to remain calm. What was I doing eating carbs? I might be getting married, and I was going to gain weight. No, that's not right. Jayla says I need to be body-positive. Oh, crap.

The waitress tops off our wine then places two steaming plates of pasta in front of us.

I stab a piece of zucchini and lift it into the air with a swish, "It's been many years since I've had such an exemplary vegetable."

Tom looks up from his plate, "What?"

"It's from Pride and Prejudice, Tom." I shake my head, "Aren't you going to eat?"

"Yes, of course," he picks up his flatware and begins cutting into his chicken piccata. Tom is completely focused on his plate. I wish I knew what he was thinking. I hate surprises. I don't want to get engaged to him *or* get dumped over dinner, which seem to be the only two options.

Memories of my parents sitting across from me in a booth like this, telling me they didn't love each other anymore, fill my head. I try to keep my breath even as I choke down bites of pasta through a tightened throat. Oh no, this can't be happening again.

"We've been dating for four months." Tom takes a drink of water and coughs.

I nod and sip more wine. Oh no. Please no.

"And we've had a lot of fun together. And you're a great girl."

I set my fork down and brace for what's coming.

"The thing is," he sputters, finally meeting my gaze, "I don't think it's going to work out."

I must look confused because he keeps talking, waving his hands around, trying to explain.

"I told you I loved you last week, and I thought I meant it. I planned out how it was going to sound and everything. But then, when I said it, even as it came out of my mouth, I knew I wasn't being honest with myself or you." The words sound like an avalanche in the relative quiet of the restaurant.

He reaches for my hands, searching my face. "And then you said it, and I felt bad. I wasn't sure what to do, so I didn't do anything, but I'm a straight shooter, and I've always been on the up and up with you, and I can't just say things that aren't true and let it stand. And if I don't love you now, there's not a big chance I will fall in love with you suddenly."

I yank my hands away and press them onto my knees. *He's* breaking up with *me*? I put up with dull Tom. I was ready to settle for boring

Tom. And *he's* breaking up with *me*? My heart races, and I feel the heat rise in my cheeks. Tears prick my eyes, and I blink them back.

Get it together, Callie. I will not meltdown in this restaurant over this guy.

Taking a deep breath, I straighten the napkin on my lap. I bite the breadstick I had abandoned earlier and chew it slowly. It's fine. I didn't like him that much anyway. Better to end it now. And at least I didn't have to be the bad guy. No, this is good. After I swallow, I raise my eyebrows, look up at him, and shrug. "Okay, can we finish dinner?"

His eyes are wide. "Is that all you have to say?"

I shrug again. "I mean, it's not like we are getting married or anything. Let's enjoy one more meal together, and then we'll call it quits." The waitress passes, and I order another glass of wine.

He frowns, shakes his head once, then picks up his fork to resume eating. He keeps looking at me as if I am a bomb about to explode at any second. I smile and pretend to enjoy my meal, even if I have to choke it down. I order an extra glass of wine.

* * *

Silence hangs between us as we drive home. He keeps opening his mouth to say something and then closes it again. Hugging my coat to me tightly, I press myself into the passenger side door as hard as possible to keep away from him.

As soon as the car stops, I jump to the curb and lean forward, "Thanks again for everything. You're a great guy!" *What? He is not a great guy. He's a jerk.* I turn around and trudge through the slush with my hands clenched inside my pockets.

I slam the apartment door shut and let out an angry groan as the macrame wall art next to me pops off its nail and falls in a puddle to the floor. Kicking off my heels, I tip my head back and sigh. At least I was home. I love our eclectic, cluttered, comfortable apartment. It is a perfect blend of Jayla's colorful personality and my love of all things vintage. My mom found the yellow glass lamp at a church tag sale and saved it for me. It is perfect on the corner table and inspired the rest of the room, a blend of gold, sage, and navy. Well, aside from the ugly red velvet couch that Jayla refuses to replace.

Jayla rushes out of her room, face covered in cream and her silk robe tied around her. "What's wrong, honey?"

"Tom and I broke up."

"Uh-oh. I thought you didn't like him that much?"

"I know," I croak. I'm laughing, crying, and shaking with anger all simultaneously.

She wraps her long, slim arms around me and pulls me in. "It's okay. We can just grow old together and raise cats."

I laugh and wipe my nose with my sleeve, and she leans back to examine my face. "Did you break up with him, or did he break up with you?"

"He broke up with me."

"Oh," she says, squeezing my arms gently and meeting my eyes, "I'm so sorry the boy you didn't like broke up with you."

I chuckle, "Shut up."

Her smile is warm. "I'm so sorry. Getting dumped is the worst."

I sniff. "It really is." I slip my coat off and head to the bathroom for a tissue.

She follows me, silently leaning on the door frame as I blow my nose.

"I'll be okay. I am not even sure why I'm so upset. Elizabeth Bennet would never cry if Mr. Collins had dumped her." I turn to give her a crooked smile. "The worst part, he did it over pasta."

Jayla sucks in her breath, "Now, that is just cruel. I think Elizabeth

7

Bennett and Mr. Darcy have ruined love for all of us."

I wipe my eyes. *Yeah, screw you, Elizabeth Bennett.*

2

The New Me

Monday, January 3

What a great way to begin the New Year. Did I actually get dumped and then proceed to stuff my face with pasta and breadsticks? I take a deep breath and throw off my duvet cover to face the day. I don't need to wallow over some guy I didn't even love.

Holding up various tops in front of the long mirror on the back of my closet door, I try to decide between the red sweater Jayla gave me for Christmas or an emerald green button-down which still has the tags on it. Deciding on the green, I head to the bathroom, determined to make sure that if I run into Tom today, he will see how big of a mistake he made. I turn on my curling iron and use my phone to play a video on contouring. I find the makeup kit I bought two months ago on a whim and get to work.

"You look great this morning," Jayla chirps as she pours herself a cup of coffee. A chic black dress hugs the curves of her dancer's body, and she easily maneuvers around the kitchen in her audaciously high heels. Jayla always looks great.

"Thank you. Tom is history, and I finally figured out how to do a decent eyebrow," I say, batting my eyelashes at her.

"Nice. And you curled your hair."

"Why, yes, I did," I say, reaching for cereal and milk, "and I'm going to have a fabulous day. I have the best friend a girl could ask for. I live in Chicago, the city of deep-dish pizza, amazing shopping, and the unlimited possibilities of big city life. What more can I ask for?"

She lifts her coffee cup in salute. "That's right, sister."

I pause in the doorway to our building and fish a pair of sunglasses out of my bag. Two days of sunshine in a row is unheard of in Chicago this time of year, and I am ready to enjoy it.

Our apartment is on the third floor of a charming old brownstone. I adore the original wood trim and tall ceilings. I head for the oak stairs, my hand skimming the railing as I walk down. The antique elevator is original to the building. It's charming to look at, but I avoid it unless I am carrying something heavy. It has a cage door you have to slide across the opening before it moves, and I am never sure if I am using it right. Even if I can get it moving, the creaking and jerking of the gears freak me out a bit.

* * *

I smile as I step onto the street and feel the bustle of the city coming alive. Trucks are parked in front of the bakery, and the smell of fresh bread fills the air. Horns blare as impatient drivers jockey around the trucks. Fluffy dogs bark at the end of leashes held by sophisticated older women wearing matching athletic wear. Young professionals in boots, long coats, and headphones hurry on their way to the train. Men and women in suits and wool coats impatiently whistle for taxis to whisk them downtown. It's an intoxicating mix of life in action and exactly why I moved to Chicago in the first place.

Luckily, there is no line at my favorite coffee shop. The bell above the door jingles as I step inside. I lightly touch the glass of the pastry case, yearning for a sugar-topped blueberry muffin. I scan the chalkboard on the wall behind the counter that lists all varieties of coffee, and even though I contemplate getting something different, I know I won't.

"Hey, Callie, the usual?" the barista asks, her blue hair tied back into a low ponytail.

"Yes, a medium vanilla latte, please."

Steam rises from the cup as the barista snaps on the lid. "Thank you, and I hope you have an amazing day!" I say, flashing her my best smile.

"Thanks," she says absently, turning her back to me.

Hmph. Well, alrighty, then. I drop a five-dollar bill in the tip jar, determined to be a ray of sunshine.

Tom made a big mistake letting me go. Not that I care much. I'm going to be fine. *Thank you, universe, for taking care of a problem I couldn't take care of myself.* And if I find real love, it will be the kind of love I fight for, not wishy-washy Tom love.

I drop my empty coffee cup into the can in the lobby of our office building. The only sound on the elevator making its way up to my cubicle on the seventh floor is the rustling of jackets and an occasional cough. I tug my phone out of my pocket while leaning against the cool, smooth handrail. I missed a call from my mom; I'll call her back later. Right now, I am busy being a ray of sunshine.

"Hi. You look great," I tell the receptionist behind the curved modern white desk, and her cheeks redden as she smiles.

"How's the new baby?" I ask, leaning into Mark's glass-walled office. He spins around from his dual screens and takes out his phone to show me pictures of the red-headed three-month-old girl he just adopted. He has circles under his eyes, and his hair is mussed, but he joyfully explains each photo, obviously a proud dad. His minimalist modern office decor is softened by framed pictures of him and his partner on various trips. A small bassinet hugs the corner of his office, ready in case of childcare emergencies. I finally excuse myself and make my way to my office.

The new me talks to my co-workers. The new me is more confident and totally happy. If word gets back to Tom that I'm doing just fine without him, that's even better.

Slipping into my sleek black and chrome office chair, I turn on my computer and check my calendar. My evening is wide open. My weekend is wide open. Maybe I should go to a museum Saturday or drag Jayla out for a drink. Not that I would have to drag her; she was always up for a night out. Whatever I decide to do, it will be fabulous. This is why I came to Chicago; freedom, adventure, excitement. The new me is ready to embrace anything this city offers as soon as the morning meeting is over.

"Something's different about you today." Simon shakes his finger at me. He taps his pencil on the stack of papers in front of him, casually facing me in his chair. He is almost six feet tall, lean, with black hair and blue eyes.

Simon was one of the first people I met at the company. And I had my eyes set on him as a possible romantic partner. After several clumsy attempts to flirt with him, he finally took me to lunch.

* * *

"*Sweet Callie,*" *he said, picking up chopsticks.*

"*Yes,*" *I smiled, leaning in over the sushi he insisted I try.*

"*If I were at all into women, you would be on the top of the list. But alas, I am not.*"

I just blinked at him, confused.

He sighed. "I'm gay. You know; likes men, dresses well, avoids three-in-one shampoo."

"*Oh,*" *I said, my eyes wide. I wasn't sure how to respond.*

"*Don't worry. It isn't contagious. I just wanted you to know so you could*

*stop your horrendous attempts at flirting." He pointed his chopsticks at me,
"That is something we need to work on if you ever want to find love."
My cheeks burned.
"Oh, don't worry about it. It just means you have good taste. And I make
a great wingman."*

* * *

"New sweater?" I ask him.

"It was a gift to myself," he says, smiling. "It's cashmere, and I got it for a steal."

"It looks great on you." I reach out to touch the sleeve.

His finger is on his lips as he plants his feet on the floor, twists in the chair, and evaluates me.

I smile at him sideways, trying to look glamorous.

"Did you cut your hair?" he says, narrowing his eyes.

"No, I did not cut my hair." I had not cut my hair in six months, but that was beside the point.

He snickers, "Well, it looks off."

I swat him on the arm. "Thanks a lot."

"Ouch! I am just looking out for you." He examines the back of my head.

Our conversation abruptly ends as people stream in for the morning meeting. As we kick off plans for the summer and fall marketing seasons, it will be a long, busy, and distracting day.

On break, I sneak off to the bathroom to double-check my hair. It does look a little wonky. Okay, back into the signature messy bun. Slipping back into my seat next to Simon, I can feel his eyes assessing me again.

He chuckles, and I stick my chin out and say, "I have a very important job and must pay attention to my responsibilities." All I can think about is hopping on the "L" after work and heading uptown.

3

After Work

Jogging down the steps to the train, I check the time. My favorite shop is uptown and is open until seven. Good, there's time to pick up the latest book in the fantasy series I devoured last month.

The "L" is always hot, even during winter. I push myself as far back into the corner of the train as I can. I have ended up with a sweaty armpit in my face or a random hand on my ass. I gaze at the overhead electric billboard advertisements as they scroll past to avoid eye contact with anyone.

Is that how people pick their bail bondsman? An advertisement on a train? Are they on the way to jail? And what does a bail bondsman do, anyway?

The sign changes again. Teased blonde hair and full cheeks peek out from beneath a *sold* sign. I can't help but chuckle. Sally Sells Chicago sounds like a stripper's name. She looks like the kind of woman who loves to bake cookies, but she wouldn't hesitate to add a little poison if the situation called for it.

A child's voice distracts me. A few seats away, a brown-haired toddler with her eyes half-closed rests her head on her mom's shoulder. Her curly-haired doll dangles from her hand. The mother stares out the window, dark circles under her eyes, lips pressed into a thin line.

The train slows and jerks to a halt, sending the doll tumbling to the floor, where it's kicked under the seat. The train is so crowded her mom doesn't seem to notice. I squeeze between a sweaty, overweight woman and a guy who has been leering at me. Reaching my fingers out, I can barely grab the hem of the doll's dress. I huff as I grab it and lift it to the little girl in one motion.

She takes it and buries her head in her mom's neck.

I smile at her and hurry back to my seat.

According to the map on the train's wall, only two more stops until I get off. I watch a couple standing nearby. The bald man in a business suit is trying to ignore a feisty bleached blonde in glasses as she glares and occasionally spits out a comment in his direction. *I would not want to be that guy.*

I notice a bright pink advertisement flashing on the electric billboard from the corner of my eye.

Are you tired of settling? Are you ready for your own Mr. Darcy? Do you think there's only true love in Indiana? Let Cupid help.

I shake my head and do a double-take. Did I read that right? Yeah, I did. There it is, up on the screen.

If so, you need to check out MyLove4Life.com, where we match you up and make sure you fall in love for good.

Right. Another scam dating website full of creepy men. But why would they mention Indiana or Mr. Darcy? I know data tracking is sophisticated, we see it in our marketing all the time, but goodness, this is a whole new level. I grab my phone and type in the web address. There's no way it will load in the tunnel, but I'll check it out later.

I slip out of the train ahead of the crowd and take the steps up two at a time. Twilight has fallen, and warm lights beckon me into the shops as soon as my feet hit the sidewalk. People mill about, laughing as they wander home after happy hour or sneak into a boutique for something unique.

My favorite place in the entire world is The Curious Bookshop, a block up from the train station. I stumbled upon it my first week in Chicago and have been a regular customer. I prefer unique little shops to the big box stores, and this one has an almost magical quality to it, right down to its old-fashioned narrow door, which is easy to overlook amid the shops surrounding it.

The familiar tinkle of the brass bell attached to the door frame greets me, and the smell of books is intoxicating. I don't know if it is the ink, paper, binding cloth, or the glue, but I love wandering the cramped shelves, running my fingers over the leather spines of the classics, and checking out the bright artwork of new fiction. I love the creaky wood floors and the comfy upholstered chairs, inviting you to sit and stay awhile. My mom used to read to me growing up, and books had filled most of the boxes I brought to Chicago. I stand in the doorway to take it all in.

"Can I help you?" A neatly dressed young woman with long silky black hair and smooth olive skin appears.

"Yes, you are holding a book for me. Callie Mcguire."

"Perfect. I will check for it in the back." She nods briskly and hustles to the storeroom. I take a moment to admire the economy of her movements; she's not one to waste time on mooning over boyfriends, I'll bet.

"Thank you. I'll just look around for a bit," I call out, heading for the new fiction shelves. Running my fingers over the shelves, I note the authors' names. Writing a book is my secret dream. I have notebooks full of ideas and characters. My laptop contains three different novels I have started but abandoned. Someday, I will finish one, and it will be amazing.

I feel a tap on my shoulder. "Here you go," the clerk says as she hands me a bag.

"Thanks." I glance at her nametag, "Marie, you must be new. I'm so excited to read this. I have the entire series."

Her eyes brighten as she ditches the professional demeanor. "Me, too! I read this in one sitting, and it's the best yet. I'm sure you're going to love it. You'll have to stop and let me know what you think."

I smile. "I will. Thanks."

I leave the bookshop carrying my little brown bag, eager to get home.

Near the train station is a flower shop in full Valentine's Day mode. It's only the beginning of January, but there is Cupid, the mischievous little cherub, swinging from a string in the window, threatening to shoot unsuspecting window shoppers with his arrow. Pausing in front of the window, I say, "Okay, Mr. Fat Flying Baby, maybe you can point an arrow in my direction this year and bring me some actual romance. Is that too much to ask?" As I turn to walk away, I swear that fat flying baby winks at me.

* * *

An hour later, I am sinking into the chair in my room with chopsticks in hand and an open carton of Chinese takeout. Just as I reach for my new book, I remember the website on my phone. Depositing the lo mein on the side table, I open the browser.

I suck in a breath because staring back at me is the hottest guy I have ever seen. He's the sort of guy who would never give me a second glance but holds court at the bar while tanned, toned, young blondes buzz around him adoringly. He's a sandy blonde with green eyes and ethnically ambiguous golden skin. He purrs, "Are you single? Are you looking for your own Mr. Darcy? Thinking you can't find love outside of Indiana? I can help."

Yeah, right, maybe you could help a girl out, but I bet every other guy on the website is a toad. This can't be real. I refresh the browser, and the same message pops up. I pick up my lo mein and start to eat, balancing the phone on my knee.

"Oh, I know you are cynical about love." He leans forward like he's telling me a secret, "I am, too. I know you've tried other dating sites. You've had disappointments, disasters, and even found yourself in dangerous situations. It's time for you to try something different. Our one hundred percent guarantee program will make sure you find your love for life."

I am mesmerized by his smile and voice. It's intoxicating, and I can almost smell him through the computer, a musky, masculine scent with a hint of coconut. His lips are full and the perfect shade of pink. His lashes are thick and long, and his strong jawline is captivating. And that accent; I am such a sucker for a British accent.

"I know you've been disappointed, but not this time," he continues, wagging a finger at me. "In fact, if you don't fall in love and stay in love, I will give you one million dollars, guaranteed. I am Cupid, after all. And finding your love is my job."

This is weird. I refresh the browser one more time to make sure I hear this right. Sure enough, the message repeats precisely as before. This has got to be a scam. Grabbing my laptop, I search for the name of the company. Okay, there are dozens of reviews, all five-star glowing. That's good.

"I would never have dated Fred, but he is perfect!"

"My family doesn't understand our love, but it doesn't matter. Our love is real, and it is forever."

Why have I never heard of this company? Why isn't everybody talking about MyLove4Life.com instead of wasting their time at other stupid dating apps? I find the website on my laptop and click through to the *Sign Up Now* button.

4

A Match

Tapping my finger on my chin, I weigh the options. Am I ready for more awkward first dates and disappointing first kisses? It's not likely that I will find a husband or even a viable boyfriend. On the other hand, if I sign up, I can tell my mom I am trying.

I set my laptop aside and focus on dinner. Then I scavenge around the takeout bag for the fortune cookie, cracking it open. Holding it in between my fingers, I read, *Take a chance on love.*

"Really?" I say out loud, looking up. "Fine. But I am not holding my breath."

I upload my standard dating app photo, enter my birth date and crucial information, and pay the ninety-nine-dollar, one-time fee. If they guarantee they're going to find my absolute soul mate, they can't charge by the month. I'm not sure it's a good business plan; maybe that is why I haven't heard of it before. I tuck my legs underneath me and prepare to slog through the questionnaire.

Blah, blah, blah, same old questions I've answered on every other site. I decided to be brutally honest this time. Maybe I can weed out some of the weirdos early.

Okay, I'm not going to get my hopes up. What's the worst that could happen? Lose a hundred dollars? Have my million-dollar heart broken? After answering the rest of the questions, I hold my breath and hit enter.

Mr. Hottie was back. "Thank you for your submission, Callie. You're not going to regret it. We use the latest technology and even a little magic to make sure you and your soul mate find each other at last."

An animated Earth slowly spins on the screen. My match is probably in Tibet or an Argentinian jail. Maybe he is a short, bald man who smells like eggs and would call me "doll." I watch the screen with low expectations.

After a few more seconds, the animated Earth stops spinning and zooms in on the United States. An arrow points to Chicago, and the name appears, *Jimmy Powell.*

I read it out loud and wait for something to happen. Was I going to get multiple choices? Or is this the one, the only one? I stare at the screen. My leg tingles and burns with numbness. I stand and shake it out, then flop down on my bed.

That's better. Blanket, comfy bed, laptop balanced on my legs, and I am ready. Let's see who you are, Jimmy Powell.

I hit continue and squint as his face appears. He has a broad smile and short dark brown hair. Every photo on the site features Jimmy Powell in various weight lifting poses. His oiled body and tight red shorts leave little to the imagination. One of the photos featured him in a black tank top, leaning his head down to kiss his left bicep. Really? This is the best they can do?

I scroll down to see what else I can find out about this guy. He works at a gym, no surprise there. He does weight lifting competitions, and that's about it. I sit up straight and let out a breath. I am not sure they could have picked someone more opposite from me. There is no way we would get along. I hate working out, and that's all he does. Maybe I should meet him because I could use that million dollars. Super. I spent a hundred dollars for another failed relationship.

I slide my computer to an open space on the bed and head to the kitchen to grab a water bottle. I need to shake off the melancholy threatening to creep in. I am being judgmental. So what if he is a bodybuilder? That doesn't mean he can't be a good guy. We might have something else in common. I'm being too picky.

Crawling back onto my bed, I pick up the laptop. "Okay, Jimmy, what's next?" I whisper to no one. Just then, a red button appears at the bottom of the page. It reads, *Swipe Right to Agree to the Terms and Conditions, Finalize match, and Schedule Your First Date.*

I move the cursor toward the button. Wait. *Am I ready for this?*

The website has promised this was going to be my soul mate. Like, my real soul mate, the person I would be with for the rest of my life. What if it is just another disappointment? What if he makes me work out?

Do soul mates even exist? I want to think so, but I doubt it. Heck, Jayla thought she found her soul mate but got dumped on her wedding day by the jerk. If she can't find her soul mate, as beautiful and confident as she is, how will I find mine?

I might puke.

"Jayla!" I shout from my bedroom, "I need you."

My bedroom door swings open dramatically, and Jayla's hands on her hips, chest puffed out. "I'm here to save the day!" she declares. Her hair is covered in conditioner and a plastic cap.

"Good," I say, patting the bed for her to join me.

"What's this?" she says, lying down and eyeing the picture of Jimmy.

"Apparently, he's my soul mate." I hand her the laptop, throw my hand over my face, and groan.

Jayla takes the laptop to my chair and sits down. "Okay, you had better start at the beginning and tell me what happened."

I tell Jayla about the train, the website, and the ninety-nine dollars.

"His name is Jimmy, and he's supposed to be my soul mate," I say, gesturing to the computer.

"Honestly, Callie, I don't see what the problem is. I mean, he likes to work out, so he is healthy. He is easy on the eyes. Soul mate? Not likely, but he might be fun to hang out with."

"He's probably married. Or using the site as a front to lure victims in and kill them."

She looks at me with her eyebrows raised. "Uh-huh, any other concerns?"

"Yeah. He could be incarcerated in a maximum-security prison, looking for a pen pal and conjugal visits. I can't risk falling in love with some guy and becoming a jailhouse widow. And what's with that fake parrot?"

Jayla turns to face me. "First, you are being irrational. Second, what did the reviews say? I know you researched the reviews, right?"

"Of course. The reviews were great. They said everybody's happy, and it works, blah, blah, blah."

"Okay, so you have a decent-looking guy who is supposed to be your soul mate. They have a guarantee that you're going to be together forever and all of your dreams will come true. What's the problem?"

I slide off my bed onto the floor and lay on my back, gazing at the ceiling. "Am I supposed to fall in love with a health-obsessed bodybuilder? This can't be serious."

Rolling over onto my knees, I grab the computer from her and point at Jimmy's picture, "I mean, look at him. I bet he hasn't read a book since high school."

Jayla sighs. "You have no idea if that is true or not. Why are you so afraid of actually being happy?"

"How many couples do you know where happiness lasts? It doesn't. People get sick of being single, settle for someone mediocre, and eventually split up."

"Wow, you are cynical." She runs her hand over her hair.

"I am not cynical; I am realistic. And I have everything I could need, good books and an amazing best friend."

"Look," Jayla says, standing up, "Are you going to meet him or not?"

"I don't know. I think I'm just going to wait a few days in and see how I feel. I have a huge project due at work, anyway. So I'm way too busy to be worrying about some guy I've never even met."

"Okay, well, in the meantime, you want to go have a glass of wine with me in the living room and watch our show?"

I smile, close my laptop, and reach my hand in the air for Jayla to help me up. Jimmy Powell will have to wait.

5

On the Town

Tuesday, January 4

At breakfast, Jayla gives me sidelong glances as she waits for me to bring up Jimmy; but I don't feel like talking about it and steer the conversation to her instead.

"Any more news about that buying trip you want to go on with your boss?" I say, pouring milk over my granola in the vintage bowl from the set I found in the cabinet above the fridge when I was home last.

"No," she says, picking at her toast, "I've been dropping hints, but she isn't picking them up."

"She should take you. You've been there for five years and know what she likes." Why did I get granola? It takes forever to chew.

"Right? I love my job, but I can't just run her shop forever. I thought I would be married by now and maybe staying at home or working part-time...."

She didn't bring up Mason very often. It was still too painful. He was a dentist, and she had met him at a club, instantly hitting it off. But their whirlwind romance had flamed out just as dramatically when he sent her a text on the morning of their wedding day and told her he couldn't marry her and was getting on a plane to California.

I reach across the table to touch her hand. "I'm sure she knows how important you are. If not, you are so amazing; you could easily find a new position as a buyer." I give up on my cereal and take my bowl to the sink.

"Maybe." Jayla finishes the last bite of toast and brushes crumbs off her dress.

As I load the dishwasher, I say, "You should sign up for the website with me so we can suffer together."

She shakes her head vigorously. "No way. I'm not ready for that scene again. Nope, I'll live vicariously through you."

"You might be disappointed if that's your plan," I say, walking back down the hall.

Standing in front of the bathroom mirror, I smack my lips. Lip gloss is the final step in my minimally acceptable makeup routine. Jayla is constantly trying to teach me makeup tips. She loves to look glamorous. I manage to look a step above a homeless person most of the time. I like to think of myself as a fashion minimalist, even if I failed at minimalism in every other area.

I fish out black pants and a gray sweater from a jam-packed drawer, promising myself to tidy up another day. Jayla once said the gray made my blue eyes sparkle. I scoop my shoulder-length light brown hair into a messy bun and am ready.

"Bye," I tell Jayla, who is watching TV and drinking coffee. She doesn't have to be at work until eleven.

Jayla waves over her shoulder. "See ya. Let me know what you decide about you-know-who."

"Okay," I reply, closing the door closed behind me.

* * *

Throughout the day, Jayla sent me texts about going out tonight.

I manage to ignore her for the most part. Now I lean against her bedroom door frame, my arms folded for emphasis, and say, "I don't want to go out tonight."

"You're my best friend, and I need you to go out with me. Please?"

I move towards her bed. "It's horrible outside, and I have to work tomorrow," I say, dragging a stack of magazines off her bed and sweeping back the brightly colored fabric canopy hanging from the ceiling.

Jayla is seated at her dressing table like a movie star, with the bright, round bulbs surrounding the trifecta of mirrors like something from a Hollywood set. "It stopped raining an hour ago, and on Tuesday's, there's a live band." She leans toward the mirror to brush silver eye shadow on her lids. "Come on. I need a pick me up. Work sucked today; we busted a shoplifter who used her stroller and baby to steal. I need some fun."

I shake my head. "People suck."

"True, but you know who doesn't suck? People who go to the bar with their best friends," she laughs.

"Fine, but you're buying me three drinks, and we're leaving when I say."

"Deal!" She leaps at me, throwing her arms around my neck.

"Ugh, okay, okay," I untangle myself from her arms, and she kisses me on the cheek and starts rummaging through her closet.

"You won't regret this, I promise," she says.

"Yeah, right." I snort.

"What do you think of my new project?" she asks, pointing to the dress form standing patiently in the corner with part of her new creation gracefully draped over its contours. The bodice for her latest design sits, clamped under the sewing machine foot, ready to be stitched and added to the layers of satin already pinned to the form.

I pick up the sketchpad on the floor, the contours of a ball gown taking shape. "You are amazing."

"I know," she says, "Now, be off. You need to get ready so that we can have some fun."

I retreat to my room and dig out my favorite pair of dark jeans and a white fitted, button-down shirt from the laundry hamper. I pat the wrinkles and roll up the sleeves; *nobody likes a freshly ironed shirt, right?* Crawling around the closet, I find black boots to complete the outfit.

Not bad, I think as I put on the red lipstick I find rolling around the back of my underwear drawer.

"Oh, you look good!" Jayla is waiting for me by the front door, wearing tight black pants, heels, and a sparkly jade top.

I spin around. "Thanks. You do, too."

She smiles. "Let's go."

* * *

We walk, arm-in-arm, three blocks to Mikey's, the local bar, dodging puddles along the way. The smell of spilled beer, fried food, and stale smoke rolls over us as we make our entrance.

"You would think it wouldn't still smell like smoke in here after all these years," I say, wrinkling my nose.

"Oh, it's not that bad."

"Always the optimist," I say. "No wonder I liked you the moment we met."

"How could you not?" she says with a flip of her hair. She pushes her way up to the bar and orders a drink for each of us. Handing one to me, she leads me over to an empty table. Sliding on the stools, she surveys the room and frowns at me. "Honey, you need to get over Tom."

"No, I don't. I was never *under* him."

"Ha-ha," she says, "You seemed pretty upset when you came home the other night."

"Have I even mentioned his name since?"

"I'm just making sure you're not stuffing your feelings down and moving on without dealing with them."

I arch my neck and look down my nose at her. "Oh?"

She waves me off. "I have known you for three years, and you are fantastic at pushing those feelings way down deep, Mariana Trench deep." She moves her hands up and down in front of her as if she's pushing something hard.

"I have no idea what you are talking about."

"Center of the Earth deep, sugar."

"Stop it!" I bat her hands apart.

"Fine," she slides off her stool. "Be right back. We need another round. You better get ready to dance."

She spins around halfway to the bar, "I'm not kidding."

The band sets up, and I try to get comfortable on the hard, metal stool that seems too small for my butt.

She hurries back to the table as the first riffs of guitar fill the bar, plopping a drink down in front of me.

The band starts playing a popular song from the 1970s.

She grabs my hand, "Let's go dance!"

"No, I'm not ready. I need to finish this drink first."

She folds her arms and taps her foot as I sip my drink, slowly batting my eyelashes.

"Come on." She yanks me to my feet and drags me to the dance floor.

Two drinks worth of alcohol is barely enough to keep me on the floor, awkwardly rocking back and forth along with the beat.

Jayla wiggles her hips then swings around, her black hair bouncing in her face.

She leans in and shouts over the music, "Isn't this fun?"

"Of course," I reply, making sure my eyes widen as I smile with innocent delight.

The guys in the band are pretty good, playing classic rock and '70s funk. The banner behind them says *Nacho Average Band*.

I might need a T-shirt. But first I need another drink.

Abandoning Jayla on the dance floor, I gulp down another drink, warmth spreading through my body as I lean against the bar. Jayla is now dancing with a hulking, red-faced, bald guy doing a solo two-step. Jayla keeps him at arm's length even as he tries to move in close. She is such a great dancer, poor guy. He is barking up the wrong tree if he is looking for a hookup.

She notices me watching her and excuses herself, heading my way, wiping sweat from her brow with her sleeve.

"Your new lover?" I ask her.

"Ha! He wishes." She orders another drink and leans against the bar next to me. "Uh-oh," she says.

"What?" I crane my neck to see what she looks at with such concern.

"Not what, who."

I see Tom standing next to an older woman with teased blonde hair and way too much makeup.

"Who is that girl?" Jayla asks.

"No idea. Maybe a cousin or something?"

Tom leans over and passionately kisses the mystery girl, tongue and all.

"Eww. I hope not."

"Is he carrying a motorcycle helmet?" I say, trying not to be obvious. He was the most cautious person I know. How can he have bought a motorcycle?

"Apparently. And he has a mustache." Jayla puts her hand over her mouth to stifle her laugh.

"What? None of this makes sense. Maybe he has an evil twin brother he doesn't know about or something."

Tom sees us and gives me a quick wave, snaking his other arm around the mystery girl's waist and whispering into her ear.

She tips her head back and laughs loudly, snorting and shaking her head.

Jayla scoffed, "Didn't he just tell you he loved you like last week?"

"Yes, but then he clarified that he didn't love me, remember?"

"Still. He's a dick. Come on, let's go show him what he's missing."

"Worst idea ever. I don't care how he feels." I shake my head, and she turns to face me.

"Do you want to go?" She asks seriously, brows knitted.

I stand up and take a deep breath, "No. I need another drink, though."

She takes my arm and steers me back to the bar.

"We need two doubles, please, and I'll be back for two more." Jayla smiles at the bartender, who raises his eyebrows and gives us a head shake and a half-smile.

Two doubles later, I'm enjoying the music and happily ignoring Tom's mustache. Sweat is dripping down my back, and my feet would ache if I could feel them. The band gets better as the night goes on.

"Oh, look, that guy is cute," I lean in and slur the words into Jayla's ear.

"Go ask him to dance," she says, pushing me toward the table next to where our coats are waiting for us. Three guys are sharing a pitcher of beer. The one in the middle smiles as I walk up, a little unsteady, trying to look sexy.

"Hey, guys, does anyone want to dance? Maybe you?" I point to Mr. Smiley.

He wordlessly slides off his stool and grabs my hand, leading me back to the floor. He spins me around and then presses himself to me. We sway to the music, and I sink into him, and he kisses my neck, then my lips, his tongue sliding into my mouth, my rum mixing with his beer, the lights and music pounding in the background. Between kisses, he tells me his name is Ben, and he works as a tow truck driver. I don't care. With no commitment, I want to feel his hands on me, with the music and lights and his lips distracting me for a while.

Finally, Jayla grabs my arm and yanks me away from Ben and off the dance floor.

"Come on, dancing queen—time to leave the ball. Want to get some pizza?" she asks.

My stomach growls. "Can we go downtown to Malnati's?" I give a quick goodbye to Ben, whose name I'll probably forget in the morning. A taxi ride downtown delivers Jayla and me to our favorite pizza joint.

A half-hour later, a medium "Lou" with its signature spicy spinach, Roma tomatoes, and three different kinds of cheese is delivered to our table, and I dig in.

"Mmm, butter crust; this was a great idea." Cheese drips from the slice as I lift it gingerly to my mouth.

"Maybe you can avoid a hangover tomorrow." She winks at me. "Ouch! Did you just kick me?"

"Yes, and you deserved it," I say.

6

Maybe I Should Get a Cat

Wednesday, January 5

Grabbing a cup of coffee, I head back to my desk. There's no time to run out today, so it is a granola bar and coffee. At least it is quiet. Simon is on vacation and insists on sending me stock photos of him lying on the beach, drinking, and generally living his best life.

My phone buzzes. It's Jayla. "How are you feeling today?"

"Fine. The pizza helped," I say.

"Ha! Pizza is always the fix," Jayla says. "So, did you decide what you are going to do?"

"Besides eating my granola bar for lunch?"

"Okay. First, that isn't healthy. And second, don't be a smart ass."

"I don't have any idea what you are talking about."

"So you are not going to meet him? Or are you going to meet him and not tell anyone?"

"I don't know."

"I think you are stupid if you don't meet the fun guy who is guaranteed to love you. Just saying."

"Yeah, yeah." I decide to change the subject. "You still want me to stop and pick up stuff for dinner?"

"Yes, please."

"Okay, I'll see you later."

Looking around behind me to make sure I am alone, I log onto the Cupid website.

"Welcome back, Callie." I shift uncomfortably under his gaze. "I have missed you. Alas, you are meant for another," he smiles seductively, "Let's not keep him waiting, eh, love?"

"Hey, Callie."

Shoot. I slap my laptop shut and spin my chair around. "Hey, Felicia." Felicia was one of the administrative assistants and self-appointed enforcer of rules. She looks different, I think. New highlights, a vacation tan, and, wait, is that a nose piercing? I try to meet her eyes but get drawn back to the tiny gemstone twinkling in the fluorescent light.

"Do you have your supply request forms done yet?" She peers over my shoulder with one arm on my cube wall. I am still staring at her nose.

I drag my eyes to hers, "Yes, they should be in your email."

"Oh, good, I am just returning from vacation and have a thousand emails to sift through." She rolls her eyes, then fans her face with the file folder she is carrying and waits. Does she want me to ask about her post-divorce vacation? There is no way I want those details.

"Um, I can resend it for you if that helps," I say, trying to get her out of my cube.

"That would be great." Her shoulders relax, and she smooths her hair.

"Of course." I put on my best professional smile.

"Thanks a bunch, Callie. You're the best. So how are things with Tom?"

And there it is. "I don't know." I start to turn in my chair, looking busy.

She frowns. "Are you two not together anymore?"

"Nope." I don't want to talk about it, especially with her.

She audibly sighs, "Well, that's a shame. You looked so cute together."

I don't respond. Instead, I shuffle random papers on my desk.

She stands there awkwardly for a moment. Rocking back on her heels, she says, "Okay, better get to those emails. Thanks again, Callie."

Whew. I'm pretty sure she didn't see what I was doing. I don't want anyone else to know about this ridiculous situation I have signed myself up for. And if she, the office gossip, knows, everyone will.

I spend the rest of the day proofreading promotional materials for the Chamber of Commerce. Not my favorite activity, but at least the afternoon goes by quickly.

* * *

Damn, I think, stepping off the elevator and hearing the rain pattering against the windows. I forgot my umbrella, so I have to flip my hood up and keep my head down against the freezing rain. I duck for cover under overhangs as I make my way home. My phone buzzes in my pocket; it's my mom. I stop under an awning in front of a bank and slide my phone inside my hood.

"Hey, honey, it's Mom; how's it going?"

"Walking home from work, and it's freezing rain."

"I hate it when you walk home from work; it's dangerous in the city."

"Trust me; no criminals want to be out in this. Besides, it's not dangerous. I live in a safe area, and it's light outside."

"Well, I hope you're at least carrying the mace I sent you."

"Of course, Mom." I fight the urge to roll my eyes.

"Have you heard from your father recently?" I hate it when she asks about Dad. It's weird, and I don't want to talk about him.

"Yeah, last week," I lie, "he seems to be doing fine." My dad hasn't called me in three months. He is too busy with his mid-life crisis to bother with his kids. But if I tell my mom that, it will send her off on a rant I don't feel like hearing again.

"Have you been busy with Tom?"

The wind whips at my legs. "Mom, Tom and I broke up."

"Oh."

I can feel her disappointment through the phone—no impending marriage or grandchildren just around the corner. "Yeah, Mom. It just didn't work out." I know I sound harsh, but I don't feel like rehashing the breakup.

"Oh, honey. I had so much hope for him, and you don't need to use that petulant tone with me."

"Mom, please, stop. My relationship status does not define me."

"Don't get snappy." She pauses as if to reconsider her words. "Anyway, how's work going? How's that new project?"

I have to fight to keep my teeth from chattering, but at least she is asking me about something interesting. "Work is good. There's a new architecture firm downtown, and I'm the head designer for their new ad campaign; I'm pretty excited."

"Oh, does that mean you're getting a promotion?"

"Not right now, but being a lead designer is the first step." I turn towards the building to shield my face.

"Congratulations, honey. I'm so proud of you. I tell all my friends about my daughter with the fancy job in advertising, who lives in a fancy apartment in Chicago and works at a big, fancy building."

"Yeah, Mom, if you come to visit this summer, you'll realize that my apartment is not fancy. Charmingly cramped and timelessly stuffy might be a better description." I need to change the subject.

"So, have you been dating anyone new, Mom?" I put my head down and jog down to the next awning in front of a liquor store, pressing myself against the wall to get out of the wind and rain.

"No, honey. After that disastrous experience with Kent, I think I'm off men for good."

"Is there something you're trying to tell me, Mom?" My teeth are definitely chattering now.

"What do you mean?" she asks innocently.

I swallow a laugh. "Never mind. You need to get out of Indiana more often. Come to Chicago. You could find a place, eat pizza, and hang out with me."

"Oh, Callie, what would I do in Chicago? Follow you around? No, I have friends and a routine here, and I don't feel the need to have new adventures."

"Well, I think that's a mistake, Mom. You're not that old, and everybody should have new adventures."

"I'm old enough to be a grandma."

"I know," I relent. "Don't worry. I'll find somebody before I'm too old to give you grandchildren."

"Can I get that in writing?"

"Bye, Mom, love you!" I tap the phone to hang up before she can say anything else.

A guy brushes past me, exiting the store with a paper bag tucked under his arm. "Hey, baby. It looks like you could use a hot body, I mean, hot toddy to warm you up."

I shake my head, flip-up my middle finger, and then step into the rain. Maybe I should just get a cat.

7

What Could Go Wrong?

Thursday, January 6

The cheery clerk is behind the register again. Pulling the door to the shop closed behind me, I say, "Hi, I was in here the other day to pick up a book. I've already finished it. Now, I need something else to read."

"Oh, I would love to help. What are you in the mood for, Romance? Thriller? Fantasy?" Her eyes light up as she skirts out from behind the counter.

I bite my lower lip, "How about something that has nothing to do with love? Maybe something with ghosts or fantasy?"

"My kind of reader," she nods approvingly. "I've got a great idea for you." She leads me to the stacks and plucks out a book I don't recognize.

She holds it up with both hands to give me a clear view of the cover. It is beautifully drawn with dragons and swords. "This book is super fun, and I think it'll be perfect for you."

I take the book from her and read the inside cover. "It looks interesting," I agree. "Do you have anything else that you recommend?"

"Actually, I do. There is a fantastic local author," she taps her cheekbone as if accessing memory banks. "I just finished his second book about the history of ghosts in Chicago. It is quite a page-turner."

I wrinkle my nose, "Is it bad?"

"Not at all. He does a ton of research and weaves in historical facts. I loved it."

"All right, let me take a look." I'm not really interested in ghost stories, but I also have difficulty saying no to people. She leads me back up to the front of the store to a little display of paperbacks and hands me one; on the cover is the Chicago skyline with a gloomy fog layered on top. *Death in an Ally: The James M. Nederlander Theatre.* Hmm, Interesting. I have walked by the theater a dozen times and even been there with Simon to see a play.

"Who did you say the author is again?"

"Oh, Gabriel Perez. He's a teacher at a local college and writes books in his spare time."

He's cute. Maybe I should read the book and then we can meet over coffee to discuss it. Then perhaps he can take me on a ghost tour, and we can fall in love. "Okay, I'll take this one, too."

* * *

"Uh-oh," I walk out of the kitchen, holding an empty bottle and stifling a laugh, "We drank all the red wine."

"Oh, no," Jayla giggles, "Whatever are we going to do?"

"Good news," I exclaim, presenting the bottle of white wine to her as a trophy.

Jayla claps her hands like a child. "Yippee."

"Remember, no stupid boy talk tonight." I fill her glass with the wine. It mixes with a bit of leftover red, turning the entire glass pink.

"Okay," she says, nodding with complete seriousness.

"Unless you want to talk about your love life," I say, sitting on the floor cross-legged and planting the bottle on the coffee table next to the open bag of chips.

Jayla shakes her head, "Oh, no, no way."

"Come on; you can't just be my wingman forever. You need to get back out there," I say, dragging a chip out of the bag.

"We can only handle one love life at a time." She laughs. "And right now, it's yours."

"Oh," I give her my best puppy dog eyes. "You're the best friend a girl could ever have."

She laughs again and heads for the kitchen. "We should make nachos."

"How can you eat like that and not gain weight?"

She shrugs. "I inherited a good metabolism, I guess."

"Yeah, that is so not fair. If I even *think* about nachos, I gain weight."

"Oh, stop, you're adorable," she says, opening the refrigerator. "One more thing, friend of mine, you deserve love."

"So you say. When are you going to get back out there? Your perfect guy is probably waiting right here in Chicago. And I am hopeless. If I can't even keep boring Tom on the line, I am packing up my fishing pole and going home. But you haven't even tried."

She pauses and drops her chin, "Okay, fine, I did meet this cute guy at work yesterday."

"Really?" I lean forward so I don't miss any details.

"Yes. He was so cute. Big brown eyes, lashes for days. He was wearing this great trendy blue outfit. He even brought his mom to shop. So sweet." She gestures excitedly.

"Did you get his number?"

Jayla flashes a Cheshire cat grin. "I tried, but when I leaned over his stroller, his mom told me to get away from her baby boy, so I don't think it will work out." She shrugs.

I groan. "All right, I've had enough wine," I say, standing up and grabbing the book out of the bag on the kitchen table. "Time for me to get to know Gabriel Perez." I flash the book at her and head to my room.

Tomorrow is going to be painful.

* * *

Fortunately, Fridays are typically slow at work, so after spending the morning recovering from a minor hangover, I settle into a chair in the office break room and begin to read the ghost hunting book. After a few pages, I turn it over and look at the author's photo on the back. He is cute. Why couldn't I have been matched with him? I bet he has a fantastic library; most writers do. I need to marry this kind of guy, not some bodybuilder. Gabriel Perez...Callie Perez.

Get it together; I scold myself. You are supposed to be matched with Jimmy Powell. So why am I so drawn to this stranger on the back of a book?

I finish the first two chapters of the book. I love his writing style. Maybe he had a *ghost*writer. I chuckle out loud at my pun. I'm such a dork. I set down the book and turn to my computer, typing his name into the search bar. I hit enter and wait.

A list of results comes up. The first is a story from fifteen years ago; House *Fire Kills One, Injures Two*. I click on the link, and there is a picture of Gabriel, much younger, but it's him. He holds a plaque and stands with a man in a suit and the fire chief. I skim the article. Gabriel's house caught fire, and his younger brother Xavier, thirteen years old, was killed. Gabriel and his dad were injured trying to get everyone out.

"Gabriel Perez was honored by the City of Chicago as a hero for his efforts to get his sisters out of the house."

Gabriel looked to be about fifteen or sixteen years old in the photo. I try to imagine losing my only sister, or Jayla, and sadness washes over me.

How horrible. It doesn't say anything about Gabriel's injuries, but I can see he has bandages on his shoulder and arm sticking out from underneath his shirt. His lips are pressed into a tight smile that doesn't reach his eyes.

I close the browser and slide the book into my bag. Standing, I stretch my back and peek over to see what Simon is doing. He is on the phone with someone. I shake out my hands and head to the vending machine. A coke and chocolate bar will help get me through the rest of the day. Jimmy would be appalled. I giggle as I flatten my dollar bills and slide them into the machine.

8

Ikea on a Saturday

Saturday, January 8

"What in the world was that?" Jayla appears with folded arms and raised eyebrows. Green face cream covers her rich mahogany skin, and her lilac silk robe is wrapped around her. She smells like a mint julep.

"That stupid book." I flick my chin at the book lying injured in the corner by the closet.

"Which book are you trying to kill now? You own every book in Chicago," she says, pointing to the color-coded bookshelves lining one wall of my bedroom.

"The one about the tidying up; it's a bunch of BS." I am sitting cross-legged in the middle of the only clear spot on the floor, sorting through twenty-three pairs of jeans. "Bestseller, my ass."

"At least your empty closet is tidy." She smirks. "Maybe you should lie down and make snow angels." She motions to the piles of clothing scattered all around.

I pick up a pair of pink lacy underwear and slingshot them at her.

"Hey, eww." She turns away, shielding herself.

"Oh, stop. They're clean, I think." I sigh and flop back on the pile of jeans. "I need to get my life in order, and I'm supposed to figure out what brings me joy. How do I know?"

"Obviously, you were embracing getting rid of stuff," she says, waving her hand at the clothing and shoes. "So what happened?"

"The author of that stupid book said to sort through your clothing, kitchen, and bathroom. And apparently, she thinks I should throw out most of my books." I point to the wall of bookshelves, overflowing but organized. "Now I am just overwhelmed."

Jayla sucks in a breath. "Oh, that would be a deal-breaker."

"Yup. My books are the only part of my life that is in order. Oh, but I am getting rid of one book, though." I crawl across the clothing and retrieve the softcover book. "Hers. You want it?"

Her throaty laughter fills the room. "Heck, no. I don't need that kind of negativity in my life." She pats the door frame. "At least you have all day to wade through this mess."

"Don't you want to help?" I call out. "It'll be fun."

"Nope," she replies from the other room. "Stop complaining and start cleaning."

"Those who do not complain are never pitied," I say loud enough for her to hear.

"And stop quoting Jane Austen," she calls back, laughing.

* * *

Two hours later, I have shoved most of my clothes back into the closet and headed towards the living room. Being tidy is overrated. I have other plans. "Let's go to IKEA."

Jayla looks up from folding clothes on the coffee table. "IKEA? On a Saturday? No way."

"Come on, there's meatballs and throw pillows." I wiggle my eyebrows and smack my lips.

"I'm not hungry, and we don't need another throw pillow."

"There is Swedish furniture you can put together without any other tools besides a little wrench thing that it comes with."

"Oh, well, that convinces me," she says, frowning at me.

"Come on; it'll be fun."

"What do you need to buy there?"

"Maybe a new duvet cover and a pillow and...." I lower my voice, "a new bookshelf."

"Where are you going to put a new bookshelf?" She motions around the living room.

I dramatically prance around the room. "I declare, after all, there is no enjoyment like reading! How much sooner one tires of anything than of a book! When I have a house of my own, I shall be miserable if I have not an excellent library."

"Let me guess, *Pride and Prejudice?*"

"Of course." I walk over to the TV stand and point. "If we move this, there's more than enough room.

She sighs, "You need an intervention."

"It could be worse."

"I don't know what's worse than you dragging my ass to an IKEA on a Saturday."

"It's important to me that all my bookcases match. And I got the rest of them at IKEA. I've already checked online, and they have some in stock, so we need to go."

"Fine, can I take a shower first?"

"Yes. But I want to leave in an hour."

* * *

This may have been a bad idea.

"Everyone in Chicago is here today," Jayla hisses as we look for a

46

cart.

I smile widely. "That's what makes it so much fun."

She rolls her eyes and grabs a random cart parked at the end of an aisle.

We follow the arrows on the floor and stop to look at random displays of pillow covers, plastic cups, and office chairs.

Sure, it's crowded, but that's just part of the experience, and at least everyone is moving in the same general direction.

"What do you think this does?" I hold up a white plastic contraption. Jayla looks perplexed, and I drop it back in the bin.

I tug her down next to me on the slip-covered couch. "I think we should buy a new couch."

"No way, I love our velvet couch."

"But it's so tacky."

"What?" Jayla looks sincerely offended. "That couch has been in my family for thirty years."

"Exactly. It might be time for a new one."

"You don't appreciate vintage. That couch has *history*."

"I don't think I want to know the 'history' of that couch," I say, wrinkling my nose.

"Come on." Jayla tugs me to my feet.

"What do you think of this table?" she asks and then stands back next to me, looking at the display.

"Excuse me." A woman with a stroller pushes between the two of us. As I step backward to avoid getting run over, I realize too late, someone is behind me. My feet hit theirs, and I fall, taking the poor stranger down with me.

I lay there for a second to make sure nothing is broken. Then, I roll over and scramble to my feet. The contents of my purse are scattered across the aisle, and shoppers have paused in their frenzy to view the carnage.

Jayla reaches to help me up. "Are you okay?"

"I'm okay," I say and turn to whomever it is I assaulted. "I am so sorry."

I know those golden-brown eyes. It's the guy from the ghost books. He has an easy smile, dark wavy hair that hangs to his ear lobes, soft brown skin, and a quirky half-smile with a hint of mischief. Oh, no. My face flushes with heat. He's staring at me as he jumps to his feet and brushes the dust off his pants.

"Hi," he says in a husky voice.

"Hi." My voice sounds raspy; I need a drink of water. I try to smooth out my shirt and my hair.

"Hi," he says again, combing his hair out of his face and smiling.

My cheeks are on fire, and I can't help but grin back. My heart flutters as his smile widens. His shoulders are broad, and he is at least six inches taller than me. I feel breathless and dorky. I suddenly realize I've been staring at him and drop my eyes, realizing I need to gather my spilled things.

"Nice to meet you," he says, kneeling to help me.

"I-I'm so sorry for knocking you down."

"It's okay," he says in a deep, smooth voice as we stand up and look at each other, awkwardly, "This happens every time I come to IKEA," he looks around, "but usually my attacker isn't so pretty."

He laughs softly as I blush again and blurt out, "Well, everyone knows IKEA is dangerous. I would judge you for coming to IKEA on a Saturday, but I made the same mistake." *Oh, my God, I sound like a dork.*

"Yeah, well, most of Chicago is here, so we aren't alone. I'm Gabriel Perez."

"Callie Mcguire and this is my best friend and roommate, Jayla Johnson."

"Nice to meet you both."

"We were just heading over to the cafeteria." Jayla smiles at me. "Since Callie tried to kill you, at least let us buy you lunch."

9

Lunch

"So, what do you do for a living?" Jayla asks Gabriel over the din of the busy cafeteria. I'm twisting my napkin on my lap, wondering if my hair is sticking up and gauging whether my breath is fresh.

"I am a History professor at Northwestern. What about you, Jayla?"

"Oh, I am a manager at a small boutique uptown. And Callie here is in marketing."

"Oh, really?" he says, looking at me.

"Yeah, but it's not anything special," I say, taking a drink of my Coke.

"She's modest," Jayla says, pointing her fork at me. "You've probably seen some of her campaigns."

Some part of me realizes I need to join the conversation. "Anyway," I clear my throat, "what made you want to be a professor?"

"Well, I love history and have always been a nerd."

"Nerds in my high school did not look like you," Jayla says, shaking her head and cutting a meatball in half with her fork.

Gabriel looks at me. "Well, I have certainly earned the label. And girls didn't find me all that attractive with my nose stuck in a book." Rubbing his hands on his jeans, he continues, "And try telling a date you write books on ghosts. It's a great pick-up line."

"Ghost hunting?" I try to hang an innocent look on my face.

"Yeah. I know it seems weird, but I promise, it isn't."

"No, I think it's interesting," I respond, smiling.

"So are we talking *Casper the Friendly Ghost* or *The Ring?*" Jayla asks.

"Well, it's more about the city's history with a few ghosts mixed in." He picks up a fry, dips it in ketchup, and pops it into his mouth.

I try not to stare while he chews. He has nice teeth and long lashes. And his love of books. Maybe we *are* a match made in heaven.

Jayla is just sitting there with a stupid grin on her face.

"Knock it off!" I mouth to her as Gabriel looks down for a moment. She shakes her head and smiles wider.

"Callie, didn't you just tell me you wanted to go on a ghost tour?"

I am going to kill her later.

He smiles at me, waiting for me to respond. I want to run away, but I can't make my feet move. My heart beats in my throat as he says, "As much as I enjoyed bumping into you here at IKEA, I would like to take you out to dinner."

"Okay." The word pops out of my mouth before I can stop it.

"Why don't I pick you up tonight, at seven?"

Tonight? I feel like every light in the store has been turned to focus on me. My face is hot, and my plastic, hard chair is suddenly very uncomfortable.

He folds and unfolds his hands on the table, watching my reaction. "Let's go on a date, and if it's terrible, we'll call it off."

He's awfully forward. I search his face for signs of sarcasm or joking, but sincerity is all that is reflected in the soft brown eyes with gold flecks. I gather my wits and manage to say, "Sure, that sounds nice," with a pleasant but tepid smile.

"Great!" He breaks into another big smile, and I can't help but return it. This is crazy. What's wrong with me?

Jayla has already written my phone number down on the back of a flyer, and then she slides it across the table to Gabriel.

He scans the paper then carefully folds it into his front pocket. "All right, Callie Mcguire, I will text you later and finalize plans." I might throw up. He dumps his trash into the receptacle and slides the tray on the stack, and then he's gone.

I sink back into the hard plastic, "Oh, my gosh."

"He's hot!" Jayla says, smacking my arm.

"This is insane."

"What's insane is that we're sitting in IKEA when you need something to wear tonight." She grabs the tray, scoops their lunch debris, and heads for the trashcan. "We're going shopping to buy you something gorgeous."

* * *

Standing in the middle of a chic boutique, I groan under the weight of Jayla's choices. "I can't possibly hold one more thing," I say as Jayla throws one more thing into my arms.

"I don't want to come back out here, so we're going to get everything in one trip. It's called efficiency."

"And you're called crazy."

"True, I have been called crazy. I wear it as a badge of honor," she says with her chin in the air. "It's time for you to stop wearing gray and black just because I told you once that it made your eyes stand out."

"Hey! That's not very nice. It does make my eyes stand out."

She rolled her eyes. "They would stand out no matter what you were wearing. And that's what makeup is for."

"You know I'm a makeup minimalist."

She smirks. "I know you made up that term to make yourself feel better for not taking time to apply makeup." She brushes past toward the dressing room. "I think that's enough for now. Let's go make some magic."

Jayla gasps as I model the royal blue dress she's picked out. It has three-quarter length sleeves that brush just below my elbow. The neckline plunges to a deep V. If my boobs were any bigger, it would be inappropriate. A little black belt cinches my waist.

"It's perfect!" She cries, rushing to brush a bit of lint off the arm and smooth down the back. She then turns me around and stands behind me, glowing with approval. "You look fabulous."

I do look good. "But it's so showy," I complain, adjusting the belt.

"It's blue. It's not like I'm asking you to wear bright pink, yellow, or orange. Blue is basically black."

I pinch my lips together.

"Oh, no, don't you get an attitude with me, Callie! You're going to have fun with a nice, hot man tonight, and I'm going to make sure you look good doing it." Jayla arches her back, crosses her arms, and wags an index finger at me.

I laugh; there's nothing to be done once she wields the finger wag.

I turn around, and she gathers my hair up on top of my head, experimenting with different hairstyles. "Someday, you're going to tell your grandchildren about how you met, and this dress will be part of the story."

"Ha, you think I will remember this dress fifty years from now?"

She leans close to my ear, "I think you're going to remember how he looks at you in this dress fifty years from now."

"I know I'll remember how my best friend pushed me around." I smile and hug her tightly.

10

Date Night

"Watch it." Jayla ducks as a shoe soars over her head. "Why are you throwing things?"

"I can't find my good shoes." My nerves are humming as I look for heels that don't give me blisters.

She looks at her Apple watch, "You are cutting it close, girl; it's almost seven."

"Don't remind me," I call after her as she heads back down the hall. I hop on one shoe, trying to wrench my foot into the other one. "I'll be ready in a minute. I need to find my earrings."

"He's here," Jayla yells from the living room.

I grab my silver hoops off the dresser and fumble with them as I walk. Jayla is standing near the closed door, smiling like a Cheshire cat. I shush her. "Please, don't be weird."

I head to the closet to grab my coat. She laughs and opens the door with a dramatic curtsy. She lays it on thick with an English accent, "Welcome to our humble abode, Your Grace."

He bows deeply with an impressive English accent of his own, "Why, thank you. Is Lady Callie receiving callers this evening?"

I'm standing awkwardly, halfway in the hall closet with one arm stuck in my coat sleeve while struggling to untangle my hair caught in the hook and eye closure at the neck. I consider simply yanking my hair out when it suddenly comes loose, and my arm slides into the sleeve. I turn to face him with as much dignity as I can muster.

His smile makes my heart skip. "There she is. My lady." Another deep bow.

"Howdy, partner!" I wave my hand like Woody in *Toy Story*. Oh, no, no, no. Please, just mercy kill me now, Jayla. Out of the corner of my eye, I can see her trying to hold back laughter, a hand pressed over her mouth, her eyes merry.

Gabriel is staring at me, and I need to say something else. I gawp like an idiot.

Then, his eyes crinkle at the corners, "Alrighty, then. Giddyup, girl, time to go rustle up some grub." He loops his arm through mine and leads me out of the apartment and down to the curb. We laugh all the way down.

"Your building is nice," he says, opening the ornate antique oak door and waiting for me to pass through.

"Thanks. There are eight apartments; it used to be a single-family home. I could never afford the rent, but Jayla's boss owns the building and manages it. The discounted rent is part of her compensation."

"That's lucky for both Jayla and you."

"I know. Jayla is the reason I am still in Chicago. So where are we going?" I ask as he stands on the curb and looks for a cab to hail.

"Well, I was looking at this little Italian place; it's right down the street."

My chest tightens. I keep my face blank.

"But then," Gabriel drawls, "I remembered I tend to roll meatballs down my shirt when I'm wearing white, so I made us a reservation at a Thai place a little further out. Does that sound good?" His smile is easy, and I relax.

"Oh, that sounds great." Thank God. I did not want to revisit the scene of the breakup.

"Good," he says, and we share a smile as he helps me into the taxi and gives the driver the address.

I clear my throat, "So that's near Grant Park?"

He raises his eyebrows in surprise, "Yes, Dao Thai, have you been there?"

"No, but I've wanted to; it's got great reviews on Yelp." A sudden feeling of easiness settles over me, and I relax. We chat about chicken satay and pad thai and whether or not we'll have extra fish sauce.

* * *

The window next to our table overlooks the patio, empty except for snow piled in the corners. The legs on the tables and chairs are cut short, so I tuck my legs to one side as demurely as possible—the horns and shouts of the street mix with the clatter and hum of a busy kitchen.

Two hours later, it feels like we've sampled half the menu. "I don't know why I've never eaten here before. It's great," I say, stuffing Mango Sticky Rice into my mouth. "So, how did you discover this place?"

"I stumbled on it when I was researching my second book."

"Really?" I lean in to whisper, "Is it haunted?"

He leans close and whispers with a grin, "I could tell you, but then I'd have to kill you."

"Oh great, then my mom will be proven right. She is convinced I'm going to be killed by some big city psycho."

"Really?"

"Yes. Every conversation we have is about that or my love life. She is relentless."

"I get it. My mom is always on me about getting married."

"What is with these moms?" I say, shaking my head.

56

"It's a good thing you plowed me over in IKEA. Now we can both report back to our mothers that we are making an effort. Maybe it's fate."

"First, I didn't plow you over. I was avoiding being killed by that deranged mother with the stroller," I blurt out. "Second, I don't believe in fate. But I'm glad to have met you."

"Me too," he smiles, tapping his fingers on the table. "Why don't we get out of here."

11

Walk in the Park

After dinner, we stroll south along the river in Grant Park, hand-in-hand, and I pause to admire the architecture of the Art Institute to my right. "It's beautiful, isn't it?"

"Yes," he says, looking straight at me.

I smile with pleasure but decide to turn the conversation to him. "What are your favorite books to read?"

"Lately? Fantasy, historical fiction, and the occasional biography."

"All my favorites," I chuckle.

"Really?"

"Really. I love to read. Oh, and true crime stories. I love true crime."

"My, you do have a dark side." He wiggles his eyebrows for emphasis.

I push a wisp of hair behind my ear, turn my head slightly, and in a low voice, reveal, "Everyone has a dark side, Mr. Perez."

"Indeed. Except me. I'm a Care Bear; got it from my mom and pop." He looks a little embarrassed, "I'm from one of those big, multi-generational Mexican families where everyone hugs, like a lot. Growing up, we didn't always have much money, but there was always plenty of loud, obnoxious love." He laughs. "So what about your family, Callie?"

I shrug and fumble with the hook and eye closure at the collar of my coat as a chill runs through me. "Nothing like yours. The last time I heard, my dad had a new apartment in Florida; and my mom never left the house I grew up in. It was just me and my big sister, Shannon, and my parents divorced when I was in college. They never understood why I wanted to come to Chicago and get out of our small town. It's like I was rejecting them by pursuing my dreams."

"I'm sorry, Callie. I can't imagine not having a close family."

"It's not that bad. At least I have Jayla. I met her the first day I arrived in Chicago. I needed new clothes for my marketing job, and I stumbled on a little boutique with things I couldn't possibly afford. Jayla let me use her employee discount, and we just hit it off immediately. Now she is stuck with me." I look at him, and he seems to be waiting for something more.

Gabriel stops and takes my hand. "I don't know what I would do without my family." He looks thoughtful. "You know, my father was an orphan at five, and he never knew what family life could be like until he met my mother. He always says, 'You must build the future to replace the past.'" A shadow crosses his face as his smile fades, and he gazes toward the water briefly.

I want to ask him what caused him to get that faraway look when he talked about his father's words, but I don't.

We walk in congenial silence until he says, "My mother is pretty sick. She had breast cancer when I was in high school. She was in treatment for three years, and last year, we found out that cancer had come back, this time in her lungs and her pancreas. She's been fighting it, but...."

I squeeze his hand. "I'm so sorry; I can't imagine what your family has gone through and is going through now."

He nods and turns to me. "Yeah, it's hard. But we have learned to have faith that things will eventually work out the way they are supposed to."

"Your family sounds amazing," I say, looking around. Shadows keep catching my attention out of the corner of my eye.

He leads me forward to a coffee cart. The steaming coffee and warm cup are just what I need to settle my nerves.

We continue to stroll, chatting comfortably about his family, my job, and my favorite topic, books. Whenever he asks me about my family, I steer the conversation back to him. He may find it easy to be open, but there are some things I don't share.

Later, as we approach my apartment, my heart beats faster at every step. Will he kiss me? Should I invite him inside for a drink? I tell myself I don't want to sleep with him on the first date. It never works out. I don't want this to be a casual hookup. *I hope he kisses me. I hope he kisses me. I hope...*I bite my lip to keep from saying it out loud. We stand on the stoop, and the key is in my hand.

"Come here," he says in a low sexy voice. With one arm around my waist and the other about my shoulders, he gently draws me to him, our chests and hips pressed together. I can feel his heart beating. "Is this okay?"

"Yes," I reply breathlessly.

He kisses me without hesitation and with intensity and passion that I always hoped existed but had never experienced. I knew those lips were going to be good for kissing. I wrap my arms around him, feeling his strong shoulder muscles flex beneath my fingers, and kiss him back.

He pulls away and gently runs his hands through my hair, then traces the side of my face as his breathing slows. "Goodnight, Callie." He kisses my forehead, each cheek, the tip of my nose, and finally my lips in a final soft kiss.

"Good night," I whisper, my knees weak.

I wobble into Jayla's room, waking her up by flipping the ceiling light on abruptly. Her hair is sticking up, and she's rubbing her eyes.

Peeking through her hands, she grins. "Girl, you look like you have been kissed by someone who knows what he's doing."

"I don't know what you are talking about," I giggle, pushing hair out of my face.

"Yeah, right. So it went well?"

"It did." I can't help it. I want to be cool about it. Instead, I spin around with a smile that I can't stop.

12

Impromptu Book Signing

Sunday, January 9

A canopy of trees blots out the sun, except for the occasional ray that sneaks through the leaves to dapple the mossy ground—another *perfect date.* Gabriel lays facing me, kissing my cheeks, nose, and lips. A plaid blanket is our bed, and a picnic basket our pantry.

"Callie," his soft voice purrs, "you are the most beautiful girl I have ever met." He brushes my hair aside and kisses me on the neck. I feel his whole body pressing down on me as a fluttering in my belly warms and expands. I tug at his collar and fumble with his shirt's buttons, but I can't get any clothing off. The world slips in and out of focus, my breath in shallow gasps between kisses. Is this how it feels to be truly, Mr. Darcy, happy? It must be.

We are no longer alone. I see the trim figure of the handsome man from MyLove4Life.com sitting in a chair that has magically appeared next to us in between kisses. His face is twisted in anger. He opens his mouth and screams.

* * *

My phone rings, startling me out of sleep.

"Good morning. Wait.., too soon?"

Smiling as fragments of my dream float away with the morning sun, I roll over and snuggle down into my pillow to reply. "Good morning to you."

"Last night was pretty great."

"It was."

"Can I see you today?"

Warmth spreads through my stomach as I remember his lips on mine. "Okay." I try to hold back a smile.

"Great! Will pick you up in an hour."

"Wait, what?"

"Too soon?"

"No, just not exactly up yet."

"Oh, okay."

"But don't worry." Standing up, I grab my robe and head for the bathroom, "I'll be ready."

"Okay, see you soon."

I'm showered, dressed, and ready to go before he arrives. Jayla is fast asleep, but I sneak past her to borrow a sapphire scarf and drape it about my neck.

I read on the couch until a light knock on the door pulls me out of my book. I slip the bookmark into the text and set it on the coffee table. When I open the door, Gabriel is looking perfect in a black argyle sweater. I immediately pull him in for a kiss.

Gabriel tips his head back, breaking the lip lock first, but keeps his hands on my waist. "I thought we could go to brunch and tour one of my favorite haunted spots; The James M. Nederlander Theatre," he smiles, "they have backstage tours on Sundays. I made reservations for noon."

"Behind the scenes?" My hands rest on his shoulders.

"Yes, it is a cool experience. Does that sound okay?" His fingers flex a little, sending a shiver up my spine.

"Yes, it sounds amazing. Can we also hit the bookshop?" I lace my fingers behind his neck, and his mouth hovers over mine.

"Of course. Let's wing it after that."

"Y'all better get a room or get a move on." Jayla leans against the kitchen countertop, steaming coffee mug hiding her grin. "Nice scarf, Callie."

* * *

Light flakes continue to fall on the snow-covered ground as we leave the building. The city is muted, softly twinkling. We take the train downtown, avoiding the headache of parking.

After a quick brunch, we stroll the three blocks up to the theater. The magical white blanket has been reduced to a gray slop by traffic by the time we arrive, but it doesn't matter.

Gabriel takes my hand, and we cross the street to the theater. We laugh as we dodge a car, jumping to the curb together. Inside the theater, he helps me take my coat off and hangs it up for me. Then he pays for our tickets for the noon tour.

Gabriel and I hang out at the back of the tour group. He whispers details about the theater that the guide either doesn't know or doesn't bother to share. His warm breath on my neck is distracting. He smells like mint and pine.

The rest of the day is easy. I take him to my favorite bookshop and show him his book on display. "Look, it's your book on display." My favorite clerk looks up from a stack of books and looks to me and then Gabriel.

"Shhhhh!" he puts his finger to my lips.

She strides over, grabs a copy of the book and flips it over, comparing the photo to his face, "Are you Gabriel Perez? Maybe you could sign a couple of books right now since you're already here?" She smiles at him and bounces on the balls of her feet.

"You're in big trouble," he whispers, brushing his lips against my ear. I look innocently at him and back away as shoppers gather around, peppering him with questions. The clerk quickly sets up a little table and chair for him to use, and suddenly we have an impromptu book signing. I stand off to the side, taking photos when asked. When the crowd thins, I rescue him and promise ice cream for all his hard work. He is an unbelievably good sport about it all.

My phone buzzes and I pull it out to check my text messages.

Please complete your online registration now to avoid delay in meeting your match, Jimmy Powell.

I chuckle and slide it back into my pocket.

"What's so funny?" Gabriel says as he helps me on with my coat.

"Before I met you, I was on a dating website and matched with this bodybuilder guy. He was totally not my type. Anyway, I never finalized the match because I met you." I reach up and kiss him on the cheek. "They keep sending me stupid text messages about it."

I make a mental note to block the number.

13

Good Grief

Monday, January 10

The small cafe is packed, and the bell above the door tracks the constant flow of pick-up orders and lunch patrons. "Why do you look so happy?" Simon asks, digging through his salad for a piece of chicken. He is on another diet and isn't happy about it. Apparently, he overindulged last week.

"I don't know what you are talking about." I roll my eyes as I pick up a fry and shove it into my mouth. "It's not like *I've* been on a tropical vacation or anything." Simon is shockingly tan and wearing a pale yellow shirt that makes him look like a tropical bird far from home.

"Yeah, well, even on my vacation, I didn't look that happy." He pauses and stares into the distance, "except for that one night...."

"I'm eating," I say, rolling my eyes while picking at the remnants of a club sandwich, "I don't want to hear about your love life."

"Who said anything about love?" he smiles coyly.

"Well, maybe I am just happy about life," I say, taking a bite of the sandwich.

"No way. You are wearing a new top, and it's pink. Where did that come from?"

The harried waiter arrives with our bills, and we hand her our credit cards.

"I borrowed it from Jayla. She gets a great discount at the boutique where she works."

"I like it. Much better than the drab gray you wear all the time." Simon wags his finger at me. "Don't say it. Girl, your eyes are the color of the Caribbean ocean; any color will make them look good."

I feel the heat rise in my cheeks. "Thank you." I fold my napkin over my plate and push it away to keep from eating the stray burn fries that are definitely not worth the carbs.

"I just call it as I see it," he says, pointing his fork at me. "But seriously, did you meet someone?"

I duck my head to hide my smile.

"I knew it." Simon smacks the table. "I can almost smell the sexual tension on you."

"Eww!" I throw my hands up and look around to make sure no one heard him.

He is ambivalent. "I know. But there it is."

I fold my arms on the table and lean in, "What about you? Any love interests?"

"Have you seen a fat baby with wings flying around me? Shooting me with an arrow?" He flaps his arms then drops them to his sides. "I'm starting to believe there is no one worthy of my love in the entire city of Chicago."

"The entire city?" I say, raising my eyebrows.

"Apparently. Maybe there's a man for me on a ranch out in Wyoming, just pining to find true love with a big city boy. But there is no way I am moving out of my fabulous apartment, so he will have to come to me."

"No compromises for you?"

"Why should I compromise? I am the standard they should aspire to."

"Well, I know what I am getting you for your birthday."

"What?" He asks, grabbing his bill to sign the slip.

"A horse. Oh, and a flannel shirt. You'll need both to snag your Wyoming cowboy." I swipe the pen from him and sign my slip, tucking my credit card back in my purse.

"Good grief. No, thank you." He checks his phone. "We better get back to work." He stands up and folds his napkin on his plate. "And on the way back, I want a name."

We squeeze through the tables and push our way out onto the street. I turn and start walking, "Gabriel Perez."

He matches my stride, "Ooh, Latino, a Latin Lover, a sexy Spaniard."

I smack him on the arm, "Oh, stop it. Yes, he is Mexican-American. Third-generation immigrant. And yes, he is sexy."

"Wait," he stops short on the sidewalk. "Have you already...."

"No! No. We are taking it slow."

"Oh," his face falls. "I was excited for a second."

I start to walk again, "Sorry to disappoint."

"Have you at least kissed?" He rushes to catch up with me just as we reach the edge of our building.

I nod.

"And?"

We enter the revolving door to the building and make our way across the lobby.

"And what?"

"How was it?"

I stop and turn to him. "It was fabulous." I smile and press the elevator button.

He rocks on his feet, appraising me. "Of course, it was."

"Simon, you could find true love." He has so much to offer. I don't know why he refuses to let his guard down. However, I am hardly one to talk. But still, if I can find love, anyone can.

"There is no way I will find someone worth settling down for."

"Not with that attitude."

14

I Hate Sales Calls

Later that night my phone starts ringing from somewhere in the pile of clothing on my bed. Digging around, I finally find it and breathlessly answer.

"Hello?"

A chipper female voice on the other end says, "Good evening. Is this Callie Mcguire?"

I look at the number. Crap, I shouldn't have picked up. I hate sales calls. I'm in the middle of cleaning my room, and my fresh laundry awaits sorting.

"This is Betty from MyLove4Life—"

"The dating website?"

"Uh-huh, and we're calling because we noticed you registered for the website, and we matched you, but you did not complete your registration."

"Um..." I want to give her a snarky response but can't think of what to say.

"Is there a particular reason why you didn't finalize your match?"

I lie, "I'm quite busy at work right now—"

"Well, honestly, Ms. Mcguire, this is a rare occurrence for us, and we want to make sure that your experience is as positive as possible."

"Okay, but wait, what am I supposed to do?" I can't think clearly.

"And if you don't complete the process, then we can't guarantee you the million dollars if you don't find lifelong love. You do want to receive a million dollars if you get your heart broken, don't you?"

"Yes, but…" I sit down on the edge of my bed.

"Perfect! We want to honor our one million dollar guarantee if you get your heart broken, but how can we if you don't finalize your order? We've already invested a lot of time trying to help you with this, so let's take care of this on your phone, now, shall we?"

I hate these kinds of calls. "I'm sorry, but I have to go—"

"Oh, dear, are you not interested in meeting the love of your life? I believe his name is," I hear the sound of keyboard keys tapping, "Jimmy Powell. We can't finish the program for matching until you have completed the full registration."

Good grief, they'll probably never stop phoning and texting, so I say, "Actually, I've met someone else, so—"

"Excuse me?"

"Yeah, I don't need your services."

There is a short pause. "Did you say you met someone else before completing your registration?" Her voice sounds a bit frosty.

"Yes, I did, and we're actually dating now, so—"

"Just to be clear, you matched with Jimmy but chose to date someone else?"

"Yes."

"That is extremely unusual. In fact, I'm not sure that's happened in the company's history."

My patience is wearing thin. "Yeah, well, I mean, you guys got your ninety-nine dollars, so I'm not sure why it matters."

"We just want to make sure our clients are delighted with our service, and the best way to make sure you're delighted with our service is to have you go ahead and finish that registration right away."

Frustrated, I raise my voice. "I don't want to meet Jimmy, so it's fine." What part of this is she not understanding?

"Yes, well, again, please go in and complete your registration right away, and I'll make a note in your file that you are refusing to meet him and are now dating someone else before having completed your registration."

There's an annoying buzzing on the line, which makes my neck itch and my headache. Her voice drones on, but I'm focused on the feeling that my privacy has been invaded, and she won't stop talking.

My head starts to spin, and I slide to the floor with my back against the bed, "I don't want to." I practically shout at her.

Her voice sounds hurt. "There is no need to abuse me, ma'am. I'm just trying to do my job. There is no problem as long as you complete the registration immediately. Just go to the app and click where it tells you. Ms. Mcguire, I hate to have to call you back again or escalate this issue, so please go and finish your registration as requested." Her voice becomes hard. "Do it, now."

I fumble with my phone to end the call, my heart racing.

15

Cats are My Jam

Tuesday, January 11

Walking past Simon's desk, a familiar flash of pink catches my eye. I back up. "Hey, Simon." MyLove4Life.com is open on the browser.

He yelps and turns his hand flying to his heart. "You scared me, Callie."

"Sorry, I was just wondering what you're doing."

"Oh," he points at the screen, "My cousin told me about this website. It promises a million-dollar—"

"Wait," I lean in, pretending to see this for the first time. "Isn't this a dating website?"

"Yes. They even have this guarantee they will match you up with the love of your life. Who does that? It's crazy." He turns to me and leans in conspiratorially, "Did you see that story on the news? You know the famous actor, John Malcolm?"

I had no idea what story he was talking about, but I know who John Malcolm is; everybody does.

"Well, *he* didn't sign up, but some forty-five-year-old divorcee from Detroit did, and she matched with him. That boy left his sweet, beautiful, *pregnant* wife and is marrying; hang on." He brings up another browser and does a quick search. A photo pops up of John Malcolm, twenty-nine, dark hair, star of the blockbuster series, *My Spy*, standing next to someone.

I lean closer to the image and see a short, stocky woman wearing a sweatshirt that says, *Cats are My Jam.*

"He is marrying her," he says, pointing to the screen with both hands.

"He's leaving Gina, the model?" I ask. This has to be a joke.

Simon purses his lips. "The one who is ruining her perfect figure so she can have his baby? Oh, yes, he dumped her. He and the little lady from Detroit are madly in love." Simon shakes his head. "And if they break up, she gets one million dollars and half his money if she can get him to the alter."

How odd. I had almost forgotten about the one-million-dollar guarantee until that stupid phone call. I had muted notifications from YourLove4Life, but this morning they started popping up again every hour; *Confirm your registration! Second chance to confirm! Urgent, please reply!*

I say, "One million? Wow, that does sound suspicious." I peer at the screen again.

"Simon, why does it want you to log in, and it already knows your name?"

He taps his fingers on the desk. "I don't know what you're talking about." He tries to sound innocent.

"Right there," I say, pointing to the screen and stifling laughter. "It wants you to log in. It even says you have a match."

He spins around in his chair to face me. "Okay, Miss Know-It-All. Yes, I may have signed up out of curiosity, but I'm not going to move forward with this whole thing. And keep your voice down. The last thing I need is Felicia on my butt about being on social media during work hours." He flicks his chin in the direction of Felicia's desk, grinding his teeth.

74

"Oh, should I get you a crown, drama queen?" I say, grinning and motioning in the direction of the elevators.

"Yes. That would be nice; thank you." He sticks out his lower lip.

It's an old joke between us, and we both smile and then turn our attention back to the computer screen.

"So, what do you think?" he asks. "Is this a mistake? I know it is so stupid."

"Sounds like a scam. Their guarantee that you can find your match is pretty ridiculous. They also have a pretty aggressive follow-up campaign and terrible customer service. "

His fingers hover over the keyboard. "What are you talking about, Callie?"

"Um, you know, if you don't complete the sign-up, they call and text a lot." It sounds lame when I say it out loud.

"Well, that seems like a small price for love." He points his right index finger at the return button. "Let's see just who my Mr. Right is, shall we?"

He clicks the button, and together we watch the screen pixelate, and a single name appears under a photo, *Cody Marshall.*

Simon wrinkles up his nose. "Elkhorn, Wisconsin? What the hell kind of Midwestern, small-town name is that? And a flannel shirt, are you kidding me?" Cody is standing in a field with his face turned up to the sun and his eyes closed.

Simon leans forward with his hand on his chin, contemplating the face before him. "He isn't bad looking, though, and there's something to be said for boys in flannel."

"You wanted a cowboy," I poke him lightly in the arm, "and he probably has a farm." I stifle a laugh. "Maybe you can learn how to milk cows."

"Hey, don't rain on my parade. You aren't the only one who deserves love. How are things with your sexy Spaniard?"

"Wouldn't you like to know?" I give him a wink and turn to walk away.

"What? Spill!" he calls after me.

"Nope, I have to go; you know I'm a very busy person. I'll talk to you later." I turn to walk back to my desk.

"Girl, you drive me crazy," he mutters.

"I know; that's what I live for." I smile over my shoulder and then round my cubicle wall.

"Oh, and Callie, don't forget to finish your registration." His voice is flat and monotone.

I whip around. "What?"

He is sitting there with a blank look on his face. Then, he seems to come back to himself. "I said you drive me crazy."

"Right, but after that?"

"After that, nothing." He turns to his desk and stares at the computer screen.

16

Shannon

Thursday, January 13

I haven't talked to my sister since Christmas. We were never that close growing up, but my mom sent me a weird text today asking if I had talked to her. Now I'm a little worried.

I glance at my watch. My room is reasonably clean, and there are thirty minutes before Jayla will officially begin our regular Thursday "date night", when we watch a movie together and get caught up on girl stuff. I try calling again, and my sister picks up on the second ring.

"Hey, Shannon," my voice is chirpy, "How's it going?" I lean back on my pillows and fold one arm over my midsection.

"Hey, little sis, what's up with you?" Her voice holds no hint of impending doom or trouble.

It's always like this with Shannon; she answers questions with questions, starting each conversation with a symbolic, "Enough about me; let's talk about you first." So I play along, "Same old, same old job. Mom is always asking when I'll be getting married. The usual," I say, looking at my bedroom ceiling where a tiny spider is spinning a web in the corner.

"She is concerned about your love life, that's for sure." I can hear my niece and nephew running through the house in the background.

"I know. She should be worried about her own love life. How are things with you?"

"Um, fine. Not as exciting as Chicago, I'm sure." It sounds like she is cooking dinner, possibly chopping vegetables.

"Well, Chicago isn't exciting all the time," I say, stifling a sigh. Why does it always have to be a competition with her?

"That's not how Mom tells it; she says you've taken over the entire city and will eventually marry the most eligible bachelor in the state." She chuckles, but there is an edge to her voice.

"You know how Mom is," I say, trying to smooth things over. "She always tells me how happy it makes her that you still live in Indiana and how she gets to see her grandchildren all the time. Then she complains that if I ever get married, she'll never have a relationship with my kids."

"Well, at least she's making us both feel bad about our life choices," she laughs, and this time it is sincere.

"Seriously, though, what's going on? Mom said something was wrong, and I—"

She cuts me off. "Yeah. No. Everything's fine. Look, I have to go now. I need to bathe the kids. We'll talk soon," she says in a rush.

"Shannon?" I say, sitting up on the edge of my bed, listening intently for any clue to what is going on.

"I love you, Sis," she says.

"I love—" but the line is dead. I put on my pajamas and head out to the couch.

"Everything all right?" Jayla shuffles out of the kitchen in her bunny slippers and jammies. She's made a heaping bowl of popcorn and hands it to me.

"I don't know. My mom said Shannon was having some trouble, and Shannon sounds weird, but she won't tell me anything."

78

"Nothing new about that. The girl is buttoned up so tight I'm surprised you know her kids' names. Of course, she has difficulty sharing with you because you're her biggest competition."

This is an old argument between Jayla and me. "I am not," I say for the umpteenth time as I flop onto the couch and tuck a fuzzy blanket around me.

"Your mom compares you guys all the time, and she pits you against each other. It's manipulative."

"Whatever. I am worried, though," I say, picking up the remote to change the station.

"She's not going to tell you until she's ready," Jayla affects a British accent. "My dear, *Sense and Sensibility* isn't going to watch itself, and we have catching up to do. This is a cell-free zone." She grabs my phone and tosses it across the room.

17

Soul Mates

Friday, January 28

"I want you to meet my family," Gabriel says, his thumb running along my jawline.

We're parked in front of my apartment building after our picture-perfect eight date amid hours of talking on the phone. "Can we finish making out first?"

He grins. "I guess so."

"Has anyone ever told you," I say between kisses, "that you are a great kisser?"

He regards me with wide-eyed innocence. "I've never kissed anyone else in my life, so how would I know?"

I bite his lower lip gently. "Liar."

He eases away from our embrace and is suddenly serious. "Look, I've made a lot of mistakes in my past, and I want things to be different with you."

"What do you mean?" I ask. I can't imagine him making any serious mistakes.

"I mean, I've rushed into the physical stuff and have been hurt, so I don't want to rush. Okay, I want to rush. I want to run my fingers against your bare skin and feel you against me. But not yet."

"Well, that speech doesn't make me feel less like rushing, but Gabriel, you don't need to explain; I trust you." As I speak the words, I realize I do trust him, which brings me up short. In the past, I've trusted men only as far as I can predict their behavior. Gabriel surprises me at every turn. I realize I'm sitting still, an epiphany just beyond my reach.

"Oh, I didn't say stop. I just said, let's not rush." He reaches for me again.

"Mmm, I can get on board with that." His stubble tickles my neck, so the last part comes out with a giggle.

"You are amazing. You know that?"

"Of course, I am." I grin and suddenly realize that since I met Gabriel, a strange sense of confidence has slowly replaced the fear I thought I had learned to live with.

"It's true." His eyes are intense. "I never thought I could connect with someone this deep and fast."

"Yeah?"

"Yeah," he seems to struggle for words, "like our souls are connected."

I pull away, stroking my fingers lightly in his palm. "Really?"

Uncertainty clouds his eyes for a moment. "You don't feel the same way?"

I cup his cheek with my right hand, fingertips caressing his earlobe. "Well, I mean, I like you; you know that. It feels like I have known you for longer than a few weeks. But I don't know if I am ready to declare us soul mates. I am not even sure soul mates exist."

"Wow, you are a cynic." He tickles my ribs lightly to let me know he's teasing.

I play slap his hand then intertwine my fingers in his. "No, I'm just realistic. Isn't it enough that we like each other? Does it have to be some undeniable chemical connection over which we have no control?

My phone buzzes. "Oh, my gosh. I am so tired of these text

notifications."

"From that dating site?"

"They keep contacting me to finalize my registration so I can meet Mr. Bodybuilder." I give him a sideways grin and show him the text.

I scroll up and show him the thread of texts. He shakes his head. "This is borderline harassment."

I sit back in my seat. "I am not sure what I have to do to get them to leave me alone."

I consider explaining the weird phone call and what I thought I heard Simon say, but it seems silly to spoil the moment when he envelopes me in his arms and whispers, "Don't worry, I will protect you."

18

Valentine's Day

Monday, February 14

"Happy Valentine's Day!" Gabriel says, handing a bouquet of purple orchids to Jayla.

"Thank you!" she unwraps the pink cellophane and sniffs. "Is there chocolate?"

"Of course," he says, drawing a small box of chocolates from behind his back and handing it to her.

She turns it over, reading aloud, "Chicago is for lovers. Ah, look at that cute Cupid."

"You know, Cupid wasn't really a baby. Baby cupid was popularized in art, but he was an adult man, very good looking," Gabriel says.

"Maybe he's available," I say to Jayla.

"I prefer the baby," Jayla says, tossing the chocolates on the table.

Gabriel hands me a dozen red roses and kisses me on the cheek. "Aww, they are lovely." I retrieve two vases from under the sink and fill them. Jayla jumps in, "Hey, let me do that. You go hang out with your man."

"Thanks." I leave her to cut the stems and arrange the flowers. Gabriel is planted on the couch and pats the seat next to him. I settle down and rest my head on his shoulder, our hands intertwined.

Jayla joins us, setting the orchids on the kitchen table and the roses on top of my bookcase. She folds a leg under her and sits in our comfy vegan leather chair. Then she pops back up, "We need wine." A few minutes later, she is back with a bottle of wine and three glasses.

We share the bottle of wine and take-out from my favorite Thai place.

"Were you serious about going home with me?" I ask.

"Sure," he says, stabbing his chicken with a chopstick.

"You know that's not how you are supposed to use those," Jayla says. I laugh.

"What?" He looks shocked. "I had no idea. No wonder stabbing the rice didn't work."

Jayla looks at me, "He's a dork."

"But he's my dork," I say, batting my eyelashes at Gabriel.

"Thanks for hanging out with me on Valentine's Day," Jayla says wistfully.

"No problem," Gabriel says. "Glad to be here."

Jayla chews her food. "Not sure if she told you," she points to me, "but I was supposed to get married this year."

"Really?" Gabriel asks, his eyes wide with surprise.

"Yeah. I have the dress hanging in my closet to prove it."

"What happened?" he asks carefully.

"Besides getting dumped the morning of my wedding," she says, waving her chopsticks in the air, "I found out he had been having sex with his dental hygienist in his office after hours. Totally cliché. I did get these beautiful veneers out of the deal, though," she flashes a big toothy smile.

"Well, that is something," Gabriel says. Then, he asks, "You want me to hurt him? I need a name and address." He flexes his muscles.

She laughs, "No, he did me a favor. It would have been a disaster.

We never had the chemistry that you two have." She leans back in the chair, "and now I know not to settle."

"Maybe you should sign up for that dating site yourself," Gabriel says casually.

Jayla shakes her head, swallowing a mouthful of rice. "I am not interested in dating right now. I have way too much going on with the new store opening up, and every time I jump on one of those apps, all I get is dick pics and men who are *almost* divorced or *just living* with their wives. Yeah, right." She continues shaking her head, "No, thanks. I think you guys just got lucky."

The rest of the night passes with easy conversation. We talk about Jayla's family and the new store her boss is opening. I tell them about my latest project at work, and we grill Gabriel on everything ghost-related in Chicago.

Jayla finally excuses herself and heads to bed, leaving Gabriel and me on the couch. It's so comfortable with him. I don't have to worry about having something stuck in my teeth or sucking in my stomach. I can relax around him.

After Jayla shuts her bedroom door, there's a pause in the conversation. Then, Gabriel walks over to his coat hanging over the kitchen chair. He slides something out of his pocket. Did he get me a present? I didn't get him one. We said we weren't exchanging gifts.

He walks back with a coy smile and sits down next to me. "Didn't we say no presents?" I ask, trying not to panic.

"Guilty," he says, holding the box carefully on his lap. "I never thought I would meet someone like you. I hoped but wasn't sure."

My stomach starts to flutter. I stand up, looking at him, and blurt out, "You better not even think about proposing."

He laughs, "No." He pulls me back down to sit next to him.

"I don't mean to offend you," I say, relieved and yet mortified at my reaction. "It just, well, it would be a little weird since we just met, and

85

I don't even know if I want to get married."

"You don't say," he grins and pats my knee, "and you may be shocked, but I don't make it a habit of proposing to girls. And even if I did, so what? Heck, my parents got married after knowing each other for a month."

"My parents got married fast too. But that was what they did back then." I employ my mediocre English accent. "It is a truth universally acknowledged that a single man in possession of a good fortune must be in want of a wife."

"Oh, I am, but not right this second," he says, turning and holding out the box. "I wanted to get you something so that you know how much I appreciate you just the way you are." He places the box in my palm.

I can't help but smile because I love to get presents. "What is it?" I ask.

"I'm not going to tell you. Just open it."

I tug the little red ribbon and look inside. My breath catches. "Oh, it's beautiful," I say, lifting out the gold chain with a locket in the shape of a book. I read the engraving on the front that says, *Most Ardently.*

His face is serious as he meets my eyes. "I'm looking forward to writing this story with you. The story of us. Whatever it brings."

"That's the nicest thing anyone has ever said to me."

"Well, it's a good thing I mean it."

"Thank you." I turn around and lift my hair so he can help me clasp it. "It's perfect," I say, touching it with my fingertips.

"Happy Valentine's Day," he says, wrapping his arms around my waist and kissing the side of my neck.

"Happy Valentine's Day to you," I say, turning around in his arms and reaching up to kiss him.

19

Panic at the Museum

Friday, February 25

Gabriel and I have seen each other every day since Valentine's Day. Sometimes we wander through museums or shops downtown. But my favorite days are curled up on the couch in my apartment or his, reading in comfortable silence. He is easily one of my favorite people ever. And the more I know, the more I like. I know how he likes his coffee, and he knows I love to wear his old university sweatshirt when his apartment gets chilly. It feels like we have known each other forever. And aside from the occasional text, I haven't heard much from the dating website. Hopefully, they have moved on and matched Jimmy with someone else because I'm happy with Gabriel.

I squeeze his hand and thank the universe for bringing him to me. We are strolling through the Natural History Museum and a chattering group of excited elementary kids brushes past us to the robot exhibit. For a moment, we are awash in a sea of smiling cherubs.

"Let's go see the chicks hatch." I tug him toward the glass box filled with rocking eggs, some with cracks and even little beaks sticking out. A few soggy chicks are drying out amid other little yellow fluff balls hopping around under a heat lamp. "They're so adorable that I could sit here all day and watch them peck, peck through their little shells."

He regards me with a smile. "So, do you want little chicks of your own?"

"What?" I turn to face him with a chuckle. "Where did that come from?"

He shrugs. "I don't know. Maybe I'm inspired by these fluffy little guys." I look at his face to see if he is joking, but there's no hint of mischief in his eyes.

I turn to fix my gaze on the chicks. "I don't know," I say as casually as I can, "I haven't thought too much about it."

Liar, I tell myself. I had thought about it. I had researched the cost of raising children and the impact of multiple siblings. I had even read What to Expect When You're Expecting, just in case I ever got pregnant. I had Pinterest boards for my engagement, wedding, children, and house. All I was missing was the husband.

He shifts his feet and looks down. "It's not a deal-breaker, but our kids would be cute."

I playfully nudge him with my shoulder. "Gabriel, we haven't known each other that long."

"But it feels like we've known each other forever. In those Jane Austen books you love so much, we would already be married."

I know, I think. "That's just because it's new and exciting. But I am not your Elizabeth Bennet and you are not my Mr. Darcy. You barely know me, and what if you get to know me more and decide you don't like me?" I stick out my lower lip and pretend to pout.

He rolls his eyes dramatically. "Gee, most women would pay a million dollars just to have a guy interested enough to talk about chickens."

"Maybe. But I didn't exactly come from a big, loving home like you did, Gabriel." He knows I hardly talk to my sister and haven't seen my dad since he moved away.

He touches my cheek gently, and I close my eyes, "But we are not your parents. We can make our own rules. Who knows, maybe I am your Mr. Darcy."

I don't know what to say. The old familiar feeling of panic returns, and for a moment, I want to run out of that room and down the street, screaming.

I say to him softly, "Three. I want three children. Or maybe four, so there are even numbers. I want them relatively close together so they can play. But not too close together because I don't think I could survive it. They will need a house, in a suburban neighborhood, with a fence. And a dog."

I can't say more because I'm shaking, and for some reason, tears are gathering at the corners of my eyes, and I'm afraid I might start blubbering right there in the museum, in front of all the chicks.

Gabriel wraps his arms around me and holds me close.

I bury my face in his chest and pretend we are alone.

"I can't wait to start working on that project," he whispers. So, of course, I start to laugh, and he gently laughs along with me as he dabs the tears on my cheeks with a clean handkerchief he likes to keep in his pocket.

I'm blushing in embarrassment, and I try to pull myself together. A few museum patrons are glancing at us with interest.

"You're cute when you blush; you know that?"

"I think we should check out the human body display and see what we're getting ourselves into."

"Sounds good to me," he says looking lost in thought.

"Hello, Earth to Gabriel." I flash my hand in front of his face.

He sighs, "Callie, I've been looking for someone serious for a while. But it had to be the right person."

"What do you mean?"

He starts walking again, keeping my hand in his. "I'm the youngest of five, and all my older siblings are already married. Her one wish was that she would see all of us married before she died."

I keep my mouth shut and let him continue.

"So I promised her I'd make it happen or find my future wife, if possible. But it's not like you can easily find your soul mate." He runs a hand through his hair.

"That's true," I say. Where is he going with this?

"But you are such a surprise; I'd almost given up finding someone."

"Okay." The wider he smiles, the more warning bells go off in my head. Danger. Danger. We have only been dating for a little over a month. That is nothing. We don't even know each other that well. Why is he talking about marriage? I keep walking, tugging him along and hoping to distract him with exhibits we pass by.

Undeterred, he stops me and turns me to face him. "I guess what I am saying is I love you, Callie. And maybe not now, but soon, well…" He trails off as he looks into my eyes.

My heart beats in my ears. Is he trying to find a wife to hurry up and marry before his mom dies? I let go of his hands. "So the only reason we're here is that your mom got cancer, and you promised her you would find someone before she dies?" I choked on the last word, feeling awful for saying it aloud.

He looks like I smacked him, and I despise myself for blurting out more words.

My breath is coming in spurts. "I'm sorry. I didn't mean that. I don't understand what you are trying to say."

He puts his hands on his hips and looks away. "I was trying to say that I love you and can see a future with you. But maybe you don't feel the same." He turns his head to meet my gaze.

"I think this is a mistake," I whisper, feeling nauseous and dizzy.

"What are you talking about, Callie?"

"We hardly know each other, and we need to slow this way down. I don't think I can do this."

"Come on, Callie. Don't make a big deal out of this. I was trying to be honest. I thought you felt the same. Was I wrong?" He's standing there with a broken look on his face, waiting for a reply.

I can't explain the fear that grips my heart. It makes no sense. It feels like the walls are closing in, and I can't breathe. I have to get out of here. "Please, take me home, Gabriel."

His eyebrows are furrowed, but he nods.

We don't speak on the drive home, though he glances sideways at me. I don't return the gaze, and I feel myself pressing into the car door.

I try to jump out on the curb for a quick goodbye, but he catches up and walks me to the entry door to the apartment building. "Callie, please, let's talk about this."

As I brush his cheek with a light kiss, my heart is pounding in my ears. "Sure, sure. I'll call you." I rush inside and don't look back.

20

A Visit

Monday, February 28

I didn't call him the next day. Or the day after that. I wasn't planning to call him at all. But sipping coffee at my desk, I hear my phone buzz in my purse. It's a text from Gabriel.

> Gabriel: Can we talk?
> Callie: About what?
> Gabriel: Come on, Callie. I want to explain.
> Callie: I can't handle this right now. I have a meeting in five minutes.
> Gabriel: Okay, can I come over tonight night so we can talk?
> Callie: Fine, come over at seven.

I sigh as I drop my phone back onto my desk. It's better to end it before we both get hurt. He can get over me and move on to some other girl.

After lunch, my phone rings. My sister's number pops up on display.

"Hey, Shannon," I try not to sound surprised, even though I am.

I can hear the fear in her voice when she says, "I don't have much time to talk, but I'm sure Mom told you what's going on."

"No, she didn't. She was concerned, though. What's wrong?"

"Last night, Henry was arrested."

I suck in a breath. I can hardly comprehend what she just said. Henry? That makes no sense. There must be some mistake. Shannon clears her throat and pulls me back to the present. "Are you sure? There must be some mistake." I stand up and walk toward the conference room. Her computer programmer husband is the most strait-laced guy I've ever met. I doubt he has ever had even a parking ticket.

She lowers her voice to whisper, "I can't talk about it over the phone because it might be bugged."

Stepping into the conference room, I shut the door. "Who would be bugging your phone?"

She ignores my questions. "There are media outside my house right now, and I have to get my kids out of town. I thought we could come to see you."

"Okay, yeah, sure. I'll text my roommate, and we'll figure it out."

She exhales. "Thank you. I'll see you later this evening. I really appreciate it. And if the media calls you or anything like that, please, don't say anything about anything."

"That's easy because I don't know anything, do I?"

* * *

I dialed my mom several times back at my desk before she finally answered. "Oh, honey, what are we going to do?" She's sobbing into the phone, and it takes a few moments for her to calm down.

"Mom, Shannon called me. Are you okay?" I can feel Simon's eyes on me.

"Yes, but Henry got arrested. I guess I don't know, something to do with his work."

"Are you safe?" I hear Simon get up and head over in my direction.

"Yes, I'm hunkered down here at home. Margaret from next door is staying with me."

"Should you go somewhere else? Get out of town?" This is surreal. My boring family is now talking about phone tapping and media camped out on their lawn. How is this even possible? Simon walks over and puts a hand on my shoulder. I look up and give him a small smile, patting his hand.

"Don't worry. I have the shades drawn, and my car's in the garage with the door shut; they don't even know that I'm here. I've got plenty of groceries and, if need be, I'll make a run for it in the middle of the night."

I chuckle. "That would be quite dramatic, Mom." I roll my eyes at Simon, who is waiting for an explanation.

"Well, sometimes life is like that, I guess. I'm just worried about your sister and the kids. And Henry, of course. He won't last a minute in prison."

"I'm sure he's not going to end up in prison," I assure her. "There must be some misunderstanding. He's Mr. Goody Two Shoes, Mr. Hall Monitor."

"I know. I think so, too, and if he did something, there had to be a darn good reason for it. I'm sure everything will come out in the wash, but your sister is pretty bent out of shape."

"Well, she's on her way here, so I'll make sure she's okay." I grab a piece of paper and write on it, *More coffee, please* and hand it to Simon, who skims it and marches off toward the break room with my coffee cup in hand, knowing coffee is the price he has to pay for my info.

"Oh, good, she said she might be heading up there. Have her call me from your cell when she gets there; she doesn't want to use her phone. I know she's worried about them tracking her."

"All right, Mom. I love you, and I'll talk to you later."

I quickly text to Shannon,

> Callie: Hey, you might want to ditch your phone and pick
> up a burner.

Wait, burner phone? What in the world do I know about burner phones? My phone vibrates with Shannon's answer,

> Shannon: I already thought about that. I'll call you when I'm
> on the road.

Well, all right, then. Simon returns with my coffee, and I fill him in.

"Apparently, Indiana isn't boring after all," he says before giving me a quick hug and patting me on the back.

"I have to go," I say, "Can you cover for me this afternoon?"

"Of course, I can."

"Thank you, Simon; you are a good friend." I grab my purse and coat and head home.

Jayla is used to chaos, having grown up in a big family. Plus, she is the most understanding person I know, so announcing that we are about to have a whole family stay with us makes her smile.

She helps me set up the kids' inflatable mattresses and ready the fold-out couch. We pile up all the extra pillows and blankets in the only open corner while we wait for Shannon and the kids to arrive.

I run down to the corner store and grab some more groceries because I'm pretty sure they'll want more to eat than vodka, eggs, and the emergency frozen pizza we keep, just in case.

As I put away groceries, I remember Gabriel and dial his number. I tell him quickly, "Hey, Gabriel, I hate to do this to you, but my sister is in a crisis and is on her way right now. I do you want to talk, but I can't talk tonight."

His voice is soft and rough at the same time. "Yeah, sure. Of course. Is there anything I can do? Do you want me to pick up groceries for you? Do you need to borrow a mattress or anything? I know she has two kids, right?"

"That's so thoughtful. I think we're all set, so I'll text you tomorrow morning, and thank you."

Silence hangs between us.

"Okay," he breathes. "If you think of anything I can do to help, let me know. I'm available anytime day or night."

"Yeah, okay." I bite my lip. I hate this. I miss him. Why couldn't he have just kept it light? Why did he have to get all weird? Why did I have to get all weird?

* * *

Shannon arrives just after 8:00 p.m. with kids in tow. The kids look tired and are tugging little suitcases behind them with stuffed animals tucked in the handles. My sister parks her suitcase by the door, deposits bags of McDonald's food on the floor, and throws her arms around me. "Thank you so much for letting us come. I'm exhausted, and I didn't want the kids around any of that."

It's been a long time since I've been this close to my sister. She was the one who always got good grades, played tennis, was on the homecoming court. I was the awkward little sister who hid in my room with my nose in a book. But the worry in her eyes was new. "I'm so sorry, Sis. Let's take care of the kids, and when they're in bed, you can fill me in."

She nods gratefully.

An hour later, the kids are asleep, and Jayla is pouring us wine then retreating to her bedroom so we can talk privately.

Shannon perches on the fold-out with her legs tucked under her and pillows bunched up around her.

I sit on the floor with my back against a chair. I wait in silence for her to start. She swirls her wine.

"Crazy day," she says.

No kidding, I think.

"It's probably on the news all over town. I left my phone at home; it must be blowing up right now." She cradles her head in her hands.

I sip my wine.

"Two years ago, Henry got a new job." She lifts her head to gaze at the city lights through the window, and her hands tremble a little as she raises the wine glass to her lips. "It was a good job at a startup; the pay was amazing, and the investors were solid, so we knew it wouldn't go belly up in six months." She took a breath. "But in the last couple of months, he became withdrawn and secretive. I could tell something was going on, but he wouldn't tell me anything. He said he didn't want me to get involved.

"He started to work long hours, he wasn't sleeping, and when he came home, he would drink way more than usual. At first, I worried he was having an affair. I tried to do some amateur investigating." She looks at me with a twisted smile. "I should've asked you to help me; you would've figured it out in fifteen minutes. You were always the smart one."

"Oh, Sis." I lean over to squeeze her hand. "We'll work together if there's a next time." She smiles, and I hope that things will be different between us no matter what happens.

She takes a deep breath and then lets it out. "From what I could find out, he is not having an affair. But I knew something was wrong. He refused to talk about it and got angry every time I brought it up, so I stopped. He was trying to protect me from something and trying to solve it on his own, which was irritating, but what was I going to do?

Last night, he told me he had quit his job. I was shocked, and we got into a big fight. I went to bed mad, and he slept on the couch. In the morning, the police came and took him away."

Her eyes start to fill with tears. "It was awful. All of our neighbors watched, and he didn't even have any shoes on. I tried to ask the police what was happening, but some guy stuck his arm out and wouldn't let me through.

"Just before they stuffed him into the police van, he shouted to me., 'I'm sorry, I had to do it.' Oh, Callie, he just looked broken, and there was nothing I could do." She hugs a pillow and weeps softly into it.

Nothing like that ever happened in Columbia City. "Shannon, what did he do?"

She raises her tear-stained face and whispers, "I don't know."

"Did you find out what the charges were?"

"One of the officers told me it was for computer tampering and cybercrime or something, but it doesn't make any sense. I just want him to tell me it's all a big mistake."

Her last words are broken, and she starts to cry again, so I jump up with a box of Kleenex and put my arms around her shoulders.

"It's going to be okay, Sis. We'll figure it out, and it'll be okay."

"I don't know what to say to the kids, and I don't want to face my neighbors, the teachers at their school, or anybody."

"Well, the good news is Chicago's full of crime, so nobody's paying attention to what happens in Fort Wayne."

She chuckles softly, wipes her eyes with the back of her hand, and smiles weakly at me. "Thanks for letting us come. Are you sure your roommate's okay with it?"

As if on cue, Jayla opens her bedroom door and tiptoes out. "You guys need some more wine?"

"Thanks so much for letting us invade your apartment. I know we are a lot with all this drama," Shannon says.

"Oh, honey, your drama has nothing on my family drama. I have seen it all and heard it all. You couldn't shock me if you tried."

She pours each of us another glass of wine, grabs one for herself, and sits down in the chair I had vacated. "Now that you're in the big city, what are you and the kids doing tomorrow for fun?"

I turn to my sister. "I can take the day off, and we can go to the children's museum or the aquarium; does that sound good?"

"That sounds amazing. I have to make some phone calls in the morning and figure out what I have to do next. But distraction will be good."

"I will help any way I can, Sis."

Her eyes sparkle with tears, and she nods, pressing her lips together.

21

I'm Sorry

Tuesday, March 1

I have fought the urge to call Gabriel all day. He would know how to help. He would have words of wisdom or at least be able to hold me and make me feel better. Maybe I was too harsh? Perhaps he was just caught up in the moment. Once again, I sabotage a perfectly good relationship. I need to call him and tell him about my sister before he shows up on my doorstep.

I pace the hallway in my apartment, waiting for Gabriel to pick up the phone. As soon as he does, I blurt out, "Hey, my sister is going to stay for a couple of days. I'm so sorry about how I reacted at the museum. It was so stupid. I just got scared." He doesn't reply right away, and I stare at my feet, nausea rising as I wait.

Finally, he sighs deeply. "I'm sorry, too. I shouldn't have put that much pressure on you. I tend to do that. I assume people feel the same way I do, so I want to shout it to the world. Even if that dating website had matched you with me, we would've met at IKEA. And hey, everyone knows that relationships that start at IKEA last a lifetime."

Relief washes over me. "You're a dork," I smile.

"I know," he chuckles. "This might be too much, and I don't want to scare you away again, but my family's having a get-together this Saturday, and I want you to come with me to introduce you to them." He pauses. "You can say no, and we can go back to first date stuff again."

"Okay. I want to meet your family. Just don't propose or anything, you promise?" Seriously, I can't deal with another surprise.

"Darn it. Now, I have to change my plans."

"Yeah, right." The tension breaks, and we laugh together.

"All right, I'll pick you up Saturday at one o'clock."

"It's a date," I say, smiling. I take a deep breath. I need at least one area of my life to be solid. And yes, we have some things to figure out. But at least we can work on it.

* * *

On Wednesday, after confirming the press had moved on to the next big scandal to hit the Fort Wayne area for the moment, my sister packs her things to drive back home. Saying goodbye is a lot harder than I thought it would be. I give each of the kids a little survival pack for the road; juice boxes, fruit snacks, coloring books with crayons.

They give me big hugs.

Her car is idling at the curb in front of the apartment building. "Call me when you get home." I look into Shannon's face and think about all the time that we've wasted. "I know it wasn't under great circumstances, but I am glad we got to spend some time together."

"Me, too," she says, squeezing my hands. "I will let you know what I find out. Thanks for being here, Sis."

We wrap our arms around each other and rock for a moment.

"Thank you," she whispers.

I wave goodbye until the car disappears in traffic.

Jayla is splayed in a chair when I return. "Having kids is exhausting!"

101

"No kidding. I don't know how my sister does it all the time."

"Speaking of kids, what's happening with you and Gabriel?"

"I don't know. After my epic freak out at the museum, he might be a little leery of getting serious again, but I told him I was sorry, and he's invited to meet his family."

"Really? Girl, he's a good guy, and if he wants to take you home to meet his family, he must be serious." She pursed her lips. "At our age, we don't have time for not serious."

I roll my eyes. "Speaking of not having time for not serious, when are you getting a boyfriend?"

"When I find someone worthy of being my boyfriend, though I don't know how I'm going to meet him now. The only men I ever see are with their girlfriends or wives shopping. Single guys who visit the boutique are picking out something nice for a lover." She gets up and walks to the kitchen, retrieving a glass and bottle of water.

"Maybe we should head back to IKEA."

"Ha!" She walks back to the living room and stands next to me, surveying the living room, still full of blankets and pizza boxes from last night.

"Come on." I nudge her shoulder. "There are many ways to meet guys in the big city." I pick up a blanket and start folding.

"You mean like MyLove4Life.com?" she says, walking back to the kitchen to deposit her glass in the sink, "I'm waiting to see how that turns out for you first; you need to confirm your match, Callie."

I look up sharply. "What did you say?"

She walks back into the living room and picks up a blanket to fold. "That I'll try the website if it works for you first. What's wrong?"

I can't talk, so I turn and walk into my room.

I might be going crazy. I don't have a history of mental illness, except for anxiety. At what age does schizophrenia start? I might have to get evaluated because I am hallucinating or subjected to a cruel prank by the people I love.

22

Lunch Confessions

Thursday, March 3

A sandwich from the deli and a cup of coffee sit untouched while I research schizophrenia and take an online assessment. Auditory hallucinations, paranoia. Great. I could be going crazy.

"Guess who I went out with last night?"

I jump. "Simon! Don't sneak up on me like that." Then, I ask, breathlessly, turning to him, "Who?"

"Mr. Midwestern Flannel," he says, sliding into the chair across from me and dropping his bag on the floor under the table.

I am grateful for the distraction, and he can barely contain his excitement. "Really?"

"Yup. And let me tell you, that boy was all hat *and* all cattle," he sighs, leaning back in the chair. "But I'm not sure it's going to work out."

"I have no idea what that means, but why wouldn't it work out?" I close my laptop and take a sip of my tea.

Simon shrugs. "He isn't my type." Simon breaks off a piece of my sandwich and pops it into his mouth.

"Is it because he's a cowboy?" I ask although I have no idea what that has to do with anything.

"No," he says, shaking his head.

"Well, then, what? If Cupid himself brought you together, how can it be wrong?"

"Cupid? He didn't have anything to do with this," he says with a wave of his hand.

I open my laptop back up and check the website. "Yeah, the CEO for the dating website calls himself Cupid." I point to an image on the screen.

I turn the screen so he can see it. "The hot guy?"

"Yup. It's Cupid who brought you together, so we should be planning your wedding, 'cause, apparently, pretty much everyone who uses this website ends up getting married."

"Girl, I am never getting married," he says, hearing his name called and getting up to grab the coffee he ordered.

"Why not? Don't you want someone to grow old with?"

He wrinkles his nose and sits back down. "And be wrinkly and gray? No, thank you. I prefer an early exit."

He can be so gloomy. "Not me. I want to live for a long time."

"Of course, you do, sweetie." He reaches over and pats my hand.

I fold my arms. "What's that supposed to mean?"

He leans in, his coffee cup in his hands, "It's just that you are a cynical romantic, and I'm a selfish aristocrat born in the wrong century and wrong country, destined to live fast and die young."

"But aren't we all cynical romantics?" I rest my chin on my hand.

He shakes his head, "You want love, but you don't believe in love, not for you."

"I'm not sure that's true," I say and stick out my lower lip.

"Oh, it is. That's why you pushed poor Tom away. Perfectly good marriage material. You choose the boring ones to prove that romance and love aren't possible for you." He taps his chin. "But maybe, just maybe, you're picking the wrong guys."

I suck in a breath. The comment stings. "I am not the problem."

He raises his eyebrows and stares at me.

I wave him off. "Whatever. We don't need to talk about me. When are you going to see Cody again?"

"I don't know that I will." He studies the floor for a moment. "There are differences between us I'm not sure I can live with." His voice is vulnerable and tentative.

I reach out to take his hand. "You should call him, you know, and give him another chance."

The moment passes, and he says, "*I* don't call boys. *They* call me."

"Okay, seriously, what is the problem? Does he have a third foot or something? Is he a felon?"

"No." He sighs and turns to me. "If you must know, he is blind."

"So?" I don't see what the big deal is.

Simon waves his hand in front of his face. "He's blind, as in can't see anything, including me. He brought a service dog on our date, and you know how I feel about dogs. Anyway, he can't even see how fabulous I accessorize. How could I possibly spend my life with someone who can't honestly appreciate me in all my glory?"

"Maybe you have more to offer than your good looks?"

"You know full well that I am a prideful and shallow man, and I have no experience in the art of fine character," he says wryly.

"That's not true, and you should give him one more chance." I pause, considering. "We should all go out together."

"All?"

I look up and meet his eyes. "I think you should meet Gabriel. And I want to meet Cody."

He regards me for a moment. "I know I'm a shallow, horrible person, but I just don't think I can do it, so there's no reason for you to meet him."

"Then, you can't meet Gabriel," I say, snapping my laptop closed and sliding it into my bag.

"What? That's not fair," he says as I stand up.

"Give Cody one more chance, and I will introduce you to Gabriel," I say, finishing the last of my tea and depositing my dishes in the return area.

He stands up, shifts his weight to one leg, and crosses his arms. "Fine."

I grin at him. "Very good. I'll make a decent man out of you yet."

23

Meet the Family

Saturday, March 12

We drive down a street lined with bare maple trees and brick ranches before turning into a short driveway. There's room for only one more car if we squeeze up as far as we can behind a black pickup. Cars line the street on both sides.

"This is home." Gabriel gestures toward a red brick ranch with cement steps and a rod iron railing out front. We hop out, and Gabriel leads me by the hand to the side door, which has a little metal awning over it. The smell of spiced meat drifts out of the house onto the porch. Inside, we walk up three steps to another door with glass steamed up on the inside. It sounds like dozens of people are laughing and talking on the other side. *"¡Hola!"* Gabriel calls as we enter the kitchen, stomping snow off our boots on the door frame.

Children dash from the living room into the kitchen, laughing and grabbing cookies from a plate on the table. A woman at the stove is shaking a spoon at them. *"No más galletas para ti, pequeños niños! La cena está casi lista."* The kids ignore her with big grins and run around the corner.

She sees Gabriel and cries out, *"¡Mi hijito!"*

Gabriel flashes a wide grin as he draws me close. "Mama, this is the girl I told you about, Callie. Remember, she doesn't speak Spanish."

His mom slips off her apron and opens her arms wide. "Welcome to our home, Callie. *Inglés*, everyone, we have a special guest. Come give her the Perez welcome."

Instantly I am surrounded by his family. While his grandma squeezes my cheeks, I notice the kids sneak back in for more cookies. Gabriel's dad slips into the refrigerator, grabs a beer, then retreats before the family can drag him into the madness.

I mouth "Help!" to Gabriel, hoping he'll rescue me from the onslaught, but he just smiles and shrugs and grabs a cookie off the plate to shove into his mouth.

Finally, I break free and join Gabriel against the wall in the dining room. "I am feeling a little sick, maybe from the car ride," I announce to escape outside for a few minutes.

Instead, Gabriel's Mom, Maria, overhears and takes my elbow, guiding me to a bedroom where coats are piled up on the bench at the end of the bed. "It's hot in here, and our family can be a little overwhelming," she says as she shuts the door. "This is my room. The bathroom is over there if you need to freshen up, and you can rest here if you need. Come out whenever you are ready. I will put Gabriel to work making tortillas."

Her hospitality overwhelms me for a moment, and I hug her. "Your family is wonderful."

She quietly shuts the door, and I am grateful for the silence. Several framed photos draw me across the room—photos of Gabriel and his siblings. I run my fingertips over the glass and try to absorb the details of the photos. A boy stands next to Gabriel, not much older than he is. The next photo is Gabriel in front of city hall, getting his hero award, his dad's hand on his shoulder. Gabriel isn't smiling. Scanning the article, I see the name of Gabriel's brother, Xavier.

After about twenty minutes, there's a gentle knock on the door.

Maria leans in and smiles warmly, "Did you get a chance to relax?"

"Yes, thank you. I am not used to so much love in one home."

"We are so glad you are here. You are the first girl our Gabriel has ever brought home, so it is you who are special, my dear." Her smile suddenly fades, and a shadow passes over her eyes. She searches my face for a long moment. Then, she says, "Something is wrong."

I feel a faint chill in the air and the faint scent of roses. "What's wrong? Please, tell me."

She shakes her head. "I don't know. But I feel something is very wrong; there is danger. You and Gabriel, something is wrong. Something is unfinished." She touches her head, heart, and shoulders with her right hand, the sign of the cross.

The door opens, and Gabriel pops his head into the room. "What are you talking about, Mama?"

She shakes her head and seems to remember where she is.

"Mama, are you okay?"

She takes Gabriel's hand, "Of course. We were just talking about how pleased Xavier would be."

Gabriel ducks his head, and his voice is gravelly. "I know, Mama." He extends his hand to me. "Come on," he says, luring me into the kitchen, "let's get you some real food."

I make a mental note to tell him about what his mom said. It was so odd, but then I didn't know her well. Maybe this isn't out of the ordinary for her.

* * *

My belly and heart are full when we do our final rounds of hugs and goodbyes and head back to my apartment.

"My mom loves you, my sisters, too," he says as we stand outside my door.

"Your whole family is amazing." I cup his face in my hands. "I'm just so sorry that your mom is so sick."

"Yes, that. I was trying to tell you a few days ago that Mama's prognosis is not good, but not as bad as we originally thought. With treatment, she could live for years. I just didn't want you to think it was an emergency."

"Oh, my gosh. I'm so relieved." I lean against his arm. "Your family is so wonderful. And that food. Oh, I could eat that every day for the rest of my life." I laugh.

"It is a benefit of being Mexican. Hey, how's your sister? I was going to ask you but got distracted earlier."

"Oh, she's good. The media seem to have found something better to do. Henry is still in jail, but they hope to get him out on bail Monday."

"Crazy. What company did he work for?"

"I don't know. I think my sister told us at Christmas, but it's a long name, and I forgot." A moment passes, and I ask, "How come you never bring up Xavier?"

"My brother?" he asks, his voice even.

I nod. "After I bought your book, I looked you up. I found the newspaper article about the fire." I put my face in my hands. "I'm sorry, I should have told you before this."

"Oh," he says, staring at the road.

I reach for his hand. "I'm so sorry that happened to your family. I can't imagine. But you are a hero."

He jerks his hand back, "I am no hero. The fire was my fault."

"What do you mean?"

"If it's okay, I don't want to talk about it right now." He softens his tone, "And pretty lady, I need to get home. I would ask to come in, but I promised to go slow."

"Yes, you did." I lean in, "You can kiss me, though."

"Yes, please."

There was something I was going to tell him, but I can't remember what.

24

Let's Stay In

Thursday, March 17

Pine and eucalyptus, I think, nuzzling Gabriel's neck. He shivers and smiles at my warm breath on his neck. This is so much better than the party Jayla tried to bribe me to attend- as if green beer could beat this.

His arm is around my shoulders as we snuggle on the soft brown leather couch worn in all the right places. His feet rest on the wood table, and mine are tucked under me. His apartment is small but has this vibe that says sexy, eclectic, intellectual bachelor. The best part? Books are everywhere. Bookshelves line one wall floor to ceiling, with titles spilling out onto the floor in piles.

"I have a confession to make," I say, taking my head off his shoulder. "I read your book."

"Really?" He leans back to look at me.

"Yes. It was recommended to me by the girl at that bookshop I love to visit. She said I would like it, and when you gave me an official autographed copy, I had to."

"Which one? I can't remember."

"*Chicago After Dark,*" I say dramatically, dragging my hand across the air in front of me.

"Ah, are you impressed with the clever title?" He copies my hand motion on the words *clever title*.

"Very. You told us in IKEA that you believed in the supernatural. I want to know more about that."

"Oh, so it is my turn to confess?"

"Yes, with lots of detail, please." I get up and go to the kitchen to grab a soda from the fridge.

"What kind of details?"

"I don't know. How do you feel about God? Have you ever seen a ghost? Is there alien life out there? That kind of thing."

"So you want to know all my secrets?"

I crack open a soda and crawl back next to him on the couch, "Uh-huh."

"Okay." He reaches for the remote to mute the TV. "I do believe there is more to the world than we see. I believe in God, angels, demons, and even ghosts." He takes a deep breath and continues, "After the fire, my brother came to visit me in my hospital room. He tried to tell me that he was okay and it wasn't my fault. But it just made me feel worse. Of course, it was my fault. I am the one who left the burner on. I was trying to make a quesadilla and just forgot. I never told anyone outside my family about that. But from then on, I was sort of obsessed with the supernatural. I tried telling my parents what I had seen, but they thought it was just the pain meds I was on. And when I read the Percy Jackson series, my fascination with mythology started. So I guess you could say I have a complicated relationship with religion."

"Hmm, and I just grew up Methodist." I intertwine my fingers with his.

He laughs. "My family is Baptist. I am still trying to figure it all out."

"Yeah, too," I say, sliding my hand behind his neck and running my fingers through his hair. "How many books have you written?"

"Two, at least two that are finished. I have a few others in process."

"All about ghosts?"

"No, actually, they are about mythology."

"Yeah? About Greek gods?"

"One is. But there isn't much of a market for Greek god literature these days."

I nod as I have an inner debate about whether to tell him my suspicions about MyLove4Life.com. I don't want to seem like a conspiracy nut or worse, and he doesn't know how much they have been harassing me. "How much do you know about the mythological gods of love, like Cupid," I ask, keeping my voice even.

"I know you are my goddess of love," he says, kissing the tip of my nose.

I brush my lips against his, distracted. "Speaking of love, have I told you about Simon from work?"

"Oh, yeah," he says, searching his mind and nodding.

"He signed up for the site and met someone. I told him we could double date."

"Okay."

"But he doesn't know I signed up."

Gabriel raises his eyebrows.

"I told him about you, but not about the bodybuilder."

"Technically true, but why didn't you just tell him you signed up?"

"He would have a fit if I signed up and then didn't tell him, and I didn't want to deal with the drama."

He puts a hand up. "Okay, it's not a big deal. When is the double date going to happen?"

"Next week some time. I need to go home this weekend to ensure my sister is okay. She met with the lawyer today, but I haven't talked to her yet."

Gabriel shakes his head. "I can't imagine what she is going through."

"I know."

Gabriel's apartment is cozy if a little cluttered. But it felt like him. It felt like home. I sigh and lean back into his arms. He wraps his arms around me. "If you need to go home, I can go with you."

I snuggle back into his body. "I would like that."

25

Psycheros Industries

Friday, March 18

My sister calls the next day, and I step into the conference room to take the call.

Henry is out on bail, and things are relatively quiet for the moment. No Federal charges are going to be filed, which is a miracle. Luckily, they had been stashing money away aggressively for the past year, so they were okay for now. All in all, it was good news, and Shannon sounded relieved.

"So what happens next?" I ask, sinking into a chair at the conference room table.

"Well, there is a full trial, I guess. But it could be a while before it happens. So we wait."

"Oh, I forgot to ask, where did he work? Just out of curiosity."

"Psycheros Industries. It's a big conglomerate of companies. Tech, media, and a bunch of other stuff."

"Has he said anything about why he did it? Or if he did it?" I grab one of the scratch pads and a company pen and start to doodle.

"No. Henry just said he had a good reason for doing what he did and would be vindicated at trial. I tried pushing him, but he started saying weird things about wanting to protect me. I don't know. I'm glad he is home, but it hasn't been easy. We have had to install a security system because we keep hearing noises outside the house at night, banging on the windows, and ringing the doorbell in the night. I think it is just stupid jerks trying to scare us, and it's working."

"I bet. I'm so sorry you are going through this. How are the kids holding up?" I start writing my name, Gabriel's name, and Callie Perez.

"They are doing okay. They know something is wrong, but we are trying to shield them as much as possible. I hope the trial happens quickly so we can get on with life, and people will leave us alone. I swear, the other day, someone followed me home from the grocery store. And when I walked in, I swear the entire house smelled like roses inside."

"Yeah?" I realize what I am writing and cross it out. I frown at the ugly scratched-out name and write it again, drawing a heart around it. "Wait, did you say roses?"

"Yes, it has freaked me out. I didn't tell Henry because he has enough to worry about."

"That is so weird. Seriously, please be careful. It sounds dangerous."

"I know. I can't believe how insane it all is. I want things to go back to the way they were." Her voice quivers.

I can't imagine my perfect sister's life turned upside down for the world to see. The ladies at church must be having a field day gossiping about them. That thought makes me angry and protective of her.

"I may be heading back in a week or two. I want to visit and introduce you to someone."

"Who? I need a distraction."

"His name is Gabriel. We met...Well, it's a long story, but he is pretty great."

"Oh, I am so glad. Tom was kind of boring when we met him at Christmas," she says hesitantly.

"I know, right? Gabriel is anything but boring. I can't wait for you to meet him."

"Think he could be the one?"

"Maybe," I admit, looking down at the heart with Callie Perez writing inside, "But you know how these things go. Callie can get a guy but not keep a guy, blah, blah, blah."

"That isn't true. You just haven't found the right guy."

"Who knows? At least Gabriel seems to find my neurotic behavior charming."

"Well, that's good news. I can't wait to meet him." I can tell she means it.

I say goodbye, and then standing in the hallway across from the conference room, I slip my phone into my pocket and stretch my arms up, trying to find some energy from the natural light pouring through the floor-to-ceiling windows. This new relationship with my sister almost makes me miss Indiana. Maybe someday I will go back. But for now, nothing beats the Chicago skyline with the lake behind it.

"Hey, you," Simon says, stepping up beside me, taking in the view.

"Hey, yourself. How is Cody?" I bump him with my hip, and he feigns offense.

"Cody is good. It's so good that I am a little spooked, to be honest."

I turn to him and put my hand on his forearm. "I don't know why. From what you say, he seems like a nice guy, and you're a nice guy. I don't think you have anything to be worried about. And how could he not adore you?"

"True," he says, lifting my hand and kissing its back. "When do we have a double date?"

Walking back to our desks, I say, "I may have to go to my sister's this weekend, but how about when I get back? We can even go on a weeknight."

"Oh, that's risqué. Are you sure you can handle it?" He stops at my cube and leans against the wall.

"Shut up. I am a grown woman with a boyfriend now, so, yeah," I say, lowering myself into my chair with both hands on the armrests then spinning around to my computer.

"So there's a label, progress."

I shift back around to him. "Well, I met his parents, and hopefully, he will meet my family soon."

A smile spreads across his face, and he smacks the wall of my cube. "All right, then. I better get invited to the wedding."

"Yeah, right." I lean down to fish lip gloss out of my purse.

"Callie, someday, I hope you realize that you are worthy of love."

He pats me on the shoulder and then walks away. Why is everyone so concerned with my love life? It's annoying.

26

Going Home

Saturday, March 26

"Hey, Mom," I say, walking into the kitchen of my childhood home. The stools still sit beneath the oak island where I did homework after school every day. The countertops are still the same granite that was going out of style when we got it. But I love it. Even the rooster border pasted along the ceiling has moved from embarrassingly outdated to charming.

"Callie," she says, wiping her hands on her apron, dropping the dishcloth into the sink, turning around, and crossing the kitchen's linoleum floor to hug me. She smells like lemons. She smells like home.

"You must be Gabriel," she says, letting me go.

He gives her his most charming smile. "Yes, I am. It's nice to meet you."

She pulls him down into a hug. He smiles, looks at me, and mouths, "Moms love me."

I roll my eyes and smile.

"I have two rooms ready. Well, Callie, your room hasn't changed, but the guest bedroom is ready for you, Gabriel."

"Thanks, Mom," I say.

"Thanks, Ms. Mcguire."

She pats him on the arm. "No need to be so formal. You can call me Laura."

"Okay, then. Thanks, Laura," Gabriel says.

My mom is beaming as we trudge up the stairs with our bags.

"I can't wait to see your room," he whispers.

"Stop it. You're going to get us in trouble." Although I am not sure how much trouble we can get in at twenty-three.

He puts his hands on my hips and says, "I hope so."

I wiggle out of his grasp and open the door to my sister's old room. It's been turned into a proper guestroom with a country quilt and a little chair in the corner.

"Here is the guestroom," I say with a sweep of my hand.

"Nice," he says, walking in, running his finger across the top of the dresser like he's checking for dust. "Not too shabby. I think it will do just fine."

Turning to me, he says, "Where's your room?" He raises his eyebrows up and down, making me laugh.

What is it about men? Bring them to your parents' house and let them go into your room and all they want to do is make out.

"Come on," I say, waving for him to follow me.

Books still fill the shelves my dad made me for my twelfth birthday. The little white desk I painted with lilacs and daisies is right where I left it. There's a new comforter on my bed. But Rufus, my ragged, stuffed St Bernard, is standing guard on my pillow, just like always. "This is it," I shrug, turning to the bed and throwing my bag on it.

"Very nice. I can imagine you here, doing math homework on the bed." He flops down on the bed next to my bag.

"Eww. I hated math."

"We could make out; I know you like that."

"Yeah, right. I'm sure my mom is making us dinner, but maybe we could go out and grab a drink after?"

"I would like that. Maybe we'll run into some of your old high school boyfriends."

"Ha! I hope not."

"I'm going to clean up a bit and unpack. I'll meet you downstairs in thirty?"

"Perfect," I say, pushing my bag to the edge of the bed and flopping down on the comforter. No matter how long I stay away, it seems like the moment I walk through the door, I'm fifteen again, awkward with braces and always with my nose in a book. The braces are gone, but I am still awkward. And I still usually have my nose in a book. I take the book out of my bag and crack it open to prove the point.

Forty-five minutes later, there's a knock on my door, and Gabriel opens it.

"What are you doing? I thought we were meeting downstairs?" he asks, amused.

"Oh, shoot," I say, slamming the book shut and jumping off my bed. "I lost track of time. I'm the worst hostess in the world."

"Don't worry about it. It gave me time to hang out with your mom and the chance to hear stories about you when you were little."

"Oh, great," I say, rummaging through my bag for a brush I drag through my hair.

"You better come on; she's got dinner on the table, and it's calling my name. I'm starving," he says, rubbing his stomach.

Garlic fills the air as I walk downstairs. My mouth starts to water. I would know my mom's spaghetti anywhere. "I hope you're hungry," she says.

"We are," I reply, sliding out the dining room chair.

"Tomorrow, your sister and Henry are coming over with the kids for a visit."

Passing a plate of garlic bread to Gabriel, I ask, "How is she doing, Mom, really?"

My mom presses her lips and reluctantly says, "It's been pretty awful. The media camped out at our house for a week. I couldn't even leave my house. And even now, the rumors and speculation." She leans forward and whispers, "Everybody's still talking about it. They're just not talking about it to her."

"That's awful," I say, anger rising, picturing my sister the subject of gossip.

"Yes. Well, it's just terrible," Mom says. She shakes her head and then grabs the pasta.

"So what exactly did he do?" I ask carefully, not wanting to overstep but curious just the same.

"I don't understand all of the legal mumbo-jumbo and technical terms. But he tried to introduce a virus into the computer system he was working on, and when that didn't work, they caught him trying to shut down the mainframe, I think they call it."

"But why would he do that?" I ask.

"I don't know. His lawyer told him not to talk to anybody about it. There are rumors around town, of course."

Gabriel just silently eats spaghetti, taking in everything we were saying. He tries to look uninterested, but he meets my eyes and gives me a slight nod of encouragement.

I casually sprinkle Parmesan over my spaghetti. "What kind of rumors, Mom?"

"Oh, you know, crazy rumors. It didn't make any sense. I guess whatever he was working on caused problems for some big-name people."

"Oh," I say, raising my eyebrows in shock, "How? What was he working on?"

Mom shook her head and squeezed her eyes closed for a second, "I don't know; it's all rumors. Maybe Shannon will tell you more. But I know they're trying to keep everything quiet as the lawyer advised."

"That makes sense. After dinner, Gabriel and I are going down to the pub and grabbing a drink. Do you wanna go with us?" I ask, even though I know the answer.

Laughing, she replies, "Oh, Callie, I wouldn't be caught dead down at that bar."

"Hey, it doesn't hurt to ask," I say, twirling spaghetti on my fork.

"Just remember when you go down there, our family is the talk of the town, so you're bound to get some questions."

I pause, "I can handle it, and you know what?" I point my breadstick at her before taking a bite, "I might get some answers, too."

Gabriel nodded, and we both quickly finished our spaghetti and helped Mom clean up.

It was just after seven when we headed down to the pub. It was only three blocks away, so we walked.

"I like your mom. She's sweet."

"She is. All she ever wanted to be was a mom and a wife. She did a good job raising us. I think that's why she was so willing to stay with my dad even when she was unhappy." That distant pain creeps into my heart. I usually did such an excellent job of keeping it locked up, but being home made it harder.

27

One More Beer

I heave open the heavy door of the log tavern. It had been in this neighborhood longer than most of the houses. Inside, neon signs glowed over wood tables that usually needed a napkin under one leg to keep level. "They have great local beer here. There's a big brewery downtown."

"I didn't know Columbia City was so cool." He follows as I weave through empty tables.

"Most people don't," I say, smiling. "Oh, and if we have time, I'll take you to check out the Columbia City haunted jail. It's quite the spectacle." I slide onto a bar stool.

Gabriel plants himself on the one next to me, "That will make the whole trip worth it."

"Hey, Mr. Johnson," I say to the gray-haired man behind the bar with his back to us.

He turns around, and his eyes light up. "Well, hey, there, young lady; I haven't seen you since Christmas. What's brought you back here?"

"Oh, I just came home to drag this guy around and show him the sights," I say, slinging an arm around Gabriel's shoulders.

Mr. Johnson looks Gabriel up and down and then nods approvingly.

"Well, you've come to the right place. Let me pour you a drink on the house." Mr. Johnson grabs two frosty mugs from the cooler and fills them from the tap of local brew.

Pushing them toward us, he leans in and says, "Real shame what's happening to your family. It seems like your brother-in-law is in some real trouble."

Well, that didn't take long. I take a long swig of my free beer before I answer. "Yeah, it's not great, that's for sure." And then I lean in and ask, "What's the word on the street?"

He smiles, happy to be able to offer some inside information. "Sounds like Henry is either a hero or a crazy man, depending on who you believe."

"What do you mean?" I ask.

Mr. Johnson looks left and right then says in a low voice, "You know that dating website?"

It takes a minute for the words to register, and then Gabriel and I look at each other, "What did you say?" I ask.

"Dating website," he slowly repeats, as if I don't understand English. "Which one?" I ask.

"One of the waitresses had it pulled up the other day, and I can't remember its name, but it's pink and has some good-looking guy talking. I think it's love for something or other; I don't know," he says, grabbing a towel to dry beer mugs.

A sense of dread goes through me, and I take another swig of alcohol, trying to calm my nerves. My mouth is dry, and I look at Gabriel. His eyebrows are furrowed in concentration as if he is mentally trying to solve a puzzle.

"So why the split decision on Henry?" Gabriel asks.

"Well, some folks think he was trying to stop some new-age technology that is changing people's brains," he says, pointing to his head. "Other people say he is kinda crazy and causing problems for a nice local company. I don't know. That's just what I hear. And there is an investigation not only into your brother-in-law but into that website."

"Really?" Gabriel asks, and I make a mental note to do some research tomorrow. Then, the television screen over the bar catches my attention.

"Hey, can you turn that up?" I ask.

Mr. Johnson grabs the remote and turns it up. It's an interview on a national news station with Mr. Hottie himself.

"So you call yourself Cupid?" a well-known brunette reporter in a conservative suit and navy heels asks.

"But of course; that is my name," he says, smiling, sitting on the edge of a stool, his shiny alligator shoes resting on the lower rung.

"Of course," she said, twirling her hair and looking up at him through her eyelashes.

"And you are the god of love?" she asks, licking and biting her bottom lip.

What in the world? I huff.

"That is what some call me, yes. Tell me, do you want, love?" Cupid asks her, not breaking eye contact.

She giggles and kicks her feet back and forth. One of her shoes goes flying across the studio, and there is an audible yelp from off stage.

"Oops," she says, hopping off her stool and limping out of shot to retrieve her shoe. When she comes back, she seems to be a little more grounded.

She settles back on the stool and takes a deep breath, sounding professional. "I don't want to put you on the spot, but I would love our audience to hear what makes your website so successful."

He leans in and stares into her eyes, "Is that what you desperately want to know?"

"Um, that's what is on the cards," she says, slinking off her stool to skitter over and show him her interview cards. "See, these are the questions they want me to ask you."

"What is wrong with her?" Gabriel asks as I watch the screen, mouth gaping. "It's like watching a slow-motion car crash."

"I don't know. She isn't very professional. She looks like she is drunk or something," I say, taking another swig of beer. I can't stop watching this horror unfold.

Cupid leans into the host and whispers something into her ear. She blushes and giggles again.

"Have you ever seen anything like this?" I ask.

"No. I have seen her do plenty of interviews, and she is usually a hard-nosed investigative reporter. She even led the effort to bring down a government corruption scandal last year," Mr. Johnson says, shaking his head.

"Well, she looks like a middle school girl talking to her crush at the dance," I say.

The next forty-five minutes are embarrassing to watch, but we finish an entire pitcher of beer.

"That guy is something else," Gabriel says as Mr. Johnson switches the channel back to the basketball game.

I consider. "He is creepy. Kinda hot, but creepy."

"Should I be jealous?" he says.

I lean in and give him a sloppy kiss. "No way. He couldn't hold a candle to you." I get up to go to the restroom. On the way back, I stop to chat with a few people I know, carefully avoiding any talk of Henry.

Weaving through the tables back to Gabriel, I see some of the locals eyeing him. A group of middle-aged women gathered around a corner table, a picture of margaritas in front of them, are whispering and pointing at him. I stop in front of his stool, lean in, and whisper. "You know, there are a dozen women here wanting to take you home right now."

"Oh?" he says.

"Uh-huh. They are looking at you right now." I smile, sliding my arms around his waist. I am the perfect amount of drunk.

"Well," he says, low and husky, "maybe you should claim your territory."

He bends down slightly to meet my lips and gives me a deep, wet, slightly drunk kiss.

We are both panting a little bit as we part.

"I probably should be embarrassed, but I'm not. And who cares, anyway, because we are already the talk of the town," I say, slurring my words slightly.

Gabriel grins, "You're a lightweight."

"I know. I don't get out much." Then, I lean over Gabriel's arm and say, "Hey, Mr. Johnson, is the grill still open?"

He finishes handing a group of girls their shot glasses and heads my way, "Sure thing; what can I get you?"

"Hmm. French fries?"

Gabriel is giving me a look.

"What?" I say as he's staring at me. "I've been drinking, and I need something to soak up all this alcohol before we get home. I can't let my mom see me drunk."

"Aren't you a little old to be worried about that?"

"If you think that, you don't know my mother as well as you think you do." I wag my finger at him.

He laughs, "Okay, then, I'm having one more beer because my mom isn't here."

28

Who is Your Boss?

Sunday, March 27

The next day, we are nursing hangovers in the living room over coffee and dry toast when the doorbell rings.

"Hey, munchkins," I say as the kids run through the door, wrapping their arms around my neck.

My sister walks in holding an apple pie. Dark circles shadowed her eyes. She smiles, but I can tell that it's been a rough couple of weeks. Behind her is Henry, waiting to see how we will treat him. Poor guy.

I smile wide and throw my arms around his neck. "Hello, my favorite brother-in-law."

He is startled and stiffens but then relaxes and hugs me back. "Hey, Callie," he says. "Thanks for helping out."

"No problem," I say. I introduce them to Gabriel, who is charming as usual.

Then, we relax in the living room with my mom as the kids run out the back door to play.

"How are things going?" I ask—what a stupid question. I grit my teeth and wait for an answer.

Luckily, Shannon rescues me, "The kids are doing well. And it's nice having Henry home more." She smiles softly at her husband. Her eyes shine as he pats her knee.

"Shannon's been amazing. It hasn't been easy in a town this size, as you can imagine. Everybody knows what's going on."

Shannon looks at us. "Yeah, I'm glad he's home now. I mean, I don't know how this works, but at least he's not in jail."

Henry chuckles, "That's true. That was an experience I do not want to repeat. It was just like in the movies. You should've seen the guys who were locked up with me. Some of them were drunk. I swear there was one guy who was six and a half feet tall, a biker guy. I am lying on my cot and thinking, *Great. I'm going to get locked up with this guy long-term and have to watch my back at night and in the shower.*"

We all genuinely laugh as we picture sweet, responsible, conservative Henry locked up with a biker gang dude. I make a mental note to try and talk with Henry about the website nonsense at some point. He might have some insights. The afternoon is spent pushing kids on the swings, helping mom in the kitchen, and eating way too much apple pie.

* * *

On the way home, my phone rings. It's a Chicago number, so I answer.

"Hello?"

"Callie McGuire?"

"Yes. Who's this?"

"I am an executive assistant at MyLove4Life. It has come to our attention that you have yet to confirm your registration with a... Mr. Jimmy Powell."

I hear papers shuffling in the background. Gabriel looks sideways at me and raises an eyebrow. I shake my head in frustration.

"As I have said before, I am not interested in finalizing my match.

Your services are no longer needed."

"I am not sure I understand you correctly."

I put it on speaker so Gabriel could hear. "I do not want to finalize my match on your website. I don't need a million-dollar guarantee."

"Ms. Mcguire, our system depends on each match going through the entire process to finalize their match. We can't have singles abandoning the process once matched."

"Why? Why do you care?"

Gabriel and I share a look, and he shakes his head.

"Ms. Mcguire. You agreed to the initial set of terms and conditions. That includes finalizing your match. You are in violation of your contract."

"I..."

She continues, "And my boss will not tolerate violations of the contract. He has invested his heart and soul into this program. And you think you can walk away?" Her tone shifts into something frantic.

Gabriel speaks up, "Listen, I don't know how you are, but your attitude is unacceptable. I will need your boss's name because we will be making a formal complaint."

"There's no need for that," she says curtly.

"Oh, I think there is. What is his name?"

"I am sure you have seen his interviews. Mr.Cupid is a very busy man."

"Your boss is Cupid?" I ask, thinking back to the interview we saw at the bar.

"That's correct. And you are free to reach out to him. Unless you finalize your match, he may reach out to you directly. Good day." And with that, she hangs up.

"Wow," Gabriel says, "I can't believe that."

"I know. I don't know what to do."

He takes my hand, "You aren't going to do anything. This is

harassment."

I look down at our hands, fingers entwined. I don't know. I don't want to get in trouble if I am in breach of contract. Maybe I should talk to my mom. "But what if they come after me?"

Gabriel squeezes my hand, "No one is coming after you. This is corporate bullying, nothing more. The Better Business Bureau will probably shut them down if this is how they are treating people. Don't worry about it." He turns on the radio to a news station, "And if this Cupid shows up, you just let me know, and I will deal with it." He looks over and smiles.

I smile back, but my stomach is sour, and anxiety threatens to take hold. I practice deep breathing and look out the window at the passing fields. Maybe Gabriel is right. This is all sounding a little too much like a mediocre crime novel. It's not like the CEO of a company will track me down just because I didn't want their service, right?

29

Terms and Conditions

Monday, March 28

Standing over the printer, I wait as page after page spits out. I look over my shoulder at Gabriel sitting on the floor next to my bed. "This is the longest terms and conditions I've ever seen."

"Have you ever actually seen a set of terms and conditions?" he asks, smirking.

"I've seen the first line of lots of them."

He laughs. "Me, too."

I grab two highlighters off my desk and hand him one. "Let's both read it over, so we don't miss anything. Highlight anything that looks suspicious or dangerous."

"Yes, ma'am," he says, giving me a mock salute.

We settle down with our backs against the bed and start reading.

"What's this section here? It says the signatory agrees to abide by the terms and conditions set forth in appendix one through thirty-four," he says, showing me the section now glowing fluorescent yellow.

"I don't know. Is there an appendix in the terms and conditions forms?"

He shuffles through the papers, "Not that I can see. The rest of this looks okay, but my uncle is a lawyer, so I'm going to send it to him.

"That's a good idea. But how will we get the missing piece of the contract?"

"I don't know. I will ask my uncle that, too."

"Okay," I say, standing up to stretch.

"Let me try one more thing." He picks up his phone off the floor and starts to dial.

"Who are you calling?" I ask, kneeling on my bed and looking over his shoulder.

He shrugs. "The company. Maybe they will give it to us if we ask."

I flop down on the bed on my stomach and grab my copy of the documents, skimming the pages of the agreement I signed.

"Hi, yes, I am hoping you can help me. I need a copy of the appendix to the terms and conditions."

After a moment, he says, "Hmmm."

"Yes, I printed off the terms and conditions but realized there is an appendix referenced that isn't included."

"Ah."He taps the highlighter on his lip, thinking.

"What are they saying?" I ask him quietly.

He shakes his head and says into the phone, hesitantly, "No. It seems like those should be accessible online. Hmm. Okay. Thanks. Bye."

"Well?" I ask, wrapping my arms around his neck.

He turns his head and kisses me, "Well, apparently, part of the terms and conditions say that we can only get them by court order."

"What? Where?" I lean back and flip through the document again. "Oh, this is convenient. It's tucked into a section way in the back."

"Let me see that," he says, taking the paper from me and reading it.

"This is crap," I say.

"I know. But it could be standard practice. I don't know." He says, shaking his head.

"How the hell could they get away with this? Don't you think somebody would complain?" I roll over on my back.

"The scarier thought is how few people read terms and conditions when they sign up for stuff," he says, shaking his head.

"Yeah. Even if this is all fine and it's just a bunch of weird coincidences, I am definitely never clicking without reading again," I say, throwing the papers in the air and letting them float to the bedroom floor.

"Good plan," Gabriel replies.

30

Hello Cupid

Tuesday, March 29

I have just enough time to hit the book shop before our double date. Gabriel is meeting me at the restaurant, conveniently located in the same part of town. Stepping out of the taxi that I splurged on to save time, I remember that one of my favorite authors has a new book. *Great.* The latest release has attracted a line of teenage girls out the shop's door, and I have to squeeze my way through the crowd to get in. I wish I could join them in line, but I have other priorities.

Bypassing my usual fare, I scan the stacks until I find what I'm looking for on the top shelf. If I want to avoid another disastrous end to a relationship, I need help. Running my fingers along the spines of the relationship books, I choose an impressively thick paperback.

Keeping Control in Every Relationship: A Girl's Guide to Surviving Love

As I read the back cover, a breeze blows through the store, and it smells like fresh, lovely roses. I turn my head toward the scent, and a familiar figure steps out from behind the stack of romance novels. I would recognize those green eyes anywhere.

"Hello, Callie." A slow, lazy smile spreads across his face.

"Aren't you...Cupid?" I glance around to see where the clerk is, but suddenly the shop seems empty. My throat feels like sandpaper as I say, "What are you doing here?" I move around the table to put some space between us.

His long fingers stroke the books on the table. "Well, like you, I'm a reader, so I thought I'd check out this charming little bookstore and who do I find, but Callie Mcguire," he says, spreading his hands out in front of him.

I blink twice and feel drawn to know everything about him, "Oh, I see, what kind of books do you like?"

"Same as you, I suppose; mystery, true crime, thrillers." He opens a book from the table and casually flips through it.

"I-I thought you'd like romance, you know, because of your business." Did he come here to find me? Is he flirting with me? He is so good-looking. I wonder what it would be like to kiss him. No, that's wrong.

He smiles as I shake my head in confusion. He then slides the book back onto the table. "My dear girl, romance...well, I don't necessarily believe in love. You know all about that, don't you?"

"I don't know what you mean. I have had plenty of boyfriends. I'm dating someone now." I straighten my shoulders and lift my chin, trying to gather my thoughts.

"Oh, yes, I know you're dating Gabriel, and you think you might even be falling in love with your Gab-ri-el." He raises his eyebrows over perfect emerald eyes, and I'm dimly aware he is closer now.

"Well, uh, I don't know. I don't know if I've ever actually been in love, but I like him a lot."

"Who, Callie?"

"The guy I'm dating."

"Say his name, Callie." He is next to me, and his breath smells like fresh mint.

Don't look at him, Callie, says my inner voice. "His name. His name is…" I can't remember anything.

"And who were you supposed to be dating?"

I feel his fingertips brush my cheek, and heat rises from my knees to my lips and face. I want very much to tip my head back.

My voice sounds like I'm drunk. "Um… Jimmy?"

"Yes, but you never did finalize the lovely match I chose for you, right, Callie?"

It's hard to concentrate. "I-I ran into Gabriel at IKEA; we are dating; no need to…"

"Right, but see, Callie, that's the problem. You failed to finalize your match, and you have violated my terms and conditions."

I'm aware of the heat radiating off his body and his palm cupping my chin. He turns my face, and my body follows; his lips, close to mine, are full, and I yearn to taste them. His scent is…I search for the word, *urgent.*

"You seem to think that this is about you, Callie, and it's not. I have a reputation to uphold, and I cannot have my clients ignoring my wishes."

My heart thumps hard in my chest, and his hands caress my shoulder blades. I'm dimly aware my mouth is open, and I can feel my heart beating in my lips. I whisper into his mouth, "I don't understand."

"My system works when people cooperate, Callie and a one hundred percent success rating is required. I am a god. I will not fail. If you want to live happily ever after, you'll be a good girl and play nice. If not, then I can make other plans for you." I think he is going to kiss me. I want more than anything for him to kiss me hard, but his lips graze my cheek, and he speaks softly into my ear, and I can't help but gasp. In detail, he describes all that he will do to my body and mind, and I shiver in delight, clinging to him, all thought of other more inferior men banished.

And as I am leaning in, finally giving in to this desire, he steps away. I stumble forward, landing painfully on my hands and knees. My cell phone flies out of my hands and slides across the floor into a bookshelf.

Cupid is on one knee, playfully tapping the tip of my nose. "You know my power, girl, so you'd best obey me. I'm always looking for new toys, and I wouldn't mind adding you and perhaps some of your attractive friends to my little playpen. Jayla would be fascinating."

I'm shaking. This is ludicrous. He has serious issues, not the least being stalking. I need to say something, stand up for myself. I can't put the words together. The only thing in my mind is a quote from *Pride and Prejudice*. "You have insulted me in every way possible and can now have nothing further to say. I must ask you to leave immediately." I croak, and then I slap his hand away. The seductive spell is undone, leaving a hideous, stomach-churning humiliation in its place.

His laughter echoes amongst the book stacks as I struggle to stand, and though I try to hold it back, my stomach churns. I run to the bathroom and throw up.

31

Double Date

My reflection blinks at me, and I realize my wrists are sore. How long have I been leaning on the bathroom sink, staring into the cracked mirror? I check my watch. It's 5:00 p.m., and I don't have enough time to go home and change before the double date with Simon. My phone is now resting on the sink. I tap the cracked screen and try to restart it. Nothing. Okay, water on, rinse mouth thoroughly, splash my face, paper towel dry, deep breath, pat hair down and start walking.

It's ten blocks to the restaurant, and I try to ground myself. The visceral memory of Cupid comes in flashes then fades. To keep from screaming, I focus on the mundane; the click of my boots on the pavement, the changing of the traffic lights from red to green, the sound of children laughing as they tap on the window of a pet store, curly-haired puppies playfully pawing at the glass. I let out controlled breaths in through the nose, out through the mouth.

By the time I opened the door to the restaurant, I still knew I was humiliated, but the details were vague and muddled. I want to tell Gabriel, but shame stabs me, and I decide to try to sort through it later.

Plates of appetizers and drinks crowd the small table where Simon, Cody, and Gabriel are seated, and they greet me with cheers. Cody's service dog sits patiently under the table, his ears alert with interest.

Gabriel pecks me on the cheek and examines my face, "Callie, what's wrong? Why are you so late?"

Mustering up every bit of energy I have, I smile and say, "Oh, nothing, I was running late and broke my cell, and I couldn't call." All true. The last thing I need right now is him telling me I am overreacting or being dramatic about the website.

Introductions are made.

Cody's handshake is firm and warm, and he lets me pet his dog, a German Shepard with soft brown eyes.

The waitress scurries over to take my order.

My stomach churns. "Uh, I just want water for now; I'll nibble off my boyfriend's plate." I paste on a grin.

Simon is beaming at me. "So, Callie, I need to tell you all about Cody, starting from birth."

Gabriel and Cody groan in unison.

"Okay, maybe I'll just give you the condensed version."

I nod and try to make appropriate sounds as he reviews Cody's life in Wyoming, how he lost ninety percent of his vision after a car crash and head injury when he was eight years old, and how they connected on MyLove4Life. I am only half-listening. I take out my phone and check my text messages. "Callie, what is so important you can't just listen to my story?" Simon is frowning.

"What? I, uh, my phone is broken."

Gabriel looks concerned. "Callie, are you okay?"

"Yes, I just need to do something." I start rummaging through my purse, but I don't know what I am looking for.

"Okay, what do you need to do, pray tell?" Simon laces his fingers under his chin.

My mind blanks as I drop my bag on my lap and stare at my phone. "There was something I needed to do with an app, but I can't remember.

It's broken." I realize that I sound like an idiot. I try to grasp the memory of the bookstore attack, but the details are suddenly wispy as if I'm trying to gather up loose threads in the wind. Is this what it feels like to have a mental breakdown? Gabriel's arm is around my shoulders, and he kisses my cheek softly.

"Callie, sweetheart, what's wrong?" I look into his perfect, beautiful brown eyes, and calm washes over me. The wispy threads of memory seem to blow away, and all that is left is Gabriel. I let out a breath and slide my phone back into my bag.

"I think I just need to eat." I grin at him.

He gestures to the waitress, and I order a cheeseburger and beer.

After the waitress leaves, Simon leans in. "Remember what I told you about the website and the rumors on the Internet?

I choke on the water I was drinking.

Gabriel gives me a questioning look and pats me on the back.

I shake my head and turn back to Simon.

"Well," Simon nods at Cody and touches his shoulder, "It's worse than I thought. Cody's sister is a software engineer who builds websites, and he knows all about researching this kind of thing. Cody, tell them what you found out."

Cody's hands remain relaxed on the table as he speaks.

"Well, this dating website is owned by a corporation called Psycheros. It's a conglomeration of many different companies, one of which is in Fort Wayne, Indiana."

"Isn't that where you're from, Callie?" Simon breaks in.

I nod without speaking. Then, realizing Cody can't see me, I say too loud, "Yes."

"Sooooo everyone knows this site keeps matching up people who don't seem ideal for each other. Married movie stars and middle-aged housewives. I mean, look at us, Simon is such a hottie, and I can't even see him unless I use my hands."

They chuckle at this inside joke as Cody places his fingertips on Simon's cheek.

Simon takes his hand and leans forward again to speak in a hushed voice, "Now, this is being kept hush-hush because no one's connecting the dots, except for a few bloggers out in California. Cody and I think Psycheros is somehow hypnotizing people or chemically changing their pheromones or something. It makes sense. Otherwise, how would these total opposites like that couple in California end up together?"

I raise my eyebrows.

Gabriel jumps in. "You missed it earlier; Cody told us more about that Hollywood actor who left his wife for a fan, who turned out to be an older lunch lady from Louisiana. Also, a young accounting executive in Washington D.C. fell in love with a great-grandmother from Mississippi. And a conservative legislator who left her husband and five kids for a nineteen-year-old college student."

"I mean, how are these matches not collecting on the million-dollar guarantee?" Simon interrupts. "Callie, you're in marketing. How do they get away with not paying?"

We pause our conversation as the waitress sets a plate of steaming fries and a hamburger in front of me. She returns a moment later to fill our water glasses.

When she is gone, Simon looks at me. "Well? How is this guy getting away with not paying? At least one of these horrendous matches should have broken up by now."

This is familiar territory. "You are right. Companies often write guarantees into the brand, and manufacturers must honor them or open themselves up to lawsuits," I explain. "It's understood that even if a customer isn't satisfied, most are just too lazy to send the product back, so the cost of the returns from the guarantee is factored into the retail cost. For instance, there is a 'male enhancement' pill on the market that is just a starch in a gelatin capsule, but out of embarrassment, only five percent of customers ask for their money back."

"It's a million dollars, Callie, and no one has collected on it yet," Cody says. "Apparently, this is a product that works one hundred percent of the time. It's as if the website is a sick joke designed by an evil genius to torment the people." He taps the tabletop. "Fortunately, you guys fell in love the old-fashioned way. I'm not complaining about how Simon and I got together, but at least your fate isn't in the hand of a corporate technocrat. Simon and I have to wonder what would have happened if we met in an aisle of Home Depot or something."

Simon snorts. "We may never have met at all, so don't worry. I know how I feel, and now that I have you wearing bowties on Sunday, we will be together forever."

They both laugh.

Gabriel looks doubtful. "It does seem a little far-fetched. I mean, conspiracy theories and impulsive celebrities aren't exactly reliable sources. Maybe these couples are outliers."

Simon scoffs, "That's what they always say until the conspiracy is proven to be true. It gets worse. Other reports are coming out people who have been matched through this site are turning up dead."

I put down my cheeseburger mid-bite, and Gabriel meets my eyes and takes my hand.

"They're saying they were murdered," Simon whispers.

"But why?" Gabriel looks incredulous. "It doesn't make any sense. Who would have a motive to go after a bunch of lonely people who signed up on a website?'

"That's what we have to find out." Simon nods for emphasis and squeezes Cody's hand at the same time. "And I think the place to start is with the CEO; guy styles himself 'Cupid,' only he's grown up into a real hottie. Why, Callie, I do believe you are blushing."

"Actually," Gabriel's hand cups my shoulder, "Callie signed up for the website. They matched her with someone, but we met before she completed the process."

"What? You never told me that." Simon teases. "Gabriel here is a lucky man to have snagged you before the ink dried on that other match.

* * *

Later, as Gabriel and I stroll back to my apartment, I need to explain my behavior. "I'm sorry for being weird tonight."

"Aww, it's nice to know you aren't perfect. You can make it up to me, though."

"How?" I know exactly what he's going to say.

"A kiss."

"I think that's fair."

He stops in the middle of the street to slip his arm around my waist. He rests his other hand on my cheek then slowly tips his head to kiss me.

"Do you want to come up to my apartment?"

He smiles and cups my cheek. "We've got all the time in the world, and I want to do this right for once."

I can't find the words to tell him that I want him near, that he centers me, that sex is the furthest thing from my mind.

He gently puts a finger under my chin and lifts it until my eyes meet his. "I want to come in. I want to come in more than you can imagine. But I also promised you to take it slow, and I'm not going to let some margaritas get in the way of that promise, even if I want them to."

"Okay," I say, trying to sound casual, but he knows something is wrong.

"Callie, are you upset about the website's conspiracy nonsense? I'm

147

sure if anything is amiss, the police or even the FBI will be all over it, and besides, what can we do? You and I have nothing to worry about, anyway." He smiles. "We wouldn't be affected because we met the old-fashioned way, in an aisle at IKEA."

He envelopes me in his arms, and I lay my head on his shoulder.

"At least *our* fate isn't in the hands of Cupid or whatever he calls himself." Gabriel's hug is warm, but a cold sense of unease creeps along my backbone as I glance over his shoulder at every shadow along the street, expecting something dark to jump out.

32

Burner Phone

Wednesday, March 30

The following day I head to the I pay cash for the phone and walk several blocks to the train as I consider what to tell Gabriel. I dial his number and wait at the top of the stairs to the station.

"Hello, Gabriel Perez speaking." His voice is formal, academic.

"Hey, it's me."

"Callie? Did you get a new number?"

"Yes, so make sure you save it." Before he can ask another question, I say, "Hey, can you take a day off tomorrow?"

"I don't have class, so that should be fine. Why?" I can hear him shuffling papers in the background.

"We need to drive to Fort Wayne and talk to my brother-in-law." I hear sirens wailing in the distance and plug my other ear to hear better.

"Tomorrow?" The shuffling stops.

"Yes, it can't wait. Please, trust me on this."

"Is this about that website again?"

"It's about spending many hours in the car with the woman you adore. And it's about the website."

"Callie, I'm thrilled to spend 'many hours' with you in the car, but I'm not sure about the website. I hate to see you get drawn into a conspiracy drama; it's not healthy. I'm sure law enforcement is investigating anything illegal going on."

I bite my lip and try to keep my voice from shaking. "Yeah, well, I still think we should go check it out before more of my friends invest in it. You know, caveat emptor and all that."

"Okay, I'll pick you up at eight, but can we drop all the conspiracy talk once your questions are answered?"

"Sure," I lie.

"What happened to your phone anyway?"

"I dropped it, and it broke." Not a lie.

I dial my sister next. I have to call twice before she picks up.

"Hey, Sis. Write down this number and don't show anyone. It's a burner. And yes, I feel ridiculous for saying that."

"Callie, you sound scared."

"I am. I'm either going crazy or I'm mixed up in something bad. Either way, I need to talk to Henry. Can I drive down tomorrow?"

"I don't know if that's a good idea, Callie. Henry is not supposed to be talking about this with anybody."

"Listen, Shannon; this is bigger than Henry. Something is going on here, and we have to figure out what it is."

Shannon sighs, "Sorry. Of course, you can talk to him; we're family. This is all just so stressful. Everything's been destroyed, and I miss my old life.

I make my voice soft. "I'm sorry, I can't imagine how hard this has been on you. I know you're trying to hold it together for the kids and be strong for Henry. You're always the strong, responsible one."

"That's the problem," Shannon says, "I'm not. Callie, I've been in therapy for years. And after college, when I hurt my knee, remember? I decided it would be a great idea to try an addiction to pain pills."

"What?"

"Oh, yeah, I was an overachiever in that, too."

"I had no idea, Sis."

"Of course, you didn't; only Mom knew. It was before I met Henry." She sighs. "I'm struggling with this, and all my friends are acting weird around me because it's not something that happens in our circle. Divorce? Yes. Kids with problems? Unavoidable. But not this."

This is all new to me. Mom has not kept me in the loop probably because she is too busy asking me about my love life instead of sharing relevant family updates.

"I'm so sorry, Shannon. I wouldn't be coming over but Henry is the only one who can answer the questions I have. I promise I won't ever do anything to harm you guys. You're my family, and I love you."

"I love you, too, and I'm just glad you are opening up a little. You've managed to build the great wall of China between us over the years, and it's kinda nice to have my sister back."

"No, I haven't. Okay, maybe I have, but I didn't have a Henry in my life to melt my cold, cold heart."

She chuckles softly, "But now you have a Gabriel."

"So true, as long as Gabriel doesn't get tired of Conspiracy Callie."

"Okay, we will be home all day. I'll let Henry know you're coming."

33

Henry's Story

Thursday, March 31

"Nice," Gabriel comments as we slow down in front of Shannon's house, a chic Colonial in a newer neighborhood. Henry's Lexus is parked in the spacious driveway, and their golden retriever, Sunny, is staring out the large bay window waiting to greet us.

I sweep my arm, palm up. "Yep. Welcome to Suburbia."

Sculptured hedges and flower beds that will be alive with color in the spring are artfully arranged around young ornamental trees. Shoots of grass poke out between scattered bits of snow; the yard will be green and lush by May. We take the hedge-trimmed brick path to the front door, and I grin at Gabriel. Grasping the big gold door knocker, I bang out a pattern; da-da-da-dum-dum, dum-dum. It's so loud even Gabriel looks startled, and I explain that it was my and Shannon's secret code knock when we were young.

A moment later, I hear a commotion inside the house, and Shannon opens the door, using her arms and legs to corral the kids and dog. She looks a little better than she did last time I saw her. The dark circles under her eyes have faded, but her face is lined with worry. Still, she breaks out a smile to greet us. "You brought Gabriel! What a wonderful surprise."

Gabriel smiles broadly and steps forward. "It's good to see you again. You have a lovely home."

Their conversation is interrupted by Sunny's barking. I reach down and scratch her behind the ears.

She ushers us into the spacious front entryway, and the kids and dog scatter to pursue adventures elsewhere.

"Long drive?" Shannon asks, taking our coats and hanging them in the hall closet.

"Yeah, it was. But I made Gabriel listen to my high school playlist so he could get a taste of what the Mcguire girls were like in high school."

She laughs, "I'm so glad to see you, Sis."

I hug her. "Me, too. Is Henry home?"

"Oh, he is upstairs shaving. He's been enthusiastically embracing this unemployed lifestyle, so I'm glad you came. He was forced to clean up a bit." She laughs, and for a moment, her eyes are merry.

She motions for us to follow her to the kitchen, and she pours each of us a cup of coffee. "I'm making lasagna tonight if you want to stay for dinner."

I look at Gabriel. "Would it be okay if we eat a bit early? Gabriel and I need to be back in the city before it gets too late."

"Of course." She stretches her arms with palms up in a circular motion. "It's not like we have to follow a normal schedule or anything." She smiles weakly.

Footsteps echo on the stairs, and a moment later, Henry appears; clean-shaven, dressed in jeans and a comfortable gray sweater.

He kisses me on the cheek and shakes Gabriel's hand. "Hey, guys, good to see you. Shannon said you have some questions for me?"

I glance over to where the kids are now watching TV in the family room. "Is there somewhere private we can talk?"

Henry looks at Shannon then back to us. "Let's go to my office. It's over the garage and very private. We'll be back down soon."

"Of course." Shannon smiles at him.

He steps forward to wrap his arms around her for several quiet seconds as she lays her head on his chest. "You're the best wife ever," he murmurs into her hair.

He leads us back toward the garage entryway and up the stairs to an office with French doors. Oak bookcases line one entire wall, and a beautiful oak desk rests in front of a large window overlooking the front yard. An elegant sofa and two wingback chairs complete the room.

Gabriel and I sit together on the sofa, our knees touching. "This is bigger than my apartment," I say. I'm only slightly exaggerating.

He chuckles. "Yeah, when we were looking for houses, I saw this and realized it would be a perfect office. I was ready to write an offer, and when your sister saw the bedroom closet, she was sold, too.

"That sounds about right. Shannon always had more clothes than everyone else in the house combined." I pause. "Look, we don't want to do anything to make your situation worse. Everything we talk about today will be held in confidence, but we have some questions only you can answer, and I hope you can help us."

Henry rubs a hand over his chin and nods once. "Okay, shoot."

"I signed up for the dating website."

Henry's eyes widen. "What? When did you sign up?"

Gabriel jumps in before I can answer, "She matched with someone else just before we met by accident," he smiles, "at IKEA. Anyway, some strange things have happened, and we're concerned." He gazes at me for a moment. "It's important to us that we get to the bottom of whatever is going on at this dating website."

Henry crosses his arms and looks down at his feet. "What do you think is going on?"

"We don't know exactly."

Henry takes a deep breath, and Gabriel and I lean forward in unison, ready to hear what he has to say.

"When you sign up for this website and click the terms and conditions, it works pretty well. Everyone matched on this website falls in love, and they're a great match like you guys; did you ever wonder why that is?

Gabriel and I look at each other and shrug.

"Look," Henry's face falls, and he rubs his hands on his thighs. "My lawyer has instructed me not to talk to anybody about the case, but I don't care. If anything happens to me, someone else needs to know what is happening." He pauses to take a drink of his coffee and continues. "It's bad. The company uses optogenetics to affect the neurons in people's brains and, simply put, hypnotize them into falling in love."

Gabriel interrupts, "I'm confused. How is that possible?"

Henry shrugs. "Sorry, I'm not involved in its science; I only know that it works. Um, let's say you log onto the website, you are watching the intro video, not thinking anything of it. Meanwhile, a series of super brief flashing lights and messages alter the neurons in your brain to make you susceptible, like hypnosis through subliminal messages. The altered neurons are activated when you finalize the registration process, and your match is set."

I remember staring at Jimmy's image the first time I saw it. Was I being brainwashed?

"It's not completely new technology. They have been developing it for years. But Cupid managed to figure out how to bring the idea to fruition to use to his advantage. And if he succeeds at this technology, imagine what it can be used for. You could mass hypnotize an entire nation into doing whatever you wanted them to."

"That's ridiculous," Gabriel says, "That's completely illegal, and the Feds would be on it in a minute."

"Yes, it's completely illegal unless you agree to the terms and conditions." Henry runs his fingers through his hair.

"I didn't agree to anything like that!" I say, too loud.

"Callie, this is important," he looks at me intently. "Did you sign the terms and conditions?"

My mind is racing, and I feel nauseous. "Yes, but I never finalized our match."

Henry releases his breath in a relieved sigh. "That's great news. Unfortunately, thousands of people have 'swiped right,' and they don't even know what's been done to them. It's caused chaos and ruined lives, and I was part of it." His eyes are full of self-recrimination.

Henry regards me. "Callie, did you even read the terms and conditions?"

"No. Does anybody read the terms and conditions?" My heart is racing.

"Not often enough," Henry sighs. "And 'swiping right' makes the decision binding. I don't understand everything, but I know that the company execs are seriously invested in getting one hundred percent compliance."

"They've been on my butt for weeks to do it," I blurt out.

"What do you mean?" Gabriel says, concern shadowing his face and reaching for my hand. "I thought the texts had stopped?"

I feel breathless, but it pours out. "Well, it started with text messages and phone calls. Then I think someone followed me home a few weeks ago. And the CEO showed up at the bookstore, and I broke my phone...."

Henry's eyes get big. "You have been in touch with Cupid?"

I nod. "He threatened me."

"What? When?" Gabriel demands.

I search my mind, trying to recreate a list of offenses. Everything is blurry and jumbled together—flashes of Cupid's smile, breath on my neck, roses, cryptic notes. The best I can come up with is a rough sketch.

"He sent me notes and showed up at the bookstore when I was there. It was so strange. I was scared, and I can't remember exactly what he said. It was like, I don't know, like I was drugged or something." I look at the floor and whisper, "I thought I might be going crazy."

"Why didn't you say anything?" Gabriel is shaking his head, and I can see the hurt in his eyes. "I knew there was something wrong when we met with Simon and Cody, but you didn't say anything. I thought you trusted me."

"Gabriel, I do. But I can't even be sure what happened, and there was something so off about him, and I was so...."

"He's intoxicating," says Henry.

"Intoxicating?" asks Gabriel.

I nod. "Yes, it was like that. Gabriel, remember the TV show host we watched at the bar when we visited my mom? She was acting as if she was in a trance. What if being close to him does that to you?"

Gabriel looks from me to Henry, "Is that possible?"

"Sure. He can either use the computer algorithm or his own influence."

"I thought you had to finalize the agreement to give them access?" I say, grabbing my purse and digging out some lip gloss.

"That is only for the love match. It's like drinking the love potion number nine," Henry says, "But if you're just close to him, it's more like one too many margaritas."

"He is charismatic, I get it," I say, picturing his beautiful green eyes and then chasing the thought away.

"But how do people who don't seem to belong together keep getting matched up?"

Gabriel looks at me and then back to Henry.

Henry grabs a legal pad and starts taking notes, "Right. Good question. Have you seen ads for the website on social media or television?"

"Yes," Gabriel and I say in unison.

"As soon as one person signs up and is matched, the other person they are matched with receives the same coding in their social media feed and computer ads."

"So you tried to stop it?" Gabriel asks.

"I am not saying that, but if someone wanted to stop it, they *might* try to load a virus into the mainframe and disrupt the patterns just enough not to be noticed immediately."

He lets the declaration hang in the air while tapping his pen on his desk.

Gabriel grabs my hand, "What can we do to help?"

A shadow falls over Henry's eyes, "There's not much you can do. Pray? This is way bigger than just me, and it needs to come to light. You've done so much by letting Shannon and the kids come to stay with you. That's exactly what we needed, and it was so good for her to spend time with you." His eyes are soft as he glances at the photo of his family on the corner of his desk.

Henry's phone buzzes, and he gets up to take a call in the other room.

Gabriel leans back on the couch and lets a breath out.

I stand up and walk to the window, watching the kids play in the backyard, oblivious to how dangerous the world is.

"I came so close to being part of this mess."

"We are part of this mess," Gabriel says.

I turn, and Gabriel looks down at the floor, hands folded on his knees. I walk over and touch his shoulder. Then, I sink back into the couch.

"You know what I mean. An evil corporation could have hypnotized me, and I would be on the sidelines and cheering for bodybuilder Jimmy."

Henry walks back in and sits down in one of the wing-backed chairs, clasping his hands. "Sorry about that. Listen, I think you guys are in real danger. Cupid doesn't like it when you don't play by his rules. And if you are in love," he notices my eyes go wide, "or in a relationship without his influence, he isn't going to let up until you either submit or break up."

"What do you mean?" I ask.

He leans forward, shoulder hunched. He meets my eyes, and then Gabriel's, "You guys have to break up. Callie needs to meet Jimmy at least, and if it doesn't work out, she can claim the money. It's either that or getting married. A marriage contract would void your contract."

No one says anything for a minute as we absorb the news. Henry sits back in the chair and crosses his legs. I shift on the couch and move away from Gabriel a little, the air in the office suddenly stifling.

"Wait," Gabriel says, leaning forward, "Break the contract? She never finalized it."

"Right, but one way or another, he will force you to. Either that or he will destroy you. He has a lot of money riding on the success of this technology." Henry keeps his voice detached, even as he delivers this terrible news.

Gabriel looks around the room and stands up abruptly, moving toward the door before turning around, "This is insane." He runs his hand through his hair.

Henry leans forward again, focusing his attention on me. "I agree. But it's true, and I think you both know it."

I meet his eyes and nod, almost imperceptibly. I know he is telling the truth. It all makes sense. Gabriel is frozen in place. He folds his arms across his chest, and emotions flash across his face; pain, fury, contemplation.

Shannon gently knocks on the door and sticks her head in, looking at each of us and frowning, "Hope I'm not interrupting. The kids want to show you all their new bike tricks." She smiles apologetically.

Gabriel drops his arms to his side and moves against the bookshelf, looking at me pleading.

I don't know what to say, so I just give him a small smile and turn my attention to my sister.

Henry stands up and sighs. He stretches his arms in front of him, gathering his composure, "Duty calls. Let's go enjoy the sunshine."

I follow him out of the office.

Gabriel grabs my hand as I pass him, and I don't resist. I don't know how much longer we have left together, and I want to enjoy every moment.

Melancholy hangs in the air the rest of the day. If my sister notices, she doesn't say anything. But with everything that's happened in the past few weeks, she may be oblivious to the change in the air.

Reluctantly, we stay for dinner because my sister is so excited about her lasagna. It's good, though. After so many years of not feeling like we had anything in common, it's nice to know she's not perfect. She thinks her failures are faults, but I think they are beautiful.

She and Henry walk us out to the car. "Thanks for dinner, Sis."

She's glowing with pride, "You're welcome. I'm so glad you got to come over."

Henry steps forward and leans in. "Listen, you two, I am sorry to be the bearer of bad news. There are a couple of things you need to do. Stay away from Cupid. And be careful. He won't give up until he gets what he wants."

34

Danger Ahead & Behind

Saturday, April 2

He's been following me for two blocks. The heels of my boots echo on the quiet sidewalk as I scan both sides of the street. I've never been mugged, but I close my fingers around the canister of mace in my pocket, just in case. My purse is hanging on one shoulder, but my credit cards and phone are hidden in coat pockets. Hopefully, if I get mugged, the guy will grab the purse and run.

Remember your grounding techniques, Callie; notice the details, stay in the present, breathe deep and steady. At least the trip to Fort Wayne was productive. Maybe this is just my overactive imagination.

Saul, the grocer, waves at me from across the street as he closes for the night, rolling the metal gate down over his storefront and hurrying around the corner to head home to his wife, Shayla. A pale, red-headed man, a constellation of freckles covering his skin, watches me curiously from behind his hotdog cart, but in a moment, he is gone as well, wheeling his cart away for the night.

It's only eight blocks to my apartment from the "L," and usually, I look forward to a lovely stroll home after a long day at what is essentially a desk job, but as darkness falls without the usual foot traffic, I realize I should have called an Uber.

There is a crash and clatter behind me, and I spin on my heel to see a garbage can bouncing off the bulletproof glass of an antique furniture store, its contents spilling across the sidewalk and gutter. A man in black pants and a brown leather jacket is leaning casually against the wall nearby. He stubs out a cigarette and smiles at me lazily—what a creep.

Walking in front of the big glass panes of the closed bank building, I glance at my reflection, and I see the same man, closer now, his hands in my pockets, sauntering confidently, his face blank and hard. *What the hell? Is he following me?*

Rizzo's Bar is four lonely blocks ahead, but it's always open. I quicken my pace, and as I cross the street, I glance over my shoulder. He is still there, eyes locked on me and closing the distance between us. *Shit. He is following me.* I can maybe make it to Rizzo's if I run now before the man catches up. My breath comes in ragged gasps after two blocks. I look over my shoulder quickly, and he's closer still, walking as if he had all the time in the world. I think I see a knife in his right hand.

Great. I'm going to get killed just as I finally find someone to love me. No, no, no. I grip the mace with a shaking hand and put everything I have into a final burst of energy, reaching the door of the bar and yanking it open with a yelp.

An older man looks up from wiping a glass with a white towel, startled. "Miss, are you quite all right?" he asks in a clipped accent.

I back into the bar, my eyes on the door, mace canister at the ready. I'm breathing so hard I can't speak.

Concern clouds his eyes. "Yes, yes, of course; are you in danger?"

"I try to catch my breath, shaking my head. "I don't know; this creepy guy has been following me for a while on the street, and I didn't know what else to do."

The barkeep bustles from behind the bar gently takes my arm, and guides me behind the counter. He walks to the door, opens it slowly, then sticks his head out to look in both directions.

Over his shoulder, he says softly, "There's no one out there now. He must have gotten scared off." Then louder, "Everyone around here knows you don't mess with Rizzo," he says to the sidewalk and then shuts the door and finds his way back behind the bar.

I realize I'm still gripping the mace canister, so I take a deep breath and try to calm down. Behind the bar is a sizable mirror surrounded by fancy woodwork and lovingly arranged bottles of exotic liquors. My reflection shows my hair has gone a little wild, so I pat it down and run my fingers through it, pushing my overly long bangs behind my ears.

"Miss, would you like a drink of water, perhaps something stronger? What are you doing out there all alone after dark?"

"I need to report this to the police."

"Miss, do you know who was chasing you?"

"No, but he was wearing black. He had dark salt and pepper hair, I think. Uh, he was tall, and he had a cigarette."

The barkeep smiles sympathetically. "That description matches a lot of characters around here, so I doubt the police will be able to help you out, especially when you don't appear to be harmed." He appraises me with his head cocked to one side. "If I were you, I'd be careful not to walk around alone after dark, young girl like you, unless your boyfriend is with you."

He opens the cooler and grabs a bottle of water. "Here," he points with his chin to a bar stool, "sit for a bit and have some water so you can settle down."

"Thank you, Mr. Rizzo." I only then realize that the bar is empty and the chairs are on the tables.

He laughs. "It's just Rizzo, dear girl," he gestures at the tables. "I was closing up for the night. My niece is getting married in the morning, and I need all the sleep I can get these days. I can call an Uber for you if you like."

"No, thank you, I'm just two blocks away from home."

"Then, let me walk you to your building; it wouldn't do for you to be out alone after your scare."

I remember my manners. "I'm Callie, by the way, and thank you."

As we make our way to my apartment building, I ask about his niece. "How did she meet her fiancée?"

"Oh," he rolls his eyes. "It was one of those internet dating sites, Forever Love or something like that. They got engaged in two weeks, love at first sight, they said, and this boy isn't exactly what we expected. But then, opposites do attract, don't they?"

* * *

Later, I wake up in the night, sheets twisted around my legs. I'm thinking of the man who chased and nearly caught me but never increased his pace beyond a saunter.

35

Encounter in a Bathroom

Monday, April 4

Stepping off the elevator after lunch, I smell roses and scan the room for signs of Mr. Hottie turned Creepy. He wouldn't dare to come here, would he? Apparently, he would. There are a dozen red roses in a crystal vase on my desk, a lurid red envelope perched between the blossoms.

"Somebody got flowers. What did you do to deserve that?" Simon spins around in his chair, grinning wickedly as I approach.

"Oh, shush." I grab the card from the flowers and rip open the envelope.

Callie, the terms and conditions of our agreement are non-negotiable. I wish you would reconsider your actions- C

I throw the card on my desk. "Argh!"

"Now, that is not the proper response to getting roses," Felicia says as she walks by.

When she is out of earshot, I tear up the card, throw it into my trash bin, then grab the flowers, jamming them in. "I'm just so sick of this."

"Hey, that's a waste of exquisite flowers," Simon protests.

"Oh, shut up." I suck blood off my finger, "Stupid thorns."

"You're dripping blood on your sleeve, hon."

"Shoot." I look for a Band-Aid in the drawer and mop up the blood with a tissue.

"You need to get some soapy cold water on that sleeve before it stains."

"Right. Thanks. I'll be right back." I stride to the bathroom, my finger throbbing and seeping blood. I push the ladies' room door open with my elbow, turn on the water in a sink, and soak my sleeve. I rub some hand soap on it, and it smells like roses. Weird that I haven't noticed this before. It smells so good.

I rub the fabric until the blood is almost out. I glance up to see Cupid standing behind me, casually leaning against a bathroom stall. His arms are crossed, and he is smiling at me like an animal that's cornered its prey. I meet his eyes, and he winks.

"Hello, Callie."

My stomach flips over, and heat spreads across my chest, neck, and cheeks. "Hello. How did you find me here?"

He takes a step toward me. "I have been keeping an eye on you."

"You have?" I turn toward him, water dripping to the floor.

"Of course." He glances down at my sleeve. "What happened to you?"

"I…" Why was I in the bathroom? I notice my sleeve and bandaged finger. "I hurt my finger on something."

"Ah, what a shame. Maybe I should kiss it and make it all better?"

I lick my lips and leave them slightly parted. *Yes, please,* I think. But I can't form the words. My eyes feel heavy as he leans in.

"Callie, do you know why I bothered to create this website?"

Website? He smells so good. "Uh, not really."

He circles me slowly, brushes my hair off my ear, and leans in to

166

whisper, "Because I have a job to do. Love is my business. You, my dear, and all of your broken fellow humans have messed things up down here." His fingertips trace small circles on my upper arms, turning me toward the mirror.

"How?" I ask his reflection.

He snakes his arms around my waist and crosses them, holding me tight, and I open my mouth in a silent gasp. His chin is nestled in my neck. "I built an empire, my dear. I spent a millennium setting up the rules of dating, courtship, marriage, and love. It was a carefully crafted plan which put my work on autopilot and left time for me to do other things I find much more enjoyable." He loosens his hold, but his hands travel to my hips, thighs. "It was working just fine. And then you humans decided you didn't need love anymore. Generations of people broke the rules. So here I am. I had to come back to straighten things out."

"So, are you a god?" My mouth is dry.

"What do you think, Callie? Am I a god?" He smiles slowly.

"I-I don't know. I don't know if I believe in gods." I tear my eyes away from our mirror image, and he twists me around to face him, with my butt pressed against the sink, my hands on his chest.

"Tsk, Tsk. I am flesh and blood. You can touch me if you want, Callie."

I reach up, slowly, to trace a pulsing artery on his neck just above the collar, then drop my hand to his chest. The fine cloth of his shirt feels cool to the touch, and I rub the pearl button of his shirt between my fingers.

"Does that feel real to you?"

"Yes."

"Good. Then listen to me." He rubs his fingers roughly through my hair with his forearms tight to my back. He yanks downward hard, exposing my throat. I am helpless, my arms pinned painfully between our chests. "I don't like being here. I don't like humans, but I do like you." His lips softly brush the taut skin on the front of my neck, and I moan. "If I didn't, I would have already dealt with you. But my patience is growing thin." He nibbles my earlobe and then releases me.

I'm leaning forward into him, my open palms on his chest, my breath coming hard. "I don't understand."

He steps backward abruptly.

I fall forward and catch myself before I hit the ground.

"My system needs to work. It needs to be one hundred percent effective. And you are a glitch in my system. You and what's his name."

I straighten myself, my hands on the edge of the sink. "I-I can't think of it."

"Of course, you can't. It was bad enough you didn't complete your registration like a good girl. But now you are mucking about in my business." His eyes are cold. "And now you and that interloper are asking questions about my company and me. If you wanted to get to know me, you could have just asked."

He leans forward to box me in between his arms, his hands on the wall, his breath hot on my cheek. "We both know you're not that committed to him," he whispers. "After all, here you are, throwing yourself at me, putting your hands all over me."

Tears sting my eyes, and shame washes over me. "I...no."

He laughs. "Well, sorry. I have no interest in you that way. Now, be a good girl and run back to your desk."

He straightens, adjusts his collar in the mirror, then walks out of the restroom without another glance at me. I grip the sink, unable to move for a moment. My heart is racing, but the overwhelming desire he stirred begins to diminish. It's replaced with rage and embarrassment. Am I committed to Gabriel? How dare he make me question my relationship. I study my reflection in the mirror once more, splash cold water on my face, and rip towels out of the dispenser, blotting my face. Damn him.

36

Just Stop

Staring at my computer screen, I read the page for the third time. I can't concentrate. I press on my finger, the sting of pain reminding me that what happened in the bathroom was real. How could I have been willing to cheat on Gabriel? The memory makes my face flush. I had wanted Cupid with every fiber of my being. What did that mean? I can't bear to admit my stupidity to anyone, not even Jayla. I am with Gabriel. I care about Gabriel. Gabriel is a good kisser. Gabriel smells good. Cupid needs to stay far away from me.

I grab a soda from the vending machine, regroup, and throw myself into work for the rest of the afternoon. At least my work hasn't changed. My finger has stopped bleeding by the time I leave, and I am ready to put Cupid behind me.

* * *

That evening, Gabriel and I sit at my kitchen table, eating bowls of rocky road ice cream.

"So you said you had some news?" I ask.

"Yeah, my uncle said he could write a letter and ask for the appendix, and it should work," Gabriel says.

"That's great," I say, leaving the table with my bowl, getting some chocolate sauce out of the fridge, and drizzling it on my ice cream.

"It is. But it might take a while. I've been doing more research about this, and Simon wasn't kidding. Cupid has been very busy. He is breaking up families, matching up people who should not be together but can't stay apart," he says before slipping a spoonful of ice cream between his lips.

"Do you want some of this?" I ask, shaking the chocolate sauce bottle at him.

He shakes his head and continues. "There is an online group, mostly friends and family of these people, and they are demanding an investigation into the website."

"Wow," I say, sliding back into my chair and squeezing an obscene amount of chocolate on my ice cream while Gabriel watches me, eyebrows raised. I give him a look, and he shakes his head.

"Yeah," he says, "And honestly, I'm a little freaked out. If this maniac has the power to do that, what else can he do? He needs to be stopped."

"But what are we going to do? We have to wait until your uncle gets the documents and then see what they say."

"Not much else we can do." He sets his spoon down and sighs.

I stare down at our hands. "This is my fault. You don't deserve all this."

"What do you mean?" He lifts my chin with his finger.

I blink back tears, "You have enough going on with your mom being sick and now I have dragged you into this mess. It's not fair."

Gabriel focuses on his bowl of melting ice cream. "No, it's not. But what are we going to do?"

I get up and toss my bowl of ice cream into the sink. My appetite is gone. Leaning my hands on the counter, I swallow hard and stare at the wall. I am the one Cupid is after. If I was out of Gabriel's life, he could go back to his job and family and not worry about all of this. "I think it's best until we figure out what's going on if we stay away from each other."

"What?" His spoon clangs to the floor.

I turn to look at him, planting my feet firmly on the linoleum. "I think we should take a break. If we are apart, maybe Cupid will leave us alone."

"Are you breaking up with me?" Gabriel asks, obviously hurt.

I'm frozen in place. "I don't know. This is all too much. It's too complicated." Of course, I don't want to break up with him. But I can't see any other way. I am so tired of being afraid and feeling guilty.

Gabriel stands up and faces me, his eyes pleading. "That is crazy. We should stick together and figure this out."

He is so naive. We can't just figure this out. We have no control. I take a step backward into the kitchen. "Gabriel, stop making this harder than it has to be."

"You stop," he points a finger at me, taking a step forward. Then, he deflates and leans on the cabinet. "There is no good reason for us not to be together."

I shake my head. "You're not listening to me. I can't risk it. I can't be a part of anything that I know could result in more heartache for your mom or hurt you."

Anger flashed in his eyes. "If you want to break up with me, Callie, you don't need to make up excuses or bring my mom into it."

What? "How dare you accuse me of using your mom when all I am doing is trying to protect her."

"Why are you getting so angry? This is not my fault."

"I'm not getting angry," I shout, "I just think you're being stupid." Feeling trapped, I brush past him and go into the living room, sitting in the chair.

He follows me and sits on the couch, turning his body to face me.

172

He says gently, "I think you're scared, terrified of loving me, so you are using Cupid as an excuse to push me away. This isn't about Cupid or my mom. It's about us." He runs his hand through his hair. "And you can't let anyone in, can you, Callie? Even the people who love you the most, you keep them at arm's length. And if they try to come closer, you run the other direction." He gestures to the door.

I suck in my breath, gritting my teeth. He doesn't know what he is talking about. If he wants to blame me to make himself feel better, fine. But this is not my fault, and he is being mean. "I think maybe you should leave, Gabriel."

"Fine," he says, standing up. "You have obviously made up your mind, and you're just going to keep trying to justify it."

Folding my arms around myself, I say, "Just stop." My eyes well up with tears, and I try to blink them back, not wanting to cry.

"Callie," he says softly, getting up and crossing over to me.

"No," I say, putting my hand out to stop him. "I can't do this; you just need to go." I shift my body away from him and stare at a little red stain on the carpet, probably wine.

"Okay," he says, slipping his coat on, pausing with his hand on the door, "This doesn't need to be goodbye forever. My feelings haven't changed," he says sadly.

I don't respond, and he turns to leave.

My phone buzzes with a text notification, and I read it through tear-filled eyes.

> Jayla: Hey, girl, my boss invited me on a last-minute buying trip to New York; I'm so excited! We're leaving in an hour. I'll be home in a couple of days. Don't have fun without me.

I am shaking and I can't even muster the energy to respond. I slide down onto the floor, holding my phone in my limp hand. I roll over and stare at the ceiling. How did this happen? I yank the throw blanket off the couch and tug it across my body, curling into the fetal position.

I lay there for a long time, watching the light disappear outside my window. My eyes hurt from crying, and my hip bone is digging into the floor. I roll over to my hands and knees, standing slowly and limping into the bathroom. I turn the water on as hot as it will go and strip off my clothes.

I shiver as I step into the shower. The water stings when it hits my body and then starts to warm me enough to stop my teeth from chattering. Slipping on my flannel pajamas, I head to the kitchen. His bowl of ice cream still sits on the kitchen table, melted. I sigh as I pick it up and set it in the sink.

I make sure the front door is locked and pad back into my bedroom, crawling under the covers and pulling them up to my chin. This is for the best. Now, nobody gets hurt. I stare at the wall until my eyes get heavy. Then, I sleep.

37

One, Please

Saturday, April 9

"One, please," I say, biting my lip and slipping my coat off. I am wearing black yoga pants and a long sweatshirt. I opted for my snow boots to navigate the slushy wet streets. My hair is pulled back into a messy bun and free of makeup. My outfit screams, *leave me alone*.

"For the 2:00 show?" says the girl in the booth at the Music Box Theater. She is chomping gum and wearing a name tag, "Lindsey."

"Yes, please." It was Saturday afternoon, and I couldn't sit in my apartment alone all day again. Gabriel and I had planned to come to the Marilyn Monroe fall in love on the big screen, and why should I miss it just because he isn't here?

"Here you go. You should have your pick of seats. There is hardly anybody in there. Enjoy the show."

"Thank you." I take the ticket, not sure if it's a good thing that the theater is so empty. My heels echo on the tile lobby floor as I walk under the ornate arch. I think about getting a glass of wine or beer, but drinking alone in a dark theater is depressing.

I draw open the theater door, balancing my popcorn and drink in my arms, letting my eyes adjust to the dark. The theater is lit with dim yellow light and full of vintage charm. There are only a few groups of people in the entire theater. I head down to the left middle section.

"Callie?" a familiar voice says.

I stop in my tracks. Turning around, I confirm it is Gabriel sitting by himself. He's wearing his brown corduroy jacket and dark jeans. He looks like a Hallmark movie protagonist.

"Hi," I say, smiling weakly. It figures he would look good. I look like a "before" picture on a makeover show.

"Hey, what are you doing here?" he asks, balancing a tub of popcorn on his knees.

I shrug. "Pottery class." I don't smile.

He does smile. "Ah, I was looking for the Jazzercise class."

"Well, looks like you missed it," I say, glancing around.

"Yup. Guess I'll have to settle for a movie."

"Me, too." Oh, my gosh, this is awful. I rock on my feet, not sure if I should sit with him or not.

"You don't have to sit with me. I know it's weird," he says, his eyes flittering away from me.

"No, it's fine. Thanks." We aren't enemies. I can do this—no big deal. I slide in the row and take a seat, leaving one seat between us.

I can't remember much about the movie. I try to pay attention, but my heart flutters every time he shifts in his seat or takes a drink. It takes everything I have not to turn to him and beg him to take me back.

Instead, I eat my popcorn one piece at a time and stare straight ahead, not daring to look at him.

Neither one acknowledges the other as we get up and walk out of the theater.

The cold hits my face as I step through the door and onto the sidewalk. I pause, and Gabriel steps up beside me, facing the street.

"Are you okay?" he asks, hands shoved in his coat.

"Why wouldn't I be?" I say, tying my scarf around my neck.

"Right," he says, looking at the ground.

"Are you okay?" I sneak a glance at him.

"No," he says, barely above a whisper. "I hate this."

I turn to face him, "You know this is for the best. We'll just get hurt."

"Callie, I don't believe that's true."

I fold my arms and turn back to the street. "Have you heard from your uncle yet?"

"No. I am hoping to hear by Tuesday."

"Okay. Let me know." I rock back on my heels, wanting to leave but not wanting to leave him.

"Okay," he says. I feel his eyes on me, but I can't fully meet his gaze. After a moment, he turns, flipping his collar up against the cold, and walks away.

I want to run after him. I want to tell him that none of that stuff mattered, and we should throw caution to the wind and stay together.

But he keeps walking, and I don't move. As he crosses the street to the next block, I turn in the other direction and head home.

Jayla will be home tonight, and that will help. She would know what to do.

38

Jayla in Love

My stomach growls as I stir the potato bacon soup. As I lift the spoon to my lips for a taste, I hear a key in the lock, and the front door opens.

Jayla breezes in, lugging her suitcase behind her, and says, "I'm back from New York," she announces and notices me in the kitchen. "Do I look different? Yes?" She strikes modeling poses. "I am an official New York buyer. Oh, yeah. That's right."

I laugh and abandon my soup to hug her.

"Oh, girl, I have so much to tell you. The lights, the fashion, and the man." She fans her face with her hand.

"What man?" There is a light in her eyes I haven't seen in a long time.

"Oh, girl. The. Man." She dumps her purse on the floor and slips into a chair at the table.

"Tell me everything," I say, skittering back to turn the stove burner down to low.

"Let's pour some wine because we need to celebrate." She springs into action, retrieving two glasses and a bottle from the fridge.

"Okay, then." I can't help but smile. Her joy is contagious.

Once we each have a glass of wine in our hands, I say, "Spill it."

She leans forward over the kitchen table. "Okay, so I was sitting in New York thinking about you and Gabriel and how I want some loving like that. So I got on that website and signed up." She clasps her hands over her mouth and shrieks.

My stomach drops. "You did?" I ask, trying to keep my face even.

She doesn't seem to notice my reaction. "Yes! And it matched me up with this man. And he is a man." She says dramatically, giving me a knowing look.

"Wow," I say, swirling the wine in my glass and watching a piece of cork float around the edge.

"He is so amazing. He writes the loveliest emails. We video chatted yesterday during visiting hours. He is perfect." She leans forward, her chin on her hand, lost in thought.

"That is great." I take a big swig of wine and try to sound casual, only half-listening to her.

"But he is so amazing. I can't wait for you to meet him." She hops up from the table, takes hold of her suitcase, and heads to her room. "I need a shower; I feel travel grimy. Pour me more wine for when I get out," she says.

I ladle my soup into a bowl. My appetite is gone, but I force it down. There are so many things I want to talk to her about, but how could I? Her ex-fiancé had so broken her, and now she has a real chance at happiness. I hear the shower turn on and figure I can wait to tell her.

She is wrapped in her silk robe an hour later and tucked under a blanket beside me. She looks so happy. What happens if her heart is broken again? How will she survive it?

She looks at me, tossing a piece of popcorn into her mouth. "What?" I shake my head and bite back the tears. "Nothing."

"What's wrong? Are you about to cry?" Concern clouds her face.

"Yes, only because you're so beautiful," I say dramatically. "I mean that dark skin and wavy hair." I twirl a piece of her hair around my finger.

She bats my hand away, "Girl, either you are buttering me up for something or seriously misreading the situation."

I laugh. "I'm just kidding, but I missed you."

"Oh," she says, patting my leg and throwing a piece of popcorn at me. "I missed you, too. We need to make sure these boys don't take over our lives."

"For sure. Tell me more about what's his name."

"Oh, his name is Fat Money," she says, letting the name drip off her tongue like molasses.

"Seriously?" I say, stifling a laugh.

She purses her lips and narrows her eyes at me, "Yes. He is a musician and an entertainment facilitator." She is deadly serious.

Sitting up, I ask, "When do I get to meet him?"

"I can't wait for you to meet him." She adjusts the blanket on her feet and says absently, "But it will have to wait a bit. Visiting hours are the first Saturday of every month."

"Wait, what? Why does he have visiting hours?"

"Because, silly, we can't just show up and see him any time. They have rules."

"I'm confused. Where is Fat Money exactly?"

"Sheridan Correctional Facility," she says, her face unreadable.

"He's a criminal?"

"No, of course not. He's incarcerated, but it's not what you think."

"Oh?"

"Yes, really," she says, with an edge to her voice.

"Okay, how is it, then?"

She sighs in frustration. "He was with some friends out at a club, he was working as a DJ in a small country bar, and someone walked up and started talking to his old girlfriend, you know, getting in her face and trying to dance with her. And Fat Money, he was a hero and stopped the guy."

"He beat him up?"

"Of course not. He shot him."

"What?"

"Just once. The guy didn't even die. Anyways..."

She spends the next ten minutes telling me all about him, including describing his tattoos in detail.

Finally, there's a break in the conversation.

"Jayla, there's something I need to tell you."

"Oh, right, I have been so excited I forgot to ask how you and Gabriel are doing."

I give her a rough story of what has happened, ending with the breakup. I mention Cupid, but I don't want to sound crazy, so I tread lightly.

She leans in and hugs me, "I am so sorry, girl. I had no idea you were going through all that."

"Thank you, but this affects you, too."

"Don't worry. You need your bestie around, and I will be here for you," she gets up to pour another glass of wine.

"I appreciate that, but I'm talking about," I can hardly say his name, "Fat Money."

She peeks out from the kitchen. "What about him?"

"Well, aren't you a little surprised that you fell in love with an incarcerated felon?"

"Well," she says, walking back in and sitting down, "it is a little unconventional, but Callie, if you could meet him, you would see that he is amazing. He has this milky white skin, and he is so short it is adorable, like a little hobbit."

"Jayla, I think you have been hypnotized or brainwashed by this website, by Cupid."

"I have not. I'm exactly the same as I was."

"I don't know."

"Listen, Callie, I am sorry that it didn't work out with Gabriel, but I don't know why you are trying to ruin this for me."

"I'm not trying to ruin anything; I am just worried about you."

Jayla stands up in front of the TV, her glass of wine hanging in her hand. "Well, you don't have to worry about me. In fact, you should be worried about yourself. You push everyone away. And just because you wanted to use this stupid conspiracy theory as a reason to break up with Gabriel, it doesn't affect me. I am happy for the first time in a year, and I don't know why you want to take that from me." She turns and stomps into her room, slamming the door.

I sigh and sink back into the couch. Now what? I have managed to push away everyone I love, and Cupid is still in business. Then, I think about Jayla, my sexy, sophisticated roommate dating a hobbit named Fat Money, and I can't help but laugh.

39

Fat Money

Monday, April 11

"Great," I moan, yanking on my favorite coffee shop door, double-checking it's locked. I cup my hands over my eyes and peer into the window, looking for signs of life. The lights are off, and there is no movement. Dammit. Checking the time, I can just make it to the coffee shop near work and hopefully be at my desk before Felicia makes her rounds.

At least there's no line at Joe's Java. Yanking open the door, I'm hit with the strong scent of cinnamon and rich coffee. Scones and lemon tarts crowd the glass cases. My stomach rumbles; apparently, breakups make me hungry. "I'd like a medium chai latte and a blueberry scone to go," I tell the barista.

After giving her my name, I step to the side and wait for my order. The bell over the door jingles, and I turn to see Gabriel walking in. He doesn't work anywhere nearby. What in the world is he doing here?

He sees me and stops in his tracks, then strides over to the back of the line.

I turn around. "Hi, what are you doing here?"

"Another Jazzercise class," he says, smiling halfheartedly.

"You're a dork. Seriously, you're way out of your neighborhood."

"Yeah, I know. I have a meeting down here this morning with my uncle."

"The lawyer?"

"Yeah. His office is just around the corner."

"Oh, did you find anything out yet?"

"No, that's why I'm on my way to a meeting."

Right, duh.

"Callie," the barista calls out, and I step up to grab my scone and coffee.

"See you later," I say to Gabriel. "Let me know what you find out, okay?"

"I will," he says. "Should I call you or maybe come over?"

"Just call me," I say and then walk out the door without looking back. My heart beats fast as I walk to the office.

* * *

"Hi, Simon," I say as I walk by his desk. "How's Cody?"

He stops typing but doesn't turn around. "He took me to a country bar last weekend, so there's that."

"Wow, you must like him," I say, leaning on his cube wall.

He leans back in his chair, folding his hands behind his head, "I like him less now that he made me line dance to 'Achy Break Heart.' I'm kidding, sort of. We don't have much in common, but every time I think about ditching him, he does something cute, and I can't imagine being apart."

I chuckle and set my latte on my desk.

He gets up from his desk and comes over to me. "Have you heard any more about that dating website?"

"Yeah, we're trying to find out more information right now. Gabriel is talking to his uncle, who is a lawyer."

"A lawyer? Are we going to sue them for a bunch of money?"

"I don't know about that, but we're trying to get a hold of the terms we signed when we signed up."

Simon wrinkles his nose at me, "What does that have to do with anything?"

"We don't know. But we're not sure where else to look. Have you heard anything new?"

"Well, there's that group on the Internet, and some theories are going around."

"Like what?"

"Well, some of them we talked about already, but the most common one is a cult with mind control. I'm hoping for the cult option. I've always wanted to join a cult."

"That's terrible." I stare at him. "Why in the world would you want to join a cult?"

"I always thought I'd be the leader of the cult one day. But if I'm not the leader, I can plot a slow takeover and enjoy all the benefits along the way. In fact, we can start right now. You shall call me Supreme Universe Leader of the Chicago Metro Area."

"Yeah, I'm not calling you that."

"Well, then, you can't be in my cult," he laughs.

"Deal," I say, "Now, get out of my cube. I have to work."

"Rude," he says and strolls back to his desk.

I need to focus on work. I know that. I've been slacking for weeks now, my mind is not all here, and I have a new project due at the end of the month. I pick up my latte to take a drink, and a wave of sadness threatens to drown me. Everything is a mess. Oh, my gosh. With the shock of seeing Gabriel this morning, I totally forgot to tell him about Jayla. I fish through my bag for my phone and dial Gabriel. I get his voicemail. "Hey, please call me when you are done with your uncle. I have news."

An hour later, my phone rings, and it's Gabriel.

"Hello," I say.

"Hey, what's up? I just got out of the meeting with my uncle."

He sounds good. I wonder what he ordered at the coffee shop. Did he finish that mystery he was reading? I don't have the right to ask any of these questions, so I ask, "How did it go? What did he have to say?"

"A lot. But first, tell me what your news is."

I take a deep breath and then tell him about last night. It's good to laugh together, and he is just as shocked as I am.

"Fat Money?" There is no mistaking the incredulity in his voice.

"Apparently," I say, giggling. "She said he was cute, like a Hobbit."

"Oh, that's not good."

"I know. So what did your uncle say?"

"Well, I think I should show you. It's pretty unbelievable."

"Unbelievable bad, or just unbelievable?"

"Both," he says. "Can I come over after work?"

"I don't want to talk about it in front of Jayla; she is already upset with me. But I think she's working till 9:00."

"I get it. I'll be over about 6:30."

40

Greek Gods

My hand shakes as I apply mascara. Why am I so nervous? It's just Gabriel. And I broke up with him. Usually, I would be trying to make an ex jealous, proving they were wrong to break up with me, but this was my fault. Still, there is no use looking like a train wreck. I rescue a soft pink sweater from the back of my closet. It was a Christmas gift from Shannon. Why does everyone insist on buying me clothing? Slipping it over my head, I'm reminded she is the sister with the fashion sense. It looks perfect.

At 6:30 on the nose, there's a knock on my door.

"Hi," I say, leaning in for a kiss and remembering we had broken up. My face flushes, and I step back. We both stand there shuffling our feet awkwardly for a second before I remember myself. "Come on in," I say.

He sits on the chair, and I sit on the couch.

"Would you like something to drink?" I hate this. It's all formal and stiff. I miss our casual, relaxed relationship.

"Maybe later," he says.

"Okay." The clock on the wall loudly ticks as I wait for him to speak first.

Finally, Gabriel says, "Sooooo, I have a theory that I want to share with you," he says.

"Oh," I say, jumping right in.

"Yeah, well, it's kind of time-sensitive."

"Well, then, tell me."

He scoots to the edge of his chair, lowering his voice, "Okay, so I think this might have something to do with Cupid."

"Yes, I already know that. CEO of Psycheros."

"No, Cupid, the god of love."

My blood turns cold. I try to stay casual. "The fat baby on Valentine's Day cards and boxes of chocolate?"

"Yes and no. Long before he was the fat baby on boxes of chocolates, he was a mighty god. The Romans called him Cupid, and the Greeks called him Eros. And I think he's back."

"What makes you say that?"

"Hear me out. Cupid is the god of love. He is here for some reason, but now there are billions of people on the Earth. No way he can travel all around shooting people with arrows. So what does he do? He discovers the Internet, which allows him to use whatever Henry called it to match people up without him needing to be there."

"Okay," I say, "I'll play along. What's your theory?" Something like relief floods my heart; maybe I am not crazy.

"According to my research, mythological gods show up occasionally throughout history, and they disappear just as quickly. When they are here, they are deeply involved in the lives of humans."

"But why does Cupid even care if we fall in love? Why is he here?"

"I can't be sure. But we humans haven't exactly been doing a good job in the love department."

"True." I get up and head to the kitchen. "I'm going to need wine for the rest of this conversation. Want a glass?"

"Sure," he says, waving me off. He gets up and follows me into the kitchen. "I'm not kidding. It sounds crazy. I know it sounds crazy. I was awake all night long thinking about how it sounded so crazy."

"It does sound crazy," I say, but it doesn't sound crazy.

"Think about when you first saw the ad. Do you remember what you told me?"

I pause and set the bottle down to search my memory. "Yeah, it mentioned Indiana specifically, and there were some other things that were weirdly specific. That's true." I pick the bottle up again. "Yeah, but that was just because of big brother in metadata and all that, you know, tracking us."

"That could be it, except that they don't have any way to know what we think, what our dreams are, or what we want unless we say it out loud or search for it online. It's not like they're doing mind control."

I raise my eyebrows and look at him, saying in my best conspiracy theory voice, "Or *are* they?"

Gabriel rolls his eyes at me, "Have you heard of Occam's Razor? It's a theory that says the most obvious answer is probably true."

"And this is the most obvious answer you can come up with?" I say, handing him the glass of wine and heading back to the couch.

"Yeah, I've racked my brain trying to figure out every other option over the last week. But then we were reading about Cupid in class, and it rang true. All of a sudden, it made sense."

"Okay, you need to back up because you think this is true, and I need to be sure you're not crazy, so please start from the beginning."

He chuckles. It's so lovely being relaxed with him again. I watch his smile and brown eyes, and I have missed him so much. I hate being away from him, even if he might be crazy.

"Okay, you have to accept the premise Greek mythology isn't a myth; it exists. I don't know how it fits in with God and Jesus, but it is not a myth."

"Okay, let's say I accept that premise."

"Great. Now, which god would be messing around in the love lives of humans?"

"Fat baby chocolate box cover, god?"

"Exactly. Cupid, or Eros if you're Roman, the god of love."

"Eros is another word for love, right?"

"Exactly."

"So Cupid is up there doing his thing and says, 'Hey, those humans are messing love up; divorce, adultery, reality TV shows about love.' "

"I get it. We have messed up love for sure. But why now? Seems like a weird time to come down to Earth and start shooting love arrows."

"It's not, though," he says, pacing around the room, "because gods have always messed around in the lives of humans. It's well documented throughout literature and history. There are always tales of it. We live in such a modern world that we don't believe it."

"Okay, let's say all that's true. Let's say you're right. This is not good news. What are we going to do? Challenge him to a duel? Lure him to his death at sea? What are our real options here?"

"I know," he says, staring out the window. "I haven't figured that part out yet."

"Well, it's a pretty big part of the equation," I say as he turns around.

"I know," he says, looking dejected, and starts pacing. "I'm a professor. I'm good with my brain. I don't fight."

"Well, there's no need to resort to violence."

"I don't know," he says, "we're in uncharted territory here."

"Well, we need to do something. Jayla is practically engaged to a professional small-town DJ who is currently incarcerated on felony charges."

Gabriel shakes his head and sits down next to me on the couch. "That is some match she has."

"I should've told her. She wouldn't have signed up if I had been honest."

"It's not your fault. We don't have to have it all figured out today. But we do need to try to start researching this company. And we need the rest of those terms and conditions to see if there's a loophole. When we met, my uncle said he should have them in a few days."

"That is good news."

He turns to me, our knees touching. "Callie, I can't sleep, I can't eat; I am dying inside without you. And If I have to see you, but not be with you," he shakes his head, "I won't survive it."

He takes my hands, and I feel my resolve fading away. "Callie, you can push me away, but I am not going anywhere. I mean it. I love you and am in this for the long haul."

"I have missed you, too," I say quietly.

"What?" he says, smiling, "Can you say that louder?"

"I've missed you, too," I say, raising my eyes to his.

His eyes focus on mine, and he licks his lips and says, "Callie, can I kiss you, please?"

"Yes, please," I say breathlessly.

41

Flower Delivery

Tuesday, April 12

"They dropped the charges!" Shannon shrieks over the phone as I jerk it away from my ear.

"What?" I say, setting down the pan I had just washed to try and make some taco meat for dinner.

"They dropped all the charges! Can you believe it?"

"No. Why would they do that? I mean, it's great news. I just didn't expect it." I turn and lean against the counter, crossing my arms in front of me.

"I don't know; we were getting ready for trial, and our lawyer subpoenaed documents. I don't know if any of the details, but suddenly, they dropped the charges."

My mind is racing, trying to figure out what this means in light of everything we know. "Did you guys get any of the documents you requested?"

"What, why? I don't know, and who cares; we don't need them now."

"Yeah, I know, of course, it's amazing news, Sis. I'm so happy for Henry. He must be relieved."

"We are so happy."

"That's amazing. I'd love to talk to Henry if he has any time. Can you have him call me? So that I can congratulate him personally?"

"Sure, he's out running errands, but he'll be home later. I'll have him call you then."

"Thank you, and congratulations."

"Thanks, Sis."

I hang up the phone and jump at a harsh knock on the door. I walk over and look through the peephole, and it's a delivery guy. I open the door, and he's holding a dozen red roses.

"Callie Mcguire?" he asks.

"That's me."

"These flowers are for you."

He holds a crystal vase filled with a beautiful batch of long stem roses. I don't want to touch it. We are at a standoff, him awkwardly holding the vase and me, hands pinned to my side.

"Look, lady, I have other deliveries."

"Right," I say, shaking my head. "Can you just put them on the table?"

He looks at me and smirks but does what I ask while I look around for my purse for some cash for a tip. When I finally find a five-dollar bill, I turn, and the delivery guy is gone. I yank the card off the little stick and rip open the envelope.

See. I can be nice. But if you don't cooperate, things are going to get ugly.
-C

I flip the card over, and there's nothing on the back. I reread it. I look at the roses, unable to resist leaning down to smell them. They are the most fragrant flowers I've ever scented in my entire life. Every stem is perfect, each in different stages of blooming. I snap a photo of the card and send it to Gabriel.

> Gabriel: What's that?
>
> Callie: A card that came with a dozen red roses from you know who.
>
> Gabriel: Shit. Okay. I have a class ending in 5. I'm coming over.
>
> Callie: Okay. Would you bring Chinese for Jayla and me?
>
> Gabriel: Okay, boss.

I slide the pan back into the cupboard and return the meat to the fridge. Instead of cooking, I grab a bottle of wine and a glass.

Jayla, fresh from a shower and wrapped in a towel, walks in and reads the card, squinting her eyes as if she'll see something between the letters. "Who is C?"

I ignore her question, "Gabriel is bringing us Chinese food for dinner. I hope that's okay. I don't feel like cooking."

"I am always up for Chinese." She leans over and inhales the fragrance of the roses appreciatively. "Seriously, Gabriel is stepping up his game."

I grab another glass for her and fill them both with white wine. "They are not from him."

"Were you seeing someone else when you were broken up?" She looks puzzled.

"Of course not. It was only two days," I say, harsher than I mean to be. "I don't want to talk about it." I hand her a glass and retreat into her bedroom to throw on some clothing.

I grab the remote and flop in front of the television. Nothing looks good. I land on a rerun of one of my favorite sitcoms. It's funny and familiar.

Gabriel knocks on the door, and when I open it, he is mid-knock with one hand and balancing a large paper bag filled with food cartons.

Jayla appears at the smell of food, her hair still up in a towel. She takes her order from him. "Thank you. If you don't mind, I'm taking my Chinese food and going to my room. You guys are a bit neurotic, and I have had a long day. And I don't have any patience for conspiracy theories." Then, she's gone, and we are left sitting at the kitchen table. I fill in Gabriel on everything Shannon had told me.

"Okay, we know that the lawyer subpoenaed documents from the company, and then they dropped the charges," Gabriel says, "so maybe they wanted to avoid providing documents or testify in court? Maybe they're trying to cover something up and figure he won't talk if he lands a new cushy job? If so, then whatever they're trying to cover up must be bad."

"Well, if the company is doing what we think they're doing, that's pretty bad, don't you think? Hey, do you want a fork?" I give him a smirk. "You're not the best with chopsticks."

"Yes, please. And, yeah, that would make sense. Hey, can you find out what they had asked for in the subpoena?"

I hand him the fork and flop next to him on the couch. "I can try. My sister didn't seem to know anything. Henry didn't tell her much." After a beat, I add, "But I did ask Henry to call me tonight so that I can congratulate him. I thought he would have more information than my sister does."

As if on cue, my phone rings, and it's Henry. I answer and put it on speaker, balancing it on my knee. "Hey, Henry."

"Hey, Callie, so you heard, huh?"

"Yes, I am so happy for you. So what happened?"

"To tell you the truth, I'm not sure what's going on."

Gabriel and I look at each other, and he mouths the words, "Is he kidding?"

"Yeah. So, Henry, I'm sitting here with Gabriel, and we have some questions. Are you able to talk right now?"

Gabriel chews his food quietly.

"Sure," he says, "Shannon took the kids to swimming lessons. Now that I have been liberated, she's trying to get them back into their extracurricular activities."

"Oh, that makes sense. I'm so glad."

"What do you guys have on your minds?"

"Shannon said your lawyer was trying to subpoena something that may have prompted them to drop the charges?"

"Well, we did submit a huge list of items we wanted to subpoena, and they replied with a letter to the judge asking to drop the charges, so I guess it's hard to believe they weren't connected."

"It seems weird. Does that happen a lot?"

"Well," he chuckles. "This is the first criminal investigation I've been involved in, but no. According to my lawyer, it's very unusual."

Gabriel leans forward. "So what did you guys subpoena? Can you give us an idea of what kind of documents you asked for?"

"Yeah, yeah." Then, all we hear is the sound of rustling papers in the background. "I think I have a list here somewhere. A lot of it was just basic financial information; annual reports, my performance reviews, complaints from the Better Business Bureau, and any lawsuits they've been involved in. You might find this interesting; we subpoenaed the terms and conditions for the dating website, including the appendix."

I stiffen. "Why?"

"Well, remember I told you guys to read them over? Did you?"

"We tried," Gabriel said, "but the appendix they referenced was nowhere to be found. I even called the company and tried to get a copy of it, but no go."

"Exactly. I worked on that dating site's programming side anyway, and even I couldn't get a copy. I've never seen a system like that. Many of the matches were personally assigned by the president of the company. It wasn't some random algorithm. It was his little pet project or something."

"How did he have time to do that?" I ask.

"The system would put together matches, but he had the final say and override authority. He needed to have that ability because he wanted to guarantee the website's effectiveness and lure in as many willing participants as possible, so he gave the million-dollar guarantee."

"Huh. Is there any way to get the appendix, you think?"

"I don't know. You'd have to have somebody on the inside who could access the Intranet for the company. That's where all of the regulations and guidelines are stored. Do you know anybody else who works there?"

"No," I say with a sigh.

Gabriel leans forward again. "Do you know anybody currently working there that was sympathetic to trying to stop him?"

"I don't know. It's so weird, but I have started to forget things about the company over the past few weeks. I can't tell you my employee ID, even where my desk was. And although I know I have talked to Cupid in person, I can't recall any details from our conversation. But based on the company's reaction to me, dragging my family and me through the mud, I can't imagine too many people be willing to risk their wrath."

"But if they could just—"

Gabriel touches my arm and interrupts, "That makes sense, Henry. We don't want anybody else getting into trouble. But if the website gets sued and all this comes out, the company will go bankrupt. And a lawsuit could implicate anybody working for it in a criminal investigation. Stopping it would be a good thing, don't you think?"

"Of course," he says, "but I don't think we can stop it."

"Why?" I say, "I mean, no company is too big to fail, right?"

"That's an age-old question. And I'm not worried about the company failing as much as I'm worried about the CEO. Although I don't remember the details exactly, I know it was bad enough for me to try to crash the whole system."

I nod, relieved to know someone else who has clouded memories of interactions with Cupid. Gabriel quizzically looks at me and then back at the phone on the table.

"Why?" Gabriel asks, picking up the phone and holding it closer to our faces, listening intently.

"Because it is unethical at best. And people are getting hurt. Did you hear about the mass shooting in Florida?"

"Yes. A guy broke in and shot the family of that doctor?" I say. It had been all over my social media feed. It was awful.

"Right. You know why?"

"They said it was a robbery or something," Gabriel says.

"Nope. A woman from Vermont registered for the site and was matched."

"With the doctor?" Gabriel asks.

"Yup. But his family and friends intervened and had him locked in a cabin near the Everglades for his own good. But he gets a message to her and tells her where he is. She shows up with a shotgun and takes out three people who were just trying to help. Luckily, his wife and kids were not there at the time."

"Wow. That escalated quickly," I say.

"Indeed. And that wasn't the only match that ended up causing trouble. Reports kept coming in, but they always shut them down with offers to settle with the families out of court for distress, but without taking responsibility. Oh hey, Shannon just got home, and I'm supposed to make dinner. I've got to run, so keep me posted if you guys do get hold of those documents. I'd love to see what's in them."

"Thanks, Henry, we will. Have a good night, and congratulations again. Hug Sis from me." I hang up the phone and look at Gabriel. "What are we going to do?"

"I don't know, but I think better when eating ice cream. Sound good?"

"I don't have any, and you know ice cream can't fix everything, right?"

"Yes, but it fixes most things. Let's go out and find some. It will be good to get away from this mess and get some fresh air. Want to see if Jayla wants to come?"

"Okay, I guess. She isn't thrilled with me right now, though. She thinks I am trying to sabotage her relationship. But I will ask."

I knock on Jayla's door and ease it open; she's putting on lipstick and has her computer cracked open on her bed. "Hey, we're going to get some ice cream. Do you want to go?"

"Can't. I have a date tonight." She turns around and gives me a big grin.

"Oh," I say, "I see. Okay, well, don't have too much fun." I wink at her, grinning back.

"Eww, don't be gross." She climbs on her knees and adjusts the ring light on a stand next to her bed.

"Hey, I'm not judging!"

"I am so excited to see him." Her voice gets squeaky at the end.

"I get it," I say. "We'll be back in about an hour. Don't do anything I wouldn't do."

She pouts. "That leaves me with zero ability to have fun."

"Hey, I have fun all the time!"

"Your idea of fun is a Jane Austen book. No, thanks. Go enjoy your ice cream because I have things to do." She flips her hair and laughs.

In the living room, Gabriel is sliding on his coat.

"She has a date tonight over the computer, so she's not free tonight."

"Oh."

"Yeah, I can't wait to get a look at this guy."

"Are you doubting her taste in men?"

He stops with one arm only partway in his coat. "Are you serious?"

"That I want to get a look at this guy? Absolutely." I laugh.

"See, we belong together," he says, zipping his coat.

"Sure, as long as there's not some maniacal fat baby god behind our affection."

"Let's hope not."

42

Rizzo to the Rescue

Thursday, April 14

"Did you finish that project proposal?" Simon asks, leaning over the wall of my cube.

"Of course," I say, pushing my chair back from the desk and spinning around to face him.

He folds his arms on my cubicle wall and rests his chin on his hands. "Good, you need to get a promotion and take me along because cowboy boots are expensive."

"I will not touch that one," I laugh, "So why don't *you* get a promotion and take me along with *you*?"

"Because I'm lazy and preoccupied with my new boyfriend." He stands up and fans his face with his hand.

"Fine, you can work for me as my assistant. But you have to fan me with palm leaves and feed me grapes."

"Whatever," he says, waving me off, "not sure you can afford me, come to think of it."

I laugh. "How are things going with Cody?"

"I'd say it's going unusually well. I agreed to try milking a cow, and he agreed to stop wearing discount jeans every day."

"It's serious, then?"

"It better be. I gave him a key to my apartment."

"Wow, I'm impressed."

"I'm glad you're impressed. Now write it down in that little book you keep so you'll pay me an impressive salary when you hire me for your team."

"Will do," I say, giving him a little salute.

After lunch, I don't have much to do. They're assigning new projects in the morning, and I'm all caught up for once. I scroll my social media pages for a few minutes and recheck my email. Then, I type in the address for the dating site. I start scrolling through all the different tabs and go to the bottom of the page. I scroll through the tabs there until I see the employee contact list. It's hidden under careers and three other levels, but I find it. It's the only thing I've thought of to try and solve the riddle of the missing appendix.

They have a lot of employees; this is going to take forever. I start scanning names looking for anything that rings a bell. After all, they have offices in several locations, including Fort Wayne, so maybe somebody I knew from home works there, besides Henry, of course. I keep scrolling down the page until my eyes get blurry, and I have to stand up and stretch.

I sit down and start scanning again, and bam, there it is. One of my best friends from high school works there. Ha. I write down her name and work phone number. I will have to ask Henry about it first because I need to ensure she won't rat me out. I keep looking to see if there's anybody else, just in case. I find three more names of people I recognize and get their information. I turn off my computer and stare at the list of names. It's something. It could be something if any of these employees are willing to help. Tucking the paper down deep into my purse so I don't lose it, I gather up my stuff and head home. I dial in Gabriel on the way.

"Well, that's not very nice," he says in a syrupy voice.

I feel the magnetic attraction to him from across the foyer. Focus, Callie. Mailboxes, eight of them, my name is on the seventh. Rug, primarily blue, some red in the corners. Railing, oak with a carving of an eagle on the newel post.

I feel his eyes on me, and I look up at him from beneath my lashes. He is still smiling, and my breath catches in my throat. He is so good-looking. I can almost touch his chest if I reach out my hand. Is that what I want to do? Yes, I want that to feel him and let him touch me more than anything.

The gears of the elevator reluctantly grind into action as the elevator begins to descend. The noise is enough to break the spell momentarily, and I step away from Cupid toward the elevator. I desperately will it to move faster.

"Callie, is that any way to treat the god of love? I'm not here to hurt you; I want to have a conversation to see if we can find some common ground on which to land."

"I-I-I-I can't," I stutter, not able to form words, every ounce of concentration focused on the elevator.

After what seems an eternity, the elevator bell rings, and as it opens, relief floods through me as Rizzo the bartender is standing there.

He must see the alarm in my face because he says, "Hey, you live here? I was just making a delivery."

"I need to get out of here." I cry, rushing into the elevator.

Rizzo steps back in as I slam the cage shut. "What's wrong? Is someone chasing you again?"

Cupid stares at me coldly from the other side of the metal.

Rizzo looks at Cupid and then back at me, "Is this guy bothering you?" Rizzo asks.

"I just need to get out of here, now." I'm fighting the urge to open the cage and run over to Cupid.

205

Instead, Cupid breaches the gap, extending his hand, and my hand responds in kind, even as I will it not to.

"Why are you doing this to me?" I try to sound angry, but it comes out with a tinge of desire.

Cupid smiles seductively. "Because I can."

Rizzo growls at my side. "Listen, Bob, the lady said she wants to be left alone, so leave her alone. You got it?"

Cupid's eyes flick to Rizzo, "Rizzo, is that what they call you? Well, I'm sure you and I will meet again. Oh, how was your niece's wedding? Is he everything you wanted for your little girl?" As the elevator moves, he drops his hand to his side. "Sleep tight, Callie." He puts his finger to his lips, and I know it's a warning not to tell anyone he was here.

"What the hell?" Rizzo turns to me. "Are you okay? Who was that guy?"

"Yes, thank you so much. I'm so glad you were here. I'll be fine. I need to get into my apartment," I assure him.

I step off the elevator and walk down the hall. Rizzo stands in the opening of the elevator, and I can feel his eyes on me. I turn to give him one last wave and then unlock my door and slide in, quickly closing and locking the door behind me.

"Okay, girl, what's going on?" Jayla says, making me jump.

"Oh," I say, spinning around, "you scared me."

"Sorry, but seriously, what's going on?" Her arms folded in front of her.

"What do you mean?" I say, dropping my bag on the table and shrugging my coat off my shoulders. My pulse is still racing; I try to slow down my breathing. I can't tell her. She wouldn't believe me even if I did.

Her eyes narrow. "Something weird is going on, and you're not telling me. And you tell me everything."

"I do tell you everything," which isn't a lie. She just didn't always believe me.

"Oh yeah? Because you and lover boy have been sneaking around talking in hushed tones and acting nervous for days. Are you pregnant?" she says, deadly serious.

I start laughing out loud as I hang my coat over the back of the chair. "No, I'm not pregnant; we haven't even had sex."

With her finger in the air, she says, "We'll get back to that. But if it's not that, what is it?"

I sigh and sit on the couch, patting the seat next to me.

She comes and sits down, folding one leg underneath her.

"I know you don't believe me about Cupid," I say.

"That again?" she asks, rolling her eyes.

I shrug off her reaction. "You know what? Let's not talk about it. Let's try cooking tonight, and you can tell me more about Fat Money."

And that does it; just the mention of his name and her eyes glaze over, and all is right with the world.

43

Let's Be Frank

Friday, April 15

Gabriel and I are sitting on his couch, and he has a laptop balanced on his legs. I'm holding a list of names and numbers in my hand.

"What did Henry say again?"

"Okay, I went through all the names with him, and he said this was the only one that he trusted not to turn us in immediately."

He looks at the highlighted name. "Frank Trombley. Did he work with Frank?"

"Yes, and they've known each other for years. Even before they worked for this company, they knew each other from social circles."

"And we can trust Frank?"

"According to Henry, we can."

"Okay, that's good. But I still want to go slow because I don't want to freak him out. If we're wrong about all this, he's going to think we're crazy."

"If we are wrong about all this, we are crazy. We spent way too many hours obsessing over this to be considered sane if we're wrong."

"Well, as long as they lock us up together, I don't care." He leans over and brushes his lips against mine, and then he starts searching for Frank Trombley in Fort Wayne.

"Mid-forties, couple of kids, belongs to the Rotary. Seems like a standup guy," Gabriel says.

I watch him as he's searching. He might be better at research than I am, which says a lot. I slowly close his computer and set it on the coffee table.

"What are you doing?" he says, smiling.

I climb over his legs to sit on his lap facing him.

"Life is too short, Gabriel, and we have done way too much talking and not nearly enough kissing."

He puts his hands on my hips. "Oh, really?"

"Uh-huh," I say as he slips his hand under my neck beneath my hair and gently pulls me into a kiss.

* * *

I wait until Saturday to call Frank, partly because I'm nervous and procrastinating and partly because I don't want to catch him at work or in the middle of dinner.

Gabriel is next to me for moral support as I dial his number. We had rehearsed what I was going to say, hoping that I won't sound like a nut.

"Hi, is this Frank Trombley?"

"Yes, who is this?"

"Hi, I'm Callie Mcguire. Do you know my brother-in-law, Henry Stein? He used to work with you."

Frank is quiet for a second and then says, curtly, "Yes."

"Right, well, he thought you might be able to help me. I signed up for the website, and I have an amazing match. But I like to read the fine details, and I work for a tech company developing their terms and conditions. I'm charged with collecting terms and conditions from different companies to see what kind of language they're using."

"The terms and conditions are on the website."

"Yes, I know, and I printed them off, and it's been constructive, but you guys were so smart to include an appendix. I think it's a way to keep the actual terms and conditions to a minimum, as people have to read them on the fly, but I wanted to figure out what you put in the actual terms and conditions versus what you put in the appendix. I couldn't find the appendix anywhere on the website."

"You couldn't access it?"

"No, and I was surprised by that. So, could you get me a copy to see how you guys structured all of the disclosures? It seems like you guys have one of the best strategies around."

"Huh, Henry told you to call me specifically?"

"Yes, he told me to call you specifically. He said you would be the most helpful because of all your experience."

"What did you say your name was?"

"My name is Callie Maguire; Henry is my brother-in-law."

"Oh. He's a good man. It isn't fair what they are doing to him. But I'm not sure I should get involved."

"It's no big deal. I am sure I could find it somehow; Henry just thought you were the best person to help me get it quickly."

"Hmm."

I try to sound sincere. I will do it if it takes stroking his ego to get what I need. "Oh yes, he says you are invaluable to the company and know the program inside and out."

"I see. Well, let me see what I can do. Is this a good number to call you back at?"

"Yes," I tell him, "and I'll text you my email address, so if you find them, you can just send them to me via email if you want."

"Sure, if I'm able to find them, I will send them. I'll probably send them from home now just because my work email gets bogged down."

"Of course, that happens to me all the time. I'll also text you my email address, so neither of us will get bogged down."

"Okay, I'll see what I can do, Callie. But if I can find them and give them to you, please keep my name out of it."

"Oh, of course. I don't want to cause any trouble; I'm just trying to make my boss happy."

"Right. Okay, I'll be in touch."

"Thank you so much."

I hang up the phone, let a breath out, and then start giggling.

"You're an excellent liar," Gabriel says, "almost too good of a liar."

"I am pretty good, aren't I? Maybe we should start a detective business?"

"Oh, I'm not sure I want to be in the detective business. It's too stressful."

"You are right about that. And now we have to wait until Monday; it will take forever to get here."

"Why don't we do something fun tomorrow? My mom's been asking about you, and I know she would love to see you. Want to go for a visit?"

"That sounds perfect. I could use some Perez family and Perez food."

"Okay, well, if I tell my mom you're coming over, I'm sure she will make sure there's a feast."

44

I Love Tacos

Sunday, April 17

I love Gabriel's family, maybe even more than I like him. Well, at least as much as him. The afternoon is full of laughter, tacos, and a test in basic Spanish for me, which I am pretty sure I failed. It's as if their family lives in full color, while my childhood was in sepia tones. The unrestrained joy that echoes through the house was never present when my sister and I grew up. Muted tension and disappointment covered everything in our house like a thin layer of dust. Gabriel's family is full of life and love, and I am still smiling from the day's merriment as we walk to the car to go home.

"If I don't marry you, I think my family will disown me," he teases.

"Well, we can't let that happen," I say in a moment of unrestrained romantic optimism. "I mean, who would inherit your dad's green recliner?"

"Exactly," he laughs.

"Well, keep feeding me tacos and letting me hang out with your family; I just might say yes."

"Deal," he says.

Despite everything that's going on, I can't help but feel light today.

Maybe it's the sun shining with the promise of spring. Perhaps it's a full belly. I look over at Gabriel. It's probably him. I take Gabriel's hand, and he smiles at me as we drive down Michigan Avenue toward his apartment.

"I could use a nap," I yawn.

"A nap sounds amazing. You can sleep at my place while I work. I have a deadline this week, and I'm way behind because a certain person keeps occupying my time."

"Oh, yeah, what kind of deadline?"

"From my publisher. I'm almost done with my book, and my edit is due this week."

"Sounds exciting."

"It's brutal. But it has to be done. So I figure I'll lock myself in my room today and stay up all night if necessary to get it done, and then tomorrow you should have some news, and we can focus on that."

"You are a man with a plan," I say.

"I like to think so as long as it doesn't involve battling mythological gods. You don't have a plan that involves battling mythological gods, do you, Callie?"

"Who, me?" I say, putting my hand on my chest, "Of course not." I am telling the truth. I don't have a plan, and I have no idea where to begin. "Just for kicks and giggles, though, can gods be killed?"

"I have no idea," he says.

"If we can't kill gods, how can mere mortals deal with them?"

"Well, instead of outright trying to kill them, you're better off trying to make a deal or trick them somehow."

"Hmm. Okay. While you're working on your book, I will do another deep dive and see if I can find anything else that might help us. May I borrow your laptop?"

"Sure. What do you want to do for dinner?"

"Ugh. I think I have a taco hangover," I say, wrapping my hands around my stomach.

"You can never eat too many tacos," he laughs.

"My stomach disagrees. Maybe we can kill Cupid with tacos?"

"I won't tell my mom you said that."

45

Appendix

Tuesday, April 19

"That's your problem," Gabriel says, looking at me from across the table, a tray of glasses filled with different wines between us. "You think every love story has to be a Jane Austen book."

"No, I don't," I say, leaning back in my chair. The wine tasting bar is empty except for a fortieth birthday party in the back, the women's laughter echoing across the cement floors and high ceiling. Flames roar in a corner fireplace and the windows are steamed from the heat.

"You do, though," he says, smiling. "It has to be Mr. Darcy dramatic and all that, and when it's no longer dramatic, you push people away. Isn't that how it went with Tom?"

"Tom broke up with me, remember?" I pick up one of the glasses and sip the red blend. It's too sweet for my liking.

"I'm just saying, do you want some guy to ride in on a white horse and rescue you all the time? That's not reality."

"Why not? Why can't I dream of that possibility, even if it doesn't last?" I sample the next wine.

"What do you mean it doesn't last?" he asks, choosing a white wine to try.

"Love never lasts," I wave my hand, "at least most of the time. It either fades over time or was never there, to begin with."

"Callie, why would you think that?"

I take another sip of wine and a deep breath. "When I went away to college, my parents filed for divorce. Their commitment to us and each other was up with my first tuition payment. And it wasn't even like they had a nasty breakup. They did fight like any married couple. But the divorce was somewhat amicable, which made it worse for me. It's like they didn't even love each other enough to hate each other. What is that?"

Gabriel shrugs and nods for me to continue.

"They drove separately up to my school, sat separately, and over chicken Alfredo, they broke up our family.

"What is it about going out to eat to deliver bad news? What do they think we're going to do so they can't tell us in private? As if dessert is going to lessen the blow. But they had decided to divorce, and I had to get back to my dorm to study. So that was that." I empty the blend and pour some pinot.

"I never told my parents how I cried in my dorm room that night and many nights after, mourning the family we had been. I never told them how angry I was. They had rejected me and abandoned me just because they couldn't get along. They would've told me it wasn't true, but it was how I felt, so there it is. Eventually, I just stuffed that hurt down and locked it away."

I realize my voice is higher, and I'm talking faster, but it all comes pouring out. I only pause when the waitress comes over to take our order for wood-fired pizza.

"I did have that junior year crisis, or maybe it was just a crisis during my junior year. I wasn't sure about my major, and I still hadn't met anyone worth dating. After spending my second Christmas in two different households, I felt like burning everything to the ground.

My mom was concerned about my melancholy mood and lack of enthusiasm for anything, even my books. She insisted on making an appointment for me to go to a therapist on campus."

"You went to a therapist?" Gabriel asks me. I am not sure what he is getting at. Did he think I needed a therapist or not? I ignore the comment.

"I told the therapist all about my jealously of Elizabeth Bennet, hatred for weak women, and obsession with getting out of our small town after graduation. She stared down her nose at me with her pursed lips, hands folded over her legal pad. 'It sounds like you have a lot of pent-up anger and hurt; do you think this has a lot to do with your parents' divorce? Or your unrealistic expectations about love? Maybe you need a prescription for antidepressants.' I wasn't sure what to say, so I didn't say anything. I ripped up the 'script' on the way back to my car. Was I depressed? Maybe. Was I also in denial? Absolutely. But denial beat depression any day of the week. So instead of a healthy run of therapy and a low-dose antidepressant, I canceled my next appointment, graduated, and moved to Chicago."

I feel like a balloon that's just had all the helium whistle out. I also realize my glass is empty again, and I feel woozy.

Gabriel is quiet for a minute. "I'm sorry that your parents split up," he covers my hands gently. "But I'm glad you came to Chicago. Not everyone is like your parents. You don't have to settle, but you can have love without a dramatic rescue or calamity."

I shake my head mockingly. "I disagree. You're my Prince Charming, so you'd better go out and find a horse and declare that you love me ardently."

"Ardently?"

"Oh, yes. Have you not read *Pride and Prejudice*? It's required reading."

"Really?" he says, raising his eyebrows.

"Yes, indeed, and we shall fight and make up and fight some more."

"That sounds dreadful."

"Is not general incivility the very essence of love?"

"I suppose that is from my required reading?"

"You will have to read it and find out."

"Okay, I will."

* * *

After dinner, I crack open my computer to check my email. I scroll the page until Frank's name catches my attention. I scroll back up and click on the email,

As requested, I am attaching the requested document. Please print and delete this email.

Thank you.

I click on the attachment and download it. After making sure it opens, I delete the email and empty my email trash. I read through the appendix. I have to stop and start five or six times. This must be fake. There's no way this is real. It's a prank or something. I reread it.

By clicking the terms and conditions, the signer agrees to submit their will to Cupid, Psycheros, upon acceptance of the match. Psycheros has expressed permission to use experimental optical and auditory marketing tools through advertisements and social media. Further, Psycheros is not liable for any injury or death associated with these actions.

How is this legal? How is it legal to fool someone into clicking on this when they don't even understand what they've read? I sit back in my chair as the awful truth settles on my shoulders. It wouldn't have mattered if this was in the terms and conditions because I didn't read them. I never read them. Nobody does. I send the document to the printer just in case something happens to my computer. I then fold it up, tucking it inside my copy of *Pride and Prejudice*. I don't want to bother Gabriel with this tonight because of his big deadline, so I spend the evening shut in my bedroom, researching everything I can find on Greek and Roman mythology, Cupid in particular. I fall asleep with my computer open on my lap, and sometime during the night, Jayla must've come in and closed it because when I wake up, it's safely over on my desk.

46

French Toast

Wednesday, April 20

The smell of bleach burns my nose as I wipe down the bathroom. I strip off the yellow rubber gloves and grab my phone off my bed. It's 8:30 a.m., and I can't wait any longer.

"I hope you're done with your work because we have to meet up ASAP," I say, pressing my closet door shut to rein in the mountain of clothing straining to escape.

"You're chipper this morning," Gabriel responds. "I stayed working on my book until three in the morning, and I'm still not awake."

"You sound like you're awake." I slide a book into the shelf, alphabetized by author name. "Grab some coffee and come over. This can't wait."

"Did you get the email from Frank?"

"Oh, yeah." I smooth the comforter on my bed and fluff the pillows.

"Okay, okay; I'm getting up right now. I need to brush my teeth at least and throw on some clothes, and then I'll be over. Wait, are you cleaning?"

"Don't sound so surprised. I clean occasionally. It helps with my anxiety. You bring coffee, and I will make some eggs and French toast and have it ready when you get here."

"That's a good bargain. I'll see you soon."

I am flipping slices of French toast when Jayla comes out of her room wearing flannel pajama pants and a cropped tank top. "Something smells divine." She smiles over my shoulder at the pan.

"Breakfast. And you may want to put on some clothes because Gabriel's on his way over."

"This early in the morning?" she says, grabbing a coffee cup.

"Yes. We have some things to do."

She folds her arms and frowns, "Does this have anything to do with the email I saw printed out on your desk?"

"When did you...When you rescued my computer," I say, shaking the spatula at her.

"Yes, and I'm not sure what you guys are into, but I hope you're not planning to do something stupid," she says, turning on the coffee pot.

"Oh, we probably are, but do you know me."

She disappears into her bedroom to dress and calls out, "I do, and that's what has me worried. What kind of influence does Gabriel have over you? What was that email from, anyway? Some role-playing game or something? Seems pretty dark." I wait until she's back in the kitchen. She's wearing jeans and a soft yellow sweatshirt that accents her dark walnut skin.

"Yeah, well, it's just a book that Gabriel is working on."

She narrows her eyes, and I can hear the skepticism in her voice. "If you say so. Are you sure it isn't more about that stupid dating website?"

"No, you were right about that; we were being silly, but now Gabriel is going to write a book about it."

I'm finishing the last of the French toast and sliding it onto the warming plate when Gabriel arrives. He walks up behind me to wrap his arms around my waist. "Good morning," I say and turn around and kiss him. "You look like you've been up all night."

"Funny you should say that because I was up all night," he says, putting his hands on my hips, and nuzzling my neck."

"All right, you two, knock it off," Jayla says, rolling her eyes. "So Gabriel, what is this I hear about a new book you're writing; some dungeons and dragons god thing or something?"

Gabriel looks at me, and I raise my eyebrows, trying to signal him to go along with the program. His eyes dart back and forth between Jayla and me, and he clears his throat. "Yeah, I am working on a book about," he looks at me, "Greek gods."

Jayla's eyes narrow again, and she turns to wag a finger at us. "You two are weird. And if you are going to take another trip to crazy town anytime soon, leave me out of it."

"Okay," I say, laughing.

Gabriel drags his finger across his chest in an x shape. "We promise, cross my heart." Turning to me, Gabriel says, "My mom is so excited to see you today. She called me last night to double-check that you were coming."

"Sounds like she likes me more than you," I say.

"Ha. You might be right."

47

Gabriel's Apartment

Thursday, April 21

Gabriel turns the key to unlock the apartment and swings open the door, flipping the light switch. He stops abruptly, and I bump into his back with my whole body. I peer around him into his dim apartment to see what caused him to stop.

I suck in a breath; I'm not sure he's breathing. His books have all been pulled off the shelves. His buttery leather couch that I love so much has been mutilated, leather in jagged strips, stuffing resting like snow tops on mountains of books. The kitchen cabinet doors are all open; plates and glasses smashed, the counters littered with open containers and food everywhere. Gabriel carefully steps in, careful to touch nothing.

I clutch his arm to stop him and whisper, "What if they're still here?"

We both pause and listen for sounds that might betray an intruder, but there's nothing. He raises eyebrows at me, and I give him a slight nod. We walk into the apartment together, carefully stepping over broken glass and books. Gabriel makes his way to his bedroom, and he gently pushes open the door, which is askew.

We are met with a similar scene of clothes strewn about. The mattress is ajar, the mirrors are broken, and a framed picture of Gabriel's family he keeps on the nightstand is smashed and face up in the middle of his bed. My eyes are drawn to the corner of the room, where a single long stem rose rests on his dresser top.

"What the hell?" he says, barely above a whisper.

"I don't know. Do you think anything is missing?"

He pushes the mattress out of the way and finds his firebox that holds his essential papers, emergency cash, and his grandfather's wedding ring. He sifts through the contents.

"No. There's not much else of value here. It looks like they just came in and destroyed the place. But why? Why would someone do this to me?"

A heaviness settles over my shoulders as I realize what they were looking for in this malicious mess. "Where is the copy of the appendix we printed out?"

He strides back into the living room and picks through the mess around where his desk has been flipped over. "I don't know where it is, but my laptop is missing." He puts both hands on his hips and releases a heavy sigh.

"What about the appendix?"

Gabriel opens his mouth to respond, but his cell phone buzzes, "It's my sister," he says, taking the call.

I watch his face change from the shock of what we have just seen to horror and grief. "What's wrong?" I mouth at him silently, and he shakes his head, his hand over his mouth.

He hangs up, his expression bleak, and I wait.

"My parents have been in an accident. Someone ran them off the road. I guess they will be okay, but my mom is pretty banged up, and my dad has a broken arm."

"Oh, my gosh, that's awful. Do they know who did it? Why would someone run them off the road?"

Gabriel looks around the apartment. "Why do people do anything? Why did someone trash my apartment? Why is any of this happening?"

A sense of dread migrates from the tips of my toes up to the top of my head. "What can we do for your parents?" I ask.

"Nothing right now. My sister is with them, and they are still at the hospital, but they should be discharged tomorrow. They want to keep both of them overnight for observation."

"Do you have any idea who might have done this?"

"I have no idea. They didn't take anything. They just destroyed my apartment for God knows what reason." His eye catches the rose in the corner. "What the hell is that?" He stomps over and picks it up, holding it out to me. "Why would someone leave a rose after destroying everything I own?" Frustration flashes in his eyes, and behind that is hurt and betrayal.

I walk to his side and take his hand. "You can stay with me while we figure this out. I don't know why this happened. I don't want anybody to come back and hurt you." But I did know. It was Cupid. That was the only thing that made sense.

48

More Roses

"Gabriel's going to stay with us for a while," I say, walking into the apartment. Jayla is sitting on the couch, thumbing through a magazine.

She looks up and asks, "Did your apartment catch on fire or something?"

"No," he says, "someone broke in." He slides his coat off and lays it over the back of the chair.

She closes the magazine and turns toward us. "Wow. That's awful. Did you call the police?"

He runs his hand through his hair. "Yes, but because there is no immediate danger, the police said they would schedule a visit for tomorrow." He sighs. "It might take a few days to put everything back together, and I need to get the insurance guy out."

She frowns. "That's terrible. Stay as long as you need, but please make sure she gives you a key. I came home tonight, and the door was open. Must have been the wind or something."

"What?" I say, setting my coat down over Gabriel's.

"Yeah, probably just a fluke," she says with a wave of her hand. "But there's a box for you." She points to a long box on the kitchen counter.

"Oh?" I walk over, slip the red ribbon off the black box and slowly remove the top. Inside, lying within white tissue paper, is a dozen red roses.

"Who is that from?" Gabriel asks.

"Who constantly is leaving me roses wherever I go?" I say, fishing around for a card. There is a small envelope tucked inside.

Callie, It would be so helpful if you would cooperate. I would hate for things to get more difficult for you and those you love. -C

I read the card and hand it to Gabriel. "What the hell?" he says.

"More Roses?" Jayla asks. "Do you have a secret admirer or something? What kind of roses are those? Even when I came home, the entire hallway was filled with the smell of roses. It made me dizzy."

Gabriel and I lock eyes, and I turn to her, "Jayla, we have talked about this."

She stares at us blankly and then says, "Are you still on that Cupid kick?"

I swallow my frustration. This is the first time Jayla and I have been at odds over something serious. She can't seem to see past her obsession for her convict.

"You don't get it, Jayla. This guy, Cupid, the CEO of that stupid website, is messing with us. I can't prove it yet, but I know it's true. He's the reason Gabriel and I broke up."

She slaps her magazine on the table and stands up, "Whatever."

"I'm not crazy," I say as she looks at me sideways. "And he trashed Gabriel's apartment and probably was responsible for his parents' crash tonight."

"Crash?" Jayla's eyes widen.

"It's true. They were run off the road today and are recovering in the hospital," Gabriel says, checking his phone for text updates.

"I am so sorry. That is terrible," Jayla says. She pats his arm and ignores me on her way to the kitchen. She takes a glass out of the cupboard and turns on the tap.

"It is. But it all started with that website. And I am scared, Jayla. Between the roses, creepy notes, and what happened today, we think this Cupid guy is dangerous," I say.

"And we are pretty sure he is more than just an evil CEO," adds Gabriel.

"Not you, too," Jayla says, hand on her hip and eyes narrowed. She raises the glass to her lips.

"Hear me out. I'm a logical guy, but the things that have been happening defy logic. And Callie has had some run-ins with the guy."

"I told her," I say, folding my arms. Maybe he can talk some sense into her, but I doubt it.

She sets the glass in the sink. "So you think this guy is an evil Greek god CEO who is matching people up for some reason but doesn't like you two?" She points at us.

"Yes," I say, meeting Gabriel's eyes. "I know we sound crazy. I never believed in the supernatural." Gabriel puts his arm around my shoulders and pulls me close.

"But now you do?" Jayla says.

"Well, yes. I know it sounds crazy. But you know me. You know I am not one to jump to conclusions or buy into conspiracy theories." I plead with her to believe me.

Jayla weighs this out for a long moment, and finally, her eyes soften. "Listen. I grew up in a Pentecostal family with frequent visits to my great auntie from Haiti, who still practices voodoo. I have seen some things."

"Then, you believe me?"

"I don't know if he is *the* Cupid or whatever, but I believe he is messing with you. So what are we going do about it?"

"*We* are not going to do anything about it," I say, shaking my head.

228

"Gabriel and I will take care of it, and you are going to worry about your job and," I swallow hard, "Fat Money."

She sighs, and I bite my tongue. "Okay," she says, "don't mess anything up with my match. He is eligible for parole in four months, and I am counting the days."

"Okay," I say, looking at Gabriel, who has to cover his mouth with the back of his hand to stifle a laugh. "We are on the case." Despite the awful situation, I am relieved that Jayla is at least willing to listen. I step forward and take her hands, "Thank you, friend. Please be careful, okay? I don't want any of us to get hurt." I look at Gabriel and then back to her. She nods and pulls me in for a hug.

She whispers in my ear. "Don't worry about me. If anyone tries to hurt me, Fat Money will kill them for sure."

49

Mischievous Gods

Friday, April 22

"What did the police say about your apartment?" I ask Gabriel. Jayla is working late, so we are snuggled under a blanket on the couch.

"I met them today, and they said it looked like maybe an attempted robbery. The place is a disaster; it looks even worse in the light of day. There wasn't much they could do. No fingerprints, no evidence of who did it. The renter's insurance company called back, and they're sending someone out to start the cleanup process."

I touch his arm. "I'm so sorry."

"It was pretty bad going back there. I can't believe how much damage was done. But it could have been worse. At least we weren't home. And it did earn me an extension on my book."

"Well, that's good," I say ruefully.

"Yup, but Callie, if we would have been there, I don't know what would have happened. This is escalating." He shakes his head.

"I know. I keep smelling roses in random places, on the street, in my bathroom. I keep telling myself it is my overactive imagination, but what if it isn't?"

Gabriel gets up and grabs my laptop off my bed. He pops it open and starts searching. I watch him scan several pages before he nods to himself and sets the computer down on the table so I can see the screen. "Look at that."

I see a naked woman and a winged child lounging on a bed.

Gabriel says, "It's Aphrodite and Cupid. It reminds me of the painting by Sustris done around 1550; it hangs on a wall at the Louvre in Paris. We tend to think of Greek gods as superheroes or humans, but they are altogether different. They are terrifying if you read the history of how they behave."

"What do you mean?"

"They don't have a value set as we do. They are mischievous, manipulative, seductive, and, well, dangerous."

I get up and start pacing the living room. "Sounds like Cupid. Did you find anything out specifically about him?"

"Of all the gods, Cupid has the most inconsistent backstory. There are so many theories and legends about him." He looks at me. "Maybe it's time to bring somebody else into this conversation."

I shake my head vigorously. "No way. Our friends already think we're crazy. And Henry's already been through enough. I tried calling the police after that guy chased me, and they didn't believe me. Did you tell the police who we thought trashed your apartment?"

He frowns, "No, I didn't." I don't blame him. I thought I was going crazy, and he might think he is, too. I wish it were that simple.

"You're worried they'll think you're crazy? I get it. That's why I need to handle this. I am the one he is after."

"Okay, but you can't just do this yourself, Callie. Sometimes, you have to rely on other people to help."

"I do have other people. I have you."

I sink next to him on the couch and meet his eyes. "I don't want to bring anybody else into this unless we absolutely have to. There's got to be a solution."

"Okay," he says. "We can try to figure this out on our own. But if anything else happens, we need to bring in backup."

"Fine, although I don't know who would be considered a backup." I put my hand on top of his. "Promise you won't leave me if this gets hard."

"I'm not going anywhere, Callie. I love you."

His eyes search mine. He is so sincere, so kind, but I've heard those words many times from many different people, and most of them never meant it. And even if they meant at the moment, they always ended up leaving. But under his unwavering gaze, I suddenly realize he isn't leaving. He's here, and he loves me.

Before I can stop myself, I say, "I love you, too, Gabriel."

He kisses me deeply, cradling my head with his hands, pressing his forehead to mine.

I wrap my arms around him as he draws me in, and we hold each other for a long time, the warmth of our bodies driving out the chill of fear.

50

Jayla

Monday, April 25

"Hello! I am home, honey," I say, swinging open the apartment door and dropping my purse on the table. It's only 3:30, but a power outage at our building gave my boss an excuse to send us home early.

No answer.

I head to my room to change and peek my head in Jayla's room first to see if she has earphones on or something. With a quick scan of the room, I see a discarded outfit on the bed, her sewing machine light on with fabric ready, but she's not there. My eyes drift lower, and there on the floor, her feet stick out from the other side of the bed.

"Jayla?" I say, heart in my throat, striding across the room.

Jayla is lying on the floor, her lilac robe gracefully framing her body, her eyes wide open, not moving and not blinking.

I shake her, my vision blurring with tears. "Jayla! Jayla!" I feel for a pulse with trembling fingers and can't find one. I grab her shoulders and shake her hard, trying to rouse any sign of life from her. Inside, I'm screaming. How can this be happening? Fumbling for my phone, I dial 9-1-1, turn on the speaker, and try to remember the proper steps for CPR.

"Nine-one-one, what's your emergency?"

"I just got home, and my best friend, she's not breathing!" I shout. "I'm doing CPR."

"Okay, ma'am, stay on the line and continue CPR. We have your phone location. Someone is on their way." I silently thank God for cell phones, location services, and ambulances; then, I pray that Jayla lives. I set the phone next to me on speaker, and the operator helps keep me calm. Tears stream down my face as I repeat the cycle: two breaths, thirty chest compressions. My arms start to ache, but I won't stop.

Then, paramedics rush through the door, gently lifting me off of her and taking over compressions. I stumble backward a few steps and lean against the wall as a paramedic pulls out a defibrillator and shocks her heart.

Someone says, "We have a pulse."

As they get some quick information from me, they load her up on the stretcher and pack their gear. Oh, God, I have to call her family. How am I going to tell her family?

Through the din of my panic, I hear Gabriel's voice, "What's happening? Callie! Callie!" He's in the hall, then at the door, breathless.

"Gabriel." I throw myself into his outstretched arms and bury my face in his shoulder.

He holds me tightly, letting me sob in heaving gasps onto his shirt.

"You can follow us to the hospital," an EMT says as they wheel her out of the bedroom. "We are taking her to Northwestern Memorial."

"I'll drive her," Gabriel says, looking at me. I nod in agreement.

As they leave, I go to my bedroom, needing a moment to breathe. There, lying on my pillow is a single red rose. I rush over to the bed to snatch up the cursed flower and rip every petal into tiny pieces. How dare he do this; how dare he play these games with my life, family, and people. I ball up my fists and scream. Then, I drop to my knees. How am I going to explain this? No one will believe me. They'll lock me up.

234

Gabriel is at my side. "You okay?" he asks softly.

I look at him, everything inside me heavy. "He tried to kill her. I need to go to the hospital. I need to call her parents."

He gently takes my hand, "Who tried to kill her?"

I gesture to the ripped-up red rose petals. "Who do you think? And no, I don't know how he got in."

Gabriel helps me to my feet. "I am going to kill him. This has gone too far."

"We need to go to the hospital and call Jayla's family."

He nods and guides me out of the apartment. I grab my coat and purse on the way to the door. I agree with Gabriel. We need to kill Cupid.

51

In Too Deep

The world feels like it's moving in slow motion. Every red light is an eternity as Gabriel drives me to the hospital. I call Jayla's mom. By her reaction, I know it will be an emotional scene at the hospital. Even though I can't remember the last time I prayed, I offer a prayer for Jayla to be healed and safe.

"Did you see..." I do a double-take out the window. I could swear I just saw the guy who followed me on the street that day.

We stop at a red light, and an older woman is standing on the corner. She wears a long, tattered coat and stands next to a small cart, the kind you bring groceries home in. But it's full of roses. She meets my eyes and holds up a red rose, smiling as if she knows me. A deep sense of unease takes hold, and my stomach does a flip. The smell of roses permeates the air through the car's closed windows as she steps toward us. The light turns green, and Gabriel pulls away. I turn back, and the woman is gone.

We turn into the hospital about two minutes before Jayla's family and meet in the lobby. "Where is my daughter?" Jayla's mom wails.

Instantly, a nurse is there, "Please, calm down; what's your daughter's name, ma'am?"

"Jayla, her name is Jayla Johnson. She was brought in by ambulance; where is she? Is she…Oh, my gosh, if she's dead, I will die, too." She collapses into a chair.

I wrap my arm around her shoulders. "She's going to be okay. She was stable when they brought her in, and they will figure this out." Out of the corner of my eye, something red catches my eye. There are dozens of red roses on the counter at the information center.

Standing up, I ask, "Why do you have so many red roses on the counter?" Which earns me a very puzzled look from Jayla's family.

"Oh," the nurse says, brightly smiling, "a very generous company donated them to lift our spirits."

My mouth goes dry as sawdust. "Oh," I mumble, trying to swallow. "What is the name of the company?"

The nurse is handing a clipboard of forms to Jayla's mom, "Something like psychology or epsych, or psych…Yes, that's it, Psycheros."

"When did they donate them? When did they show up?" I say, my stomach churning.

The nurse gives me a suspicious sideways glance. "This morning." A wide smile spreads across her face, "Wait, do you work for Psycheros? Did you do this?"

I shake my head adamantly. "No. No. I had nothing to do with those roses being delivered here." I look at Gabriel, and he's looking at me, tilting his head a little bit, and I know he understands what I'm thinking.

Jayla's mom fans her face with the clipboard. "Can we please get back to my daughter? Check on my baby. I cannot lose my baby Jayla."

The nurse retreats behind double doors.

Jayla's mom plucks my sleeve. "Callie, you have to tell me what happened to my Jayla. I want to know every little detail."

I take a deep breath and retell the story.

As I describe the dramatic scene, there are collective gasps, sighs, and wails from her family. I don't mean to share so much, but I get caught up in the moment, fully describing all of the sights and sounds we had experienced. It felt cathartic to share the story. I hadn't realized how traumatizing it had been.

A nurse shows us to a private waiting room.

Gabriel quietly holds my hand and then gets us both cups of coffee.

"Thank you," I say, clutching the warm cup. I don't know who decided coffee was good for waiting, but they were right.

Gabriel pats my knee, then takes a sip and wrinkles his nose. Apparently, they didn't clarify that it needed to be *good* coffee. He sets the cup down beside him.

I laugh a little, glad for the break in the heaviness of the room.

Gabriel leans in and whispers, "You saw all those red roses. What do you think that means?"

I look down at the floor, "You know what it means. It means that whatever's happened to Jayla is my fault."

Gabriel touches my cheek, "What? No. No, it's not."

"Yes, it is. I don't know how, but Cupid had something to do with it. He wouldn't even know Jayla if she wasn't my roommate. I can't do this...."

I have to go. I turn, my feet move faster and faster until I am jogging toward the stairwell, pushing the door open, Gabriel's voice echoing behind me.

"Callie, stop. Please."

I can't stop. I need to get out of here. I let the door slam behind me and start down the stairs.

Gabriel is in the stairwell moments later. "Callie," he calls, his footsteps pounding on the stairs behind me.

My chest heaves as I run down flight after flight of stairs. Flashing through my mind are images of Cupid, Jayla, Gabriel, the older woman, Gabriel's mom with her broken arm, Simon, and roses. Those god damned roses. Finally, I am on the ground floor, and I burst through the door onto the sidewalk and into the sunlight.

I stop, bending over with my hands on my knees, trying to catch my breath. My heart is pounding through my entire body, and I might puke.

Five seconds later, Gabriel bursts out of the door and stops just short of knocking me over. "Jesus, Callie, what are you doing?"

Between breaths, I say, "You need to get away from me, Gabriel." I put a hand up to keep him away. "Everyone around me keeps getting hurt."

"Come on, Callie, I am not leaving you." He bends over and turns his head to try and meet my eyes.

I keep looking at my feet, trying to think. "I need to leave town. Maybe if I get away, he will leave our families and friends alone."

"I am already in this too deep. If you go, I go," he says.

My breath and heart rate start to even out, but my mind is spinning.

He grasps my arms and lifts me to a standing position. "I am serious; we can leave right now."

I can't speak but nod as he leads me down the sidewalk to his car.

* * *

Gabriel drives west on I-88 until the sun drops below the horizon. I'm curled up in the passenger seat, my head against the window. Neither of us speaks.

Finally, he eases off the highway and into the parking lot of a hotel. He looks at me, "This okay?"

I silently nod.

He turns off the car and opens the door for me. We don't have any bags, so we head into the hotel. I sit in a lobby chair as Gabriel goes to the reception desk to register for a room.

He gets the key card, gently takes my hand, and guides me up to the room. There are two beds, for which I am grateful. And I immediately throw back the covers and crawl into the bed, only taking time to kick off my shoes first.

Gabriel looks thoughtful. "Okay, I think I should run to the store across the parking lot and grab some supplies. Are you going to be okay here alone?"

"Yes, but can you give me my phone? I need to check on Jayla."

"Sure. Any special requests? I can grab you some snacks and a couple of big T-shirts to sleep in, and if we need to wash anything, there is laundry down the hall here."

"I need a toothbrush and a hairbrush, please."

"No problem. I will be back in thirty minutes. Then, we can figure out dinner, okay?"

"Sure. Check on your parents, too, okay?"

"Yes. I will give them a call. If you think of anything else you need, call or text." He leans over and strokes my hair, kissing my forehead. "I love you. It's going to be okay."

"I love you, too."

And then he is gone.

My phone buzzes with a text from Jayla's sister. Jayla will be okay; they think it was a mild heart attack. They did a ton of tests, and her heart looks healthy. The doctors aren't sure what happened, but they think she will be fine. With that news, I sink into the bed linens and fall asleep before Gabriel gets back to the room.

52

Crumbling Walls

Tuesday, April 26

I feel the sun on my face before I wipe my eyes and open them, blinking at the light slipping through the slit in the curtains.

Gabriel sits at the little table in our room, drinking coffee and scrolling on his phone. "Good morning, sleepyhead," he says, smiling.

"What time is it?"

"Nine. You slept hard."

"How did you sleep?" I ask, sitting up and stretching my arms.

"Not great," he admits. "I kept waking up. I usually don't sleep well in hotels. And you snore."

"What? I do not." I swing my feet off the side of the bed.

"Yes, you do. But don't worry, it's cute. Want some coffee?"

"Yes, please," I say, getting up and padding into the bathroom. "I'm going to take a quick shower," I say, grabbing the bag of supplies he had picked up for me and shutting the door.

After the shower and fresh clothing, he even picked me up some undies and a sports bra, and I feel much better. My hair is wrapped in a towel as I sip coffee and sit down across from him at the table. I check my texts.

"I went online this morning and paid for another night for the room so we wouldn't have to rush out this morning." He says.

"Good, so what now?"

"Not sure. It's been a long twenty-four hours."

I nod in agreement and tuck my foot under me, "Well, Jayla will be okay. How are your parents?"

"They are on the mend, too."

"Thank God. Gabriel," I say, my eyes glistening with tears, "I am so relieved."

He nods, pressing his lips together.

"I know this is weird, but could we just lay in bed and cuddle for a bit? Nothing funny. I want to have you next to me for a while. Then, we can figure out what to do next."

He doesn't say anything; he takes my hand and pulls me down next to him in his bed, curling up behind me. He strokes my hair and kisses my neck. "Callie."

"Hmmm."

"When this is all over, will you marry me?"

"Marry you?"

"Yes." He keeps kissing my neck and ear. "I want you with me. I want you just the way you are."

"Even if I snore?"

He nuzzles my neck, and I turn my face to kiss him. His breath is heavy, "Even if you fart in bed."

I giggle and turn my body to face him. He kisses me tenderly like he is kissing me for the first time. He strokes my hair and face, then moves to my shoulders and back. Our kisses get more fervent.

"Gabriel, I love you. I will marry you." I say breathlessly. Then, I push him on his back and climb on top of him, letting my hair fall over his face and kissing him. His hands are on my hips, and he is grinding into me.

I push his white T-shirt up, but he stops me.

"No, Callie, we can't."

"I want to see your body," I say. He knows I mean his scars. I search his eyes, "Please?"

He slowly moves his hands away and lays them on the bed, giving me full access to his chest. I slide the shirt up and press my lips together, keeping my face even as my fingers trace his skin over the burns covering his chest's left side. I bend over and kiss the right side of his chest.

He moans my name.

Then, I kiss across to the left side, kissing his scars, sacrifice, and pain as if I could take it away with my kisses. He buries his hands in my hair and moans. Heat spreads through my belly as I feel his arousal.

I sit up and take off my shirt. "If you want to wait, we can. But if your main concern was me seeing this," I run my hands gently over his burns, "you don't have to worry. I love every part of you."

He answers me with a kiss and draws me down to him, both of us full of heat and urgent need, finally ready to crumble all the walls between us.

53

Wood Chipper

We lay in bed until my stomach growls so loud he chuckles, and I roll away, groaning. "We need food," he says. "Room service?"

"Yes, please. I need some pancakes or a burger."

"You might need to pick one."

"Fine, burger and fries, please."

Gabriel orders lunch and lies back down. "How are you?" he says, wrapping his arms around me again.

"Hmm. I am incandescently happy."

"Me too, goddess divine."

"Wait," I say, turning to him, "you read *Pride and Prejudice*?"

"Does watching the Keira Knightly movie version count? Because I did do that." He gives me an Eskimo kiss.

"Yes," I say, snuggling into the crook of his body.

Our lunch arrives, and Gabriel tugs on pants to take the tray at the door, passing a bill back for a tip.

I dress and join him at the table. I am famished.

As we eat, he turns on the noon local news.

"...Reports say that the corporation Psycheros is meeting with the president next week to discuss selling the cutting-edge technology behind the controversial website Mylove4Life. The company has been accused of influencing people without their knowing consent; some even call it brainwashing. The company's CEO denies any wrongdoing, even though at least a dozen deaths can be linked directly to the website matches. The White House has confirmed the meeting but has not said how they plan to use the technology."

My cell phone buzzes. It's Simon.

Simon: Girl, where are you? You missed the meeting.

Shoot, I forgot to call into work.

Callie: I'm sick. Can you let Felicia know? You okay?
Simon: Okay. Fine, except we totaled my car last night.
Callie: What? How?
Simon: Brakes went out. Thank God for airbags and insurance.
Callie: Anybody hurt?
Simon: I'm fine. Poor Cody broke his wrist and looks like he was in a bar fight.
Callie: Oh no
Simon: Yes, but I get a new car out of the deal.

There is a knock at the door. Gabriel gets up to answer it, and a man is standing there with a vase full of red roses. I suck in a breath. Gabriel stares at the vase, then turns to look at me and back at the roses.

"These were left at the front desk for you," the clerk says.

Gabriel stands there for a moment and then seems to remember himself. "Oh, thank you," he says, taking the vase.

He fumbles in his pocket for a tip, but the clerk says, "No need, sir, I've already been tipped; very generously, too."

Gabriel closes the door and sets them on the dresser. I stare at them. Gabriel grabs the card and opens it.

You are trying my patience. You know I have the power to get what I want, even if it involves hurting the ones you care about. Please, give Gabriel my best, won't you? - C

I jump up, grab the roses, and stuff them upside down into the trash. "Come on. I've had enough of this."

"Where are we going?" Gabriel watches me rush around the room.

"To confront the bastard."

"We can't just storm into his office."

"Why not? I'm not going to sit around and wait for him to come for us. And this is ridiculous," I say, pointing to the roses in the trash. "We obviously can't get away from him, and he won't stop. And did you hear that news report? We can't let the government get hold of that system. Hang on a minute. We need a plan." I rub my temples.

Gabriel pulls out his laptop and opens a browser. I pace, waiting for him to speak again.

"So the only way to defeat a god," he reads the screen, "is to chop them up into little pieces and scatter them around." He keeps reading and then sits back. "Even that doesn't kill them because, technically, it just takes them a long time to reform. So they'll only be gone for a while." He looks up from his keyboard at me. "Even if we could figure out how to do it, that's not going to stop him forever."

I draw my leg up underneath me and tap my chin. "So you're talking like a wood chipper here? I'm not sure we can get him to go to wood chipper even if I wanted to do that."

"Yeah, that wouldn't work probably. I don't think he could be drugged or anything."

"Not to mention that it's just gross," I say.

"Yeah, it would be messy. But we could freeze the body and keep the mess to a minimum," he says, grinning at me.

I push him, "Eww."

"Right," he nods, "The wood chipper is out. Okay." He shuts the computer and slides it into his bag with a sigh. "I don't know what we can do."

I drop my head into my hands, "We need to do something. I don't know why he won't leave us alone."

He pulls me into his arms, "Is there anything else you remember him saying that might help?"

I bury my head in his shoulder and run through the conversations we had. I pull back, remembering, "The Divine Council."

"The what?"

I shake my head, clearing away the fog around the memory, "He said he had to prove something to the Divine Council."

"Anything else?"

I shake my head, "That is all I can remember."

He squeezes my arms and searches my face. "Okay, so this is a pride thing for him. Maybe we should try to reason with him?"

"No way. He will probably tell me to date Jimmy. I don't care if he picked Jimmy out for me. Even if I had not met you, I am not interested in being some hypnotized lovesick fool. I want to know that what we have is real, even if it is messy."

"Okay, I am with you." He stuffs our things into the plastic bags from his shopping trip, "So we are driving to Fort Wayne?"

"No. He's not located in Fort Wayne," I say, running a brush through my hair. "That's the satellite office for the website. The main headquarters are in Chicago."

"Oh," he says, searching his mind as if he should've known.

"You couldn't have known. It's not on the website. I only know because Henry told me last week."

"Listen, you can't keep things from me," he sighs, "So what's the plan?"

"I don't know. I don't think we should make a plan." I stuff a few bites of burger in my mouth and wash it down with water, "I think we should go for it. We confront him and demand to know what's going on. You know, the element of surprise."

Gabriel rubs his chin, considering. "Don't you think that sounds a little reckless?"

"There's going be other people around. It's not like he'll smite us in the middle of his office," I say and then add with my eyebrows raised, "right?" I open the door, and he follows me out of the room.

"I don't think he can smite people," he responds, thoughtfully, as we walk down the hall.

"Good. At least we have that going for us."

54

Confrontation

I look at the numbers above the door and the text message on my phone. "This is it."

I open the door to an empty lobby. The air is stale and oppressive, as if I am the first person to open these doors in a decade. There is no signage, just a red velvet chair standing watch in the corner. Two elevators wait directly in front of us, beckoning us in.

"Now what?" Gabriel asks.

"Well," I say, trying to sound sure of myself. "I don't know what floor he is on. But if I'm the boss, I'm on the top floor, right?"

I look at him.

He nods steps forward, pressing the button.

I shift on my feet, trying to work out the anxiety and fear threatening to overtake my courage. Finally, there is the telltale ding of the elevator doors. When the doors open, he takes my hand, and we step inside, looking at the numbers on the panel *1, 2, 3, 4, 5, 6, 7.*

Gabriel furrows his eyebrows. "I thought there were only five floors?" We had counted only five floors from the outside. That's weird. "Top floor is the top floor, whether there are seven or five…" His voice trails off as he presses the seventh-floor button. "Here goes nothing." He takes my hand as the elevator moves up, and I can feel the tension rolling off of him.

I try to smile reassuringly and squeeze his hand. He looks down at me and gives me a quick peck on my lips in solidarity.

The elevator abruptly stops, and the door slides open, revealing an ornately carved oak receptionist desk and gold foil wallpaper on every wall in the lobby. The carpet is red, and a young blonde in a trim black suit and French twisted hair looks up and smiles brightly at us. She looks like she stepped out of the 1950s. There is even a black rotary phone sitting on her desk.

"Can I help you?" she says in a singsong voice.

"We're here to see your boss, "I straighten my shoulders."

She looks confused. "Do you have an appointment?"

"No," I reply.

Gabriel squeezes my hand, and I lift my chin.

"But we need to see him right now."

Gabriel steps forward, putting his hands on her desk and smiling. "It's urgent."

"Oh, dear," she says, putting her hand over her heart and scooting back from her desk. "Let's see what we can do." She slips out from behind the desk and opens the ten-foot-tall double oak doors, slipping through and shutting them behind her.

Gabriel grabs my hand again. "This place is something else."

"I know. Red carpet?" I swallow a horrified giggle. "Gross."

The receptionist steps back into the lobby, pulls the door shut behind her, and turns around, a smile plastered on her face.

"He's finishing up an important phone call, but then he said he would see you. Please, have a seat, and he'll come to get you when he's ready."

"Thank you," I nod.

We walk over to the emerald green velvet chairs sitting by the elevator and have a seat. I notice the instrumental '70s ballads playing over the loudspeaker.

The tall oak doors open a moment later, and before us stands Cupid. He's wearing the same suit and smiling as if he expected us.

"Well, hello, Callie. Gabriel, I'm so glad to see you." He walks over and shakes our hands.

My mind stays clear, and even I won't let him get inside my head again.

Gabriel and I stand and awkwardly nod, unsure what to say.

He doesn't miss a beat. "Come into my office and let's have a chat," he winks at us and then turns around, motioning for us to follow him.

Red velvet lines the walls of the office. An ornately carved walnut desk sits at an angle facing the door, a tall leather chair behind it.

Cupid reclines on a velvet settee, picking up a crystal tumbler-filled ice and amber. He casually takes a drink. "I have been waiting for you."

Gabriel and I look around the room, our mouths gaping.

"What did you expect, a naked baby with a bow and arrow? Come on, now." He smiles venomously. "You get one good baby portrait done, which is all anyone thinks about." He sits up and walks to the bar to refill his drink.

He is looking at us like a predator. I step backward, and Gabriel moves to stand between us.

Cupid slowly moves across the room toward us, swirling the ice in his drink. He runs his thumb across his lower lip and smiles. "And it's so cute that the two of you have fallen so deeply in love. It's like it came down from the heavens." His fingers move like rain coming down.

I straighten my back and plant my feet firmly on the ground, "Why are you doing this?" I ask.

"What are men to rocks and mountains?" he says and winks. "Or should I say, what are humans to gods?"

He pauses and tips his head, considering. "You know why I am doing this, but Gabriel here hasn't been privy to our many conversations."

Gabriel looks at me and then back at Cupid.

"For heaven's sake," Cupid says, exasperated sitting up, "I have already explained all this to Callie. I set up a perfectly effective system to pursue my other interests. You, humans, have managed to ruin it. So here I am, trying to put it back together. But of course, with so many humans and limited proximity power, I needed another way for my plans to succeed. "

"So you created the website?" Gabriel asks.

"Website? Anyone can create a website. I created an empire, a legacy, redefining love in the human world. I took my power and amplified it to reach the entire world." He spreads his arms out over his head.

"And then you are going to sell the system to the government?" I ask.

"Well, it does take money to fund all of this, and I am not Midas." He shakes his head and runs his finger around the rim of his glass.

"But why now?" Gabriel asks, "It's not like this is a new problem."

"True. But you see, I have a problem of my own. My dear Psyche, my muse, my love, has left me. She had the gall to say that I had lost my touch." He stretches his arm out and flexes his hand, looking at his fingernails. "Can you believe that? After all, I have done for her." He sighs. "Alas, I do love her, so I must win her back. And do you know what she said I had to do to win her back?"

Gabriel and I stare at him blankly.

"I need to succeed. I need to have one hundred percent success in my little experiment to prove that I am worthy of her."

"But why do you match people who don't belong together?" I ask, thinking of Jayla.

"Who's to say if you belong with him or with someone else? It is just chance, you know. But since I have to be here, I thought I would have a little fun anyway. And it has been delicious to watch the mayhem."

"But people are dying," I say.

He waves me off, "Love is dangerous, my girl. That is nothing new. People have been dying for love since the beginning of time."

"So if I let Callie go and she finalizes her match, you will leave her alone?" Gabriel asks.

"Yes, you have my word." Cupid makes an "x" mark across his chest.

"You can't just run around playing with people's hearts!" I spit. Who does he think he is?

"I can't?" he raises his eyebrows and puts his hand on his heart.

"You shouldn't," I continue. "You need to undo these matches. You can't make Jayla be with a felon."

"Oh, I see, so you should get to choose who loves who?"

"Well, no…"

"What about Simon? Should I undo that match, too? Isn't Simon a better man because of the match I gave him? Should that be undone?"

"I don't know," I admit.

"Look, I am not completely heartless; after all, I am the god of love. But I can't just leave you, humans, to your own choices; that has become a mess. I am open to a bargain, though. I'll leave you two alone and let you live your long, happy life. What the heck? I'll even leave your friend, Jayla, alone. But you leave me alone to do my work. You have two days to decide. Now, if you don't mind, I have a meeting to get to, so please leave my office."

I take a step forward. "That's not good enough."

He looks up from the papers he's shuffling on his desk. "Oh." His face is a menacing smile. "And if you tell anyone about our meeting today, all bets are off. I might have to take drastic measures." He looks back at his desk, dismissing us.

Gabriel grabs my arm and drags me out of the office.

Once we are outside, he says, "We need a new plan."

"Yes. Let's go home and figure it out."

"I need to go see my parents. Let me drop you off to shower and check on the apartment, and I will meet you there later. I want to make sure my parents are safe."

55

The Idea of Love

All I want to do is climb in the bed to go to sleep and not think about any of this; I think as I open the door to our building. On the way up the stairs, I call Jayla, and she answers.

"Hey, girl, I wondered when I would hear from you."

"Sorry, friend, I had some things to do. But your family has been keeping me updated."

"Yeah, they have been driving the staff crazy. It's probably best you weren't here the entire time; they have taken over the waiting room."

"I bet. How are you feeling?"

"Much better. I think I get to come home in a day or two."

I pause on the landing and send up a prayer of thanks. "I am so glad. You scared me to death."

"I know. I am just glad you were there. You saved my life."

"I don't know about that, but I will try to come and see you tomorrow. Okay?"

"Deal. Can you bring me my silk robe? These gowns are hideous."

I laugh. She sounds like herself, which is fantastic. "Of course. Let me know if there is anything else you need."

"Love you, Callie."

"I love you, too, Jayla." It felt good to say that to her. It was true, and I had held back my feelings from the people in my life for way too long.

I unlock the door to my darkened apartment, tossing my coat and purse onto the kitchen table. I kick off my shoes and carry them to my room. I open the door to my bedroom, flip on the light, and shriek, jumping back into the hall and dropping my shoes.

Lounging in the chair next to my bed is Cupid. One leg crossed over the other, his hands folded on top. He looks at me and slowly smiles, tilting his head.

"Hello, there, Callie. What an interesting room you have. I have been perusing your bookshelves."

"What are you doing here?" I say, not moving.

"Oh, that's not very polite." He twirls his ankle slowly.

"Well," I say, pushing my shoes out of the way with my foot, "you're the one who broke into my house, so I think I have a right to ask you what are you doing here."

"All right, then," he says with a wave of his hand, "I will get right to the point. I've come to offer you a bargain."

"You already offered us a bargain." I step into the room but press my back against the wall.

"No." He puts his feet on the floor and leans forward with his hands on his thighs. "This bargain is just for you."

I fold my arms and stand up straight, my breath shallow. "Okay, what?" I meet his unblinking gaze and hold it. "Are you going to say something or just stare?"

A puzzled look passes over his face. He does not affect me. He realizes he can't use his Casanova bull crap anymore. I am immune, thank God. Then, he changes tactics.

"You know Gabriel is not actually in love with you. And even if he is, he'll never fight for you or even stick around." His voice is even, face unreadable.

I open my mouth to respond, but he puts his hand up, so I shut it, and he continues.

"Oh, you will go through the motions for a few years, maybe even have a few happy moments. You might even have a child. But eventually, it will end. It always does. You've seen it in your own family, and you've seen it time and time again. Love doesn't last."

"That's not true!" I say, my voice shaking. "Gabriel loves me. He told me he loves me."

Cupid slowly stands up but doesn't move toward me. "Are you sure? I mean, you've been sure before, and you've always been disappointed." He slides my copy of *Pride and Prejudice* off the shelf and flips through the pages. "Without my intervention, would Gabriel continue to love you? What happens if he finds out how cynical you are about love, despite your interest in romantic literature?" He looks up at me and snaps the book closed, tossing it on my bed.

"I don't know what you've done or not done, but I know that Gabriel loves me, with or without you."

"Are you willing to take that risk?" he says, tipping his head to look at me. "You might be very disappointed in what you find out. But there's another option."

"What?"

"If you are willing to sacrifice your love, if you're so sure your love is true and real, let me hit him with an anti-love arrow and see if your love can overcome it. If it does, I will admit defeat and undo my work, but it would be a shame to undo so much fun," he says, looking out my window wistfully.

"That's not fair. You know that your arrows are too strong to fight."

"But that's the point. I don't know for sure because I shoot love arrows, and you humans still break up. You still hurt each other and hit each other. So how can I be sure?" He moves sideways, walking over to my closet, standing next to it. "Actually," he says, pointing his finger to his lips and tipping his head to the side, "this is a bigger issue than my arrow's effectiveness. I wonder if you humans believe in love at all. You certainly have a hard time believing it, and your parents didn't bother to try to believe it, either."

"I do believe in love. I've always believed in love," I stutter.

"You believed in the *idea* of love, but not for you. Isn't that a little more accurate?"

Tears prick my eyes. "Why are you so cruel?"

"I'm not," he says in his singsong voice. "I'm just wondering if I can find someone on this godforsaken planet that believes in love as I do."

"How would you know they believe in love like you do?"

"Oh, love takes sacrifice, my dear. Are you willing to sacrifice for love? Are you willing to sacrifice your love to save Gabriel's life?" He runs his fingers down one of my shirts, caressing the fabric.

I swallow hard, "You're asking me if I would die for Gabriel?"

He waves the thought away, "Oh, no, death is easy. People choose death over love all the time. I'm asking you to choose Gabriel over love. He'll live and love, but it won't be you. You'll live, but you will never fall in love."

"But why do you care? I don't understand." My hands are numb. I am glued to the wall.

"I already told you," he says impatiently, "Psyche has given me an ultimatum, and if I can not prove to her and the Divine Council that my power is absolute, it will not go well for me. You are standing between me and success. And that is not very nice." He stands in front of me, sizing me up like prey.

I need to buy some time. "Can I have tonight to think about it? I mean, I wouldn't want to make a rash decision about your offer."

I see him weighing my words, and finally, he says, "All right, then. You have twenty-four hours. But tomorrow night, if you make no decision or the wrong decision, I will have to go with Plan B." He brushes past me and heads for the front door.

I rush after him, "Wait. What's Plan B?

He puts his hand on the doorknob and turns around to me. "Honey, let's hope you don't have to find out. It would be most unpleasant." And then he's gone.

As I stand in front of the closed door, I replay the conversation in my mind. Gabriel urged me to pay close attention to the wording of anything Cupid says. He didn't tell me to keep it a secret.

I peel off my clothes and slide into the warm bath. How does he know things that I didn't even know I thought and felt? And how could he be so cruel as to use them as a weapon? My pain and my loss? Gabriel loves me. We didn't rush into anything. I had broken up with him, and he still loved me. That has to mean something. He met my family. I met his family, and everything was good.

But it's also been this whole quest thing the entire time. What if life was just mundane? Would we get bored with each other when we weren't facing danger? Maybe he won't find me interesting. Perhaps I will find him annoying. Doubt begins to creep into my mind as I sink into the water up to my chin and shut my eyes, trying to blot out the world.

I wish Jayla were here. I wish I could tell her everything and get her advice, but I don't want to upset her. I could call my sister. We've been talking a lot recently but not about this. Trying to explain to her right now all of it would be too much. Reluctantly, I release the drain on the tub and grab a towel. My entire body aches with exhaustion as I climb into bed. My heart is raw from old wounds being torn open. Tears slip down my cheeks before I finally fall asleep.

56

Willing Sacrifice

Wednesday, April 27

"Calm down," I say.

Gabriel is pacing around my living room, his face red and his hands balled into fists. "I can't believe he came into your bedroom."

"I know," I say, sitting on the chair, my hands in my lap.

"What kind of...." He stops in front of me, putting his hands on his hips. "And he told you that I wouldn't stay in love with you?"

I look at the ground. "That's what he said. It was horrible. He seemed to know all of my worst fears and was happy to use them against me."

He kneels before me, meeting my eyes, "Tell me again exactly what he said about the bargain."

"He said he would undo all the matches if I were willing to live without true love for the rest of my life."

He sits back on the floor and grabs my hand. "That's ridiculous. I love you."

"I know," I say, scratching my head with the other hand, "and I love you, too."

"This isn't right. It's not fair. There has to be another option."

"You're the one who told me we couldn't possibly fight back because he's a god. And trust me, I am still considering chopping him up into little pieces."

"We have to do something," he gets to his feet and starts pacing, "this is not going to happen."

"Okay," I say, looking up at him. "Let's do something. I want to do something. I don't want this jerk to win. I don't want to have him," my voice catches with emotion, "break us up. It's taken me too long to find you."

He crosses the room and sits next to me, taking my hands and his. "I'm not going anywhere, Callie. I don't care if you were supposed to be with someone else. We get to decide who we love."

"But would we still be together if we weren't in the middle of this mess?" My doubt clouding my thoughts, I say, "Or would you find me boring and weird and a slob? And would I find you irritating and a workaholic?"

"Callie, look at me. Even if you are boring and weird and a slob and, even if I am irritating and a workaholic, it doesn't mean we don't love each other. It isn't bigger than love."

"But what is love? He said that was the problem; people didn't believe in love itself. They fell in and out of it so easily because they didn't believe in it."

He stands up and lifts me to my feet, holding my hands and looking into my eyes. "Do you know what love is? It's my parents. It's my dad standing beside my mom through three bouts of cancer. He drives her to chemo every week and holds her head while she throws up from the medicine. He tells her she's beautiful, even when she's lost weight, has no hair or eyebrows, and can't get out of bed. It's my mom sacrificing herself to care for her husband and her children. And that's love; it's not just a feeling. It's a choice and a decision. Cupid can cause a feeling with his arrows or cause somebody not to like each other, I

261

guess, with his arrows, but he can't control all of the love because love is a choice every day. And I choose love. And I will choose love with you every single day."

My eyes well up with tears again, and my lips quiver as I understand what I have to do. And I tell him, "I choose love, too, Gabriel."

He pulls me in his arms and wraps me and a big hug, and we stand there for a long time. Finally, he leans back, "When do you have to decide?"

"I have until till tomorrow night," I lie.

"Okay. I have to teach a class today. But tonight, we're going to figure something out together." He grabs my hands. "You and me, we are going to figure this out together. Just don't do anything crazy."

"Okay," I say, choking back emotion, and then I kiss him hard and long and wrap my arms around him, pouring all of the love I have for him into him, so he knows, and hopefully, somehow, he'll never forget I loved him more than I've ever loved anyone before.

He smiles, "I'll see you tonight. I'll bring Chinese food."

I nod and smile weakly. And my heart breaks into 1,000 pieces as he shuts the door.

I fall to the floor. I can't breathe. I lay on the ground and curl up, staying there for a long time. It takes every bit of energy I have left to stand up and walk to the bathroom. As I splash cold water on my face, I know what I have to do.

57

If You Must Know

I'm numb as I put on jeans and a black sweater. I run a brush through my hair and throw on some lip gloss. Then I slip my coat over my shoulders and grab my bag. Then, I lock my apartment and head downtown.

The wind whips at my face as the last breath of winter is roars down from the north. I tug my hair back into a ponytail and dig the gloves out of my pocket.

By the time I reach the office building, my cheeks are flushed and windburned. I head up to the seventh floor, nausea rolling in my stomach.

I step into the elevator, and a melancholy love song that I don't recognize is playing. I can feel my chest expand with pent-up anxiety and grief. I swallow hard as the door opens; the cheery blonde is behind the desk.

"Hello, there," she says brightly.

"Hi. I don't have an appointment."

"Oh, that's all right, he's been expecting you." She picks up the rotary phone, dials, and then speaks softly into the handpiece. She then motions to the doors. "Go right on in."

I pause before the door as an instrumental version of "Can't Help Falling in Love" plays in the background. I take a deep breath and pull the door open.

"Ah, Callie. Good to see you." Cupid smiles as he gets up from his desk. "Come in, come in. Come, sit down. I'm so sorry about the way I've been behaving. You must think terribly of me. I'm usually a much better host. Would you like something to drink? Coffee? Cosmopolitan?"

"No, thank you," I say as he leads me over to a gathering of furniture.

He sits on one of the chairs and motions for me to sit in the middle of the green velvet couch. "Isn't this just a lovely room? I love jewel tones, and it was so fun to be able to design my own space finally."

"Sure." It looks like blood was dripping down the walls with all that red velvet, but I wasn't going to say that.

"Do you know what?" He leans forward with his elbows on his knees and his hands on his face. "You should let me decorate your room. I could do something fabulous in there."

I stare at him. I'm not sure what to make of his behavior change. "Did something happen to you today?"

He purses his lips together. "Well, if you must know, Psyche has decided to come home. She is convinced that my efforts have been a success."

"Oh?" I say, sudden hope rising in me.

He gets up and walks to the bar. Turning back, he says, "Don't think this changes anything between us."

I sink back on the couch.

"Yes, she thinks I have succeeded. But if she gets wind of you, she will leave again. And I can't have that."

I'm not sure how to respond.

"So, have you made up your mind? I see you've been crying; your eyes are puffy and red. You're not looking your best."

Tears well in my eyes again, and I blink them back. I'm tired of crying. And he didn't deserve to see my tears. "Yes," I say, finally, "I have made up my mind."

He abandons his drink mixing and strides back to drop into a chair. "Well, don't keep me in suspense, girl. Tell me."

"Okay," I say solemnly.

"Okay?"

"Yes. I agree to your terms." I can't even look at him; my body feels like it weighs 1,000 pounds, and raising my head is impossible.

"You do?" he says, leaning forward to search my face.

"Yes." How many times do I have to say it? I meet his eyes. "I love him enough to give him up. And I love him enough to want that for him. He deserves it."

"Huh," he says, leaning back, "I'm surprised."

"Why are you surprised?"

He shrugs. "I didn't think you would take the deal. I didn't think you cared enough. You have pleasantly surprised me, which does not happen very often."

He sits forward, clapping once. "I think this calls for a drink, a celebration."

"I don't want anything to drink," I say, looking back at the ground. "Let's just get it over with."

"Oh, come now." He gets up, crossing to the bar to pour himself a complicated mixed drink, "There's no reason to rush, now. At least not for me. I am immortal," he says, sipping the beverage.

Outside the office, voices rise in anger. Cupid set's his drink down on his desk and tips his head to the side, waiting. I turn towards the noise; my chest starts to hurt, and sweat breaks out on my forehead.

58

All For Love

"Where is she?" I hear Gabriel's voice just before the door flies open, and he charges in, stopping in the middle of the room. His face is flushed, and his eyes are burning.

Cupid smiles, nonplussed, "Hello, there, Gabriel. How nice to see you again."

"You can't have her," he growls, his body stiff and chin defiant.

"Can't have who?" Cupid responds, innocently taking a drink.

"I know you made a deal with her. And I have a better one for you."

"Oh, really?" he asks, tipping his head, his eyes flittering to me just for a moment.

"Yes, really," he spits. "I will give you my life. I will give you my life so that she may go on and find true love."

Cupid swirls the glass in his hand, ice clinking. He slowly looks up at Gabriel and tilts his head. Then, he walks toward Gabriel, "You're willing to lay down your life so that the woman you love can go on and love another?"

Gabriel stands his ground and swallows hard. "Yes."

Cupid stops and puts his hands out. "But why would you do that?"

"Because I love her. I believe in love, and I believe in her, and I believe that she deserves to have true love in her life." His voice catches as he continues. "And I've had true love with her, and if I die now, I'll die a happy man. But I can't live without her."

I'm frozen watching all of this unfold.

"Well, now, Gabriel, you have made an interesting proposition. You know she was willing to sacrifice herself for you," he says, his eyes again landing on me.

Gabriel follows his eyes and sees me for the first time since bursting through the door. "What are you doing here?"

"Same as you," I shrug, "making a deal with the devil."

"Hey, now," Cupid says, "I am much better looking than Hades."

I hardly hear him, though, because I am staring at Gabriel, and he is staring at me. The rest of the world seems to disappear.

"Well, we have ourselves a little conundrum," Cupid says.

I stand up but don't move.

Gabriel and I both turn to stare at Cupid.

He folds his fingers in front of him. "This is interesting." He starts pacing and talking to himself. "Not at all what I expected. I could allow Callie to give up love for love. Or I could allow Gabriel to give up his life for love." He turns to us. "Such a sacrifice you two are willing to make. Maybe I should have matched you two up. It would be funny to have Callie, who doesn't believe in love, even after reading all those Jane Austen books, and Gabriel, who wears his heart on his sleeve, thrown together. But I don't care about you. And frankly, you humans don't deserve my help."

"No love," he says, pointing to me, "or no life," he points to Gabriel. "Maybe we can do both." He creates a ball of fire in his hands and throws it toward the rug on which Gabriel is standing.

I scream.

Gabriel tries to move off the rug, but the fire spreads around him, trapping him inside the flames. I can smell the singe of his hair. He is going to burn to death right in front of me. This can't be happening. Through the flames, I see Cupid sneering at Gabriel.

"Stop it!" I scream at Cupid. "Let him go!"

"Why?" he asks, his voice sounding like he's standing next to me.

"Because you were right."

He tilts his head, and the flames spread out a bit.

Gabriel is screaming, "Callie, Callie, get out of here. Forget about me."

I don't move. "You were right about everything you said about me," I scream over the flames, "but what I've learned from you is that love is hard. It's complicated. And it's worth fighting for. And you can't trick people into loving. You have to let your arrows fly," I say, searching for words, "and trust they're going to land where they're supposed to and stick more often than not because love can't be real love without a choice. Feelings ebb and flow, but real love is a choice every day."

The flames around Gabriel quiet to waist high, and I can see his face awash with primal fear. He says, "Callie, this is all my fault; just get out of here."

He isn't making sense, but I knew he must be talking about his brother. "It's okay, Gabriel. This isn't your fault. The fire wasn't your fault." I hold his gaze.

Cupid speaks up. "It wasn't supposed to happen between you two. Callie should've fallen in love with Jimmy Powell. I shoot an arrow, and you fall in love. The end."

"No," I say. "Even if you do shoot an arrow, I fall in love, and then I make a choice every single day to stay in love. Even when I don't feel it, I choose to love from the first day until the last day of my relationship."

"But if you don't feel it, why would you stay?" Cupid asks, brows knitted together.

"Because feelings are fickle. Feelings come and go. What makes love so extraordinary is choosing to stay and to love day in and day out."

I am talking to Cupid but looking at Gabriel, holding his gaze and slowing my breathing, willing him to slow his.

Cupid starts to pace, "So you're telling me that my power is limited?"

"Your power is exactly what it is supposed to be. You have the power to make sure people in a busy, complicated world notice each other. You make sure they care enough to risk it all and fall in love. That's a lot." I shift my gaze from Gabriel to Cupid. "And the choice to love, even when it gets hard, is why Gabriel is willing to die for me." Gabriel is smiling, and I smile back.

Cupid waves his hand, and the flames disappear. I rush to Gabriel, and he folds me into his arms. Cupid flops down in the chair behind his desk. "Oh, you two are disgusting."

"We know," I say, "and it's all your fault." I bury my face in the crook of Gabriel's arm. I don't ever want to let him go.

Cupid stands up. "Indeed," he says, looking at us and crossing to the bar. "I need another drink. Do you know why? Because I am amazing. I have taken two people who were a total mess and now look at you. It may have come about differently than I'd planned, but Callie has found love, and here you are." He scoops ice cubes into the glass. "United in purpose, ready to stand up against a god, and willing to risk everything for goodness sake." Shaking his head in disbelief, he grabs the crystal cravat and pours amber fluid over his ice. "And if you can learn to love," he says, looking at me, "and you can come in here like a hero, guns a blazing, and offer to die for this girl," he says, looking at Gabriel, "then I'm better than I think."

Gabriel and I look at each other, confused, but don't say anything.

"Wait till I tell Psyche about this," he says, taking a swig of his drink. "I haven't been surprised in eons, and here you two have done just that. Outstanding." He lifts his glass in a toast to us.

"So what now?" I ask.

"Oh, you two might as well be together. You've earned it."

269

"But what about your project?" I can't believe he is giving up this easily.

He shrugs. "As far as I am concerned, it was a success. You guys are proof of that."

"What about everybody else? Will you rip up those terms and conditions you made everybody sign?"

"Fine, fine. I'm not too fond of the corporate world, anyway. Too cutthroat. And the last thing your government needs is another way to manipulate people. They already have the media for that." He empties his glass in one swig.

"But if I find out you two have chosen to stop loving each other, I'll be back." He looks down at his watch, "I have a date tonight with Psyche, so please get out of my office." The smile on his face is sincere.

We don't waste any time. We rush out of the office and downstairs to the street, laughing as we push open the doors.

"I can't believe it," I say, throwing my hands in the air.

Gabriel turns to me, seriously, "You were going to sacrifice your chance at love for me?"

"You were going to sacrifice your life for me?"

"I love you." His eyes are soft.

I grin, "I love you, too. And I'll choose to love you every single day."

He wraps me in his arms and kisses me—a kiss filled with no grief or fear, just hope, and love.

59

Epilogue

Saturday, July 22

"How do I look?" I turn around to face my mom, my veil falling over my shoulders.

"Just beautiful," she says, her eyes sparkling as she straightens the veil and admires the lace trim. We're standing in the bridal room at the church Gabriel's family has attended for years. It's a neighborhood church that holds vacation Bible study every summer and potlucks once a month.

"Maybe you can use my veil when you get married, Mom."

She smiles coyly, "Hush, now, I've only been dating him for a few weeks."

"True, but you guys are so cute together. And isn't he taking dance lessons with you?"

"Yes," she says, batting her eyelashes at me, "and he's pretty good at it."

I take her hands, "Well, then, Mom, he's a keeper."

"Oh, this is your day, enough about me," she says, shaking her head.

"Hello," I hear Shannon call from the other room.

"In here," I say, looking past my mom.

Shannon walks into the room, sucking in a breath when she sees me. I smile, crossing to give her a big hug. "I'm so glad you are here."

"I wouldn't miss this for the world, Sis. And the kids are so excited to see you." It had been a month since we had been back to Indiana. We had been busy with wedding planning and the release of Gabriel's new book.

"I think it's almost time," my mom says, straightening the back of my gown, a long chiffon ballgown that makes me feel like a fairytale princess.

"I should've had somebody go with me to the bathroom," Jayla says, walking in, "It took me forever to get this dress zipped back up." She looks stunning in the pale-yellow dress, which hugs her body in all the right places. Her brown wavy hair pulled up in a twist with little yellow and white flowers pinned at the nape.

"You look beautiful," Shannon tells her.

"Thank you," she says, posing. "Callie, let me pick this out. I can't wait to pick her bridesmaid dress when I get married." She smiles at me.

"As long as you aren't marrying anyone named Fat Money." I can't help myself.

Jayla cringes, "Don't remind me. I still can't believe I thought he was…what did I call him?"

"A cute little hobbit," I say.

We share a laugh, and she hugs me. "I saw Gabriel in the hallway. He looks nervous."

"Is his mom here yet?"

"Yes, they just brought her in. She looks pretty. It seems like she's having a good day."

"Good," I say, "I am so glad." She had been getting sicker and sicker and couldn't walk anymore. We decided to get married right away because we wanted her to be there. "Did you see Simon?"

"I did. I put him to work as an usher. Cody is helping park cars."

"What?"

"Just kidding. He is saving seats."

My mom turns to me and takes my hand, "Are you ready to go and make Gabriel the love of your life?"

"Mom, he already is the love of my life. Now, we get to make it official."

There is a knock at the door, and in walks my dad. He looks good in his tux with his salt and pepper hair and Florida tan. "Oh, Callie. You look beautiful. I have missed you more than you know." He folds me into a hug, and I wipe away a tear.

"Stop it, or you will mess up the hours of work Jayla has put in to make me look like this."

My dad had flown in a week ago, and we had spent hours together visiting bookstores, touring Chicago, and reconnecting. I had forgotten how similar we are, and after this week, it feels like he never left.

It's surreal seeing my parents standing next to each other. No bitterness, no cold silence. They are both smiling with genuine joy. They are happy, I realize. My heart swells, and it feels like something broken deep inside is finally mending. My family is going to be okay.

I stand in front of our friends and families, holding Gabriel's hands. We pledge our lives to each other and exchange rings.

Gabriel kisses me deeply when the preacher pronounces us husband and wife while the pews erupt in cheers. He whispers. "I must learn to be content with being happier than I deserve."

I lean back and smile, *"Pride and Prejudice?"*

"Of course," he says, smiling. "You have bewitched me body and soul, and I love, I love, I love you."

Made in the USA
Monee, IL
13 February 2022